ENDLESS FANTASY ONLINE

BOOK 1
THE PHOENIX KINGDOM

DEVIN AUSPLAND

DEDICATION

For my wife and our four fur babies.

CONTENTS

ACKNOWLEDGMENTS

There is a list of people I want to thank but first is my amazing wife. I had to give up a lot of family time to complete this project and she continued to support me, encourage me, and help me. She is my rock and I'm blessed every day because I have her in my life. Thank you.

I want to thank my close friend Breck Borges and his father Dick Borges. They both gave me unwavering support and were the first people to read my book from start to finish. They provided amazing comments and helped not only proofread my mistakes but took the time to help me edit everything.

I want to thank the rest of my family. My siblings, my parents, my cousins, aunts, uncles, and my grandparents for encouraging me along the way. This was a huge investment of my time and they all helped me get through it by cheering me on.

Last but certainly not least, I must thank you, the readers. Thank you for coming on this journey with me and enjoying my words. I'm so glad that I was able to share this story with you.

CHAPTER ONE

Enter the Beta

Five-thousand dollars! They're paying five grand for a month of playing video games? What's the catch, thought Luke as he reexamined the college job board for the third time. According to the neon flier the company, Vortex Industries, was looking for people to join the first human trials of a new virtual reality game. Luke checked to make sure there were no other obvious choices for summer employment before ripping the flier off the board and slipping it into his pocket.

As soon as he got back to his dorm room, he called the number on the flier. "Hello? I'm interested in joining your beta program."

"That's great! I'll just need some details from you and you'll have to sign some documents" a customer service rep responded on the other end.

After their brief conversation Luke booted up his laptop and checked his email. Sure enough, there was a message marked important from Vortex Industries. It appeared to contain standard legal documents, the kind you'd see for any prerelease game testing program. There was a non-disclosure agreement, a non-compete document and a bunch of other legalese that Luke didn't fully understand. One thing he made note of was the lack of anything talking about the game. There weren't any game briefs, screen shots, videos or anything to give him information on what they would be testing. Luke still wanted to sign up, so he electronically signed all the documents and sent them back. He got a response almost instantly with an address and time to show up.

Luke ordered an auto-taxi and keyed in his destination when it arrived. The automatic display said it would take approximately an hour, so Luke pulled out his phone and did some research. Vortex Industries has been the leader in Virtual Reality gaming ever since they released their own hardware a few years ago. Luke enjoyed gaming but hadn't played any VR games. With high end VR hardware costing thousands of dollars, he could never afford their steep entry costs.

The more research he did, the more excited he became. The screen shots for their previous VR titles looked incredible. Digging around some tech sites he found a video of the head scientist, Robert Xanders, talking about the company's recent breakthroughs. He clicked the video and it began to play on the auto-taxi's viewing monitor.

"Our new VR hardware is beyond anything on the market." Robert was speaking at a keynote address in front of a large room of gamers, investors, and industry professionals. He began "The immersion that virtual reality can provide truly is incredible, but what is holding it back from feeling real?" The screen behind him displayed images of human ears, mouths, hands, eyes, and noses. "It's the lack of senses engaged. Imagine being able to go into another world, imagine tasting its food, smelling its flowers." He paused for dramatic effect, "Imagine a new life. The Vortex Capsule will transport you to a new world." Images behind Robert changed to a large white egg-shaped capsule with the Vortex Industries branding on the side.

A video started playing showing a cartoon person walking into the capsule. The cartoon person laid down inside the capsule and the camera switched to a first-person view from the perspective of the cartoon person. The man in the video closed his eyes, and the screen went dark. Oversized eyelids opened to a large medieval town. The cartoon person looked down to see that he was holding a sword and a fireball was flaring in his other hand. There was a low rumbling sound and his eyes jolted up, revealing a group of goblins that were charging him. He threw his fireball at one of them and then ran forward to drive his sword through another.

The video suddenly changed to the first-person view of a starship captain. The captain began yelling commands at his crew while engaging in an epic space battle. Massive spacecrafts were exploding all around the captain's ship. He gripped the armrests of his chair until his knuckles turned white. A missile fired from an enemy ship in his direction. Right before the missile made contact, the screen changed, and the man was sitting on a beach enjoying an exotic drink. The bubbling drink had a miniature umbrella in it. Gazing lovingly at him was a woman in a bikini with pink skin. Looking around the beach he saw a wide variety of people with purple, green, and dark blue skin. There were sounds of exotic birds chirping and crashing out of the water were large alien like creatures. "The Vortex Capsule is not just the future of virtual reality gaming – it's the future of humanity," Rob continued. "Soon you can have a family trip to Florida without ever having to go through airport security, driving for hours or having to rent an expensive hotel. Imagine tasting the drinks you order on the beach and feeling the sand under your toes. I welcome you to the future!" Rob extended his arms in a wide, welcoming gesture and the crowd went wild. They were all standing, clapping, and cheering as the video cut out.

Luke continued to research Vortex Industries as the auto-taxi pulled up to a large skyscraper. The top of the building was adorned by the words Vortex Industries in giant neon glowing letters." Luke entered the building and went to the front desk to check in. A woman wearing what appeared to be a blue stewardess's outfit gave him a warm greeting.

"Welcome to Vortex Industries." She stood up and gave him a slight bow before continuing. "You must be Lucas Patterson. We have been waiting for you."

The woman was in her late twenties and he immediately realized why she was chosen for the front desk position. She had incredible posture, was very kind spoken and had a kind smile. Luke blushed momentarily as she stood, revealing her pleasant figure.

"You can call me Luke," he mumbled while pushing up his glasses.

She smiled, handed him a badge and gestured toward the elevator as the doors opened with a whoosh. Luke stepped inside and the doors closed behind him. He began to grow a little concerned at the lack of buttons to control the elevator. Instead of buttons, there was a box to scan keycards, but he had not been given a keycard when he arrived. Before he could contemplate returning to the front desk, he heard the quiet tones of generic elevator music, and the elevator began descending.

"Welcome to Vortex Industries," a monitor in the elevator panel said as it whistled to life. "Vortex Industries is the leading provider of virtual reality experiences. With the recent announcement of the Vortex Capsule, Vortex Industries is bringing the future to the present day."

The monitor shut off as the elevator came to a stop. With the lack of buttons and a floor number display, he wasn't sure how far down the elevator had gone.

A man in a lab coat, carrying a clipboard and sporting a 5 o'clock shadow, approached the elevator. Luke recognized the man as Robert Xanders, the lead scientist behind the Vortex Capsule. "Hello Lucas. Please come with me so we can start the scanning process."

"Please call me Luke – and what do you mean by the 'scanning process'?" Luke responded, hesitation bleeding into his voice.

"We first have to scan you before we can move your consciousness into the Vortex Capsule and sync it with your brain waves. Didn't you read about this in the package they sent you?" The man rose a single eyebrow inquisitively at Luke.

Luke explained that they only sent him legal documents and wasn't sure the full extent of this offer.

"Just like those corporate goons to not send all the correct information. All about protecting our trade secrets I suppose." The man seemed to get lost in thought and stopped talking after looking upward and holding his chin.

"Sir?" Luke called out.

"I'm sorry, I'm sorry. My name is Robert Xanders, but you can call me Rob." The man started meandering down a hallway with multiple doors on either side. He waved to Luke to follow. "Allow me to add some context. You are here to test the new Vortex Capsule. We will need to perform some minor medical examinations of you before and after each of your sessions." Luke's pace began to slow as he heard this, and Rob turned to him, palms out. "Don't worry, it's all non-invasive stuff with the occasional blood draw."

Luke winced at the mention of taking his blood.

"Sorry about that, but we need to just make sure you're healthy."

Rob continued to explain the various stages of the beta test and what Luke's responsibilities would be. Everything boiled down to Luke being medically examined and put into a virtual world. He would be expected and encouraged to play the game for a couple of hours. They would then remove him from that world and, after more medical tests, he would have to talk about his experiences. He would also fill out some customer service response forms while taking a short break between sessions. He would repeat this process a few times a week until the summer was over.

The two men reached the end of the hallway and a metal door whooshed open.

"You must be Lucas," said a woman with long red hair as she stood from her seat and approached the pair. "You can call me Doctor Judy. I run the medical research department at Vortex Industries. I'm in charge of keeping you healthy and...."

"Call him Luke," Rob interrupted. "Please get his scans done and bring him to capsule room five."

Judy's face turned red as Rob interrupted her, but she kept her calm as he left the room.

"He's a genius, but not great with social interactions. Definitely the type of kid to sit in his room building models instead of going to the school dance or kissing girls," she commented with Rob gone.

Luke shrugged and pushed his glasses up to calm his nerves. Anything to hide the fact that he, too, would skip school dances as a child to build model spaceships.

"Pushing that aside, please come in and lay on the examination table."

Luke entered the room and laid on a table that looked like a futuristic version of a table he would find at his doctor's office.

Above him, hanging from the ceiling, was a multitude of metal satellite type dishes and a variety of tools attached to curled cords. After a few moments, some of the dishes started emitting a low ringing sound, and Luke felt a low heat emanating from them.

"Don't worry," Judy reassured. "The scans are completely harmless."

About ten minutes later the machines shut off and Judy appeared to be pleased with the results that appeared on her tablet. Judy requested Luke to follow her and they moved back into the hallway following a sign reading "Capsule Rooms".

Another mechanical door whooshed open when they approached. The door had a large red five painted on it. Inside, Luke recognized the Vortex Capsule from the online video he had watched, and he noticed Rob sitting at a computer that was extending out from the side of the machine.

"Luke! I told you that would be quick." Rob turned back to his computer as he finished speaking and the capsule door opened.

Judy walked Luke to the opening and gestured him inside. Luke entered the large oval shaped device and laid on the long black bed-like cushion inside. Although the outside of the capsule was primarily white, the inside was jet black.

"Now the log-in process is painless," Judy began to explain. "There are several monitors directly above you that will display basic information for you and track your vitals. We will also be monitoring your vitals from outside." Judy handed her tablet to Rob, and he inserted it into a slot on the outside of the device. "We will link this capsule to your brain waves once you create a secure account with our system and log-in. After that, the capsule will start the sleep procedure for you."

Luke pointed to several holes he noticed on the bed. "What are these for?"

"Those are for your vital measurements, IV and blood analysis. Small needles will come out of the holes after the machine puts you to sleep. The needles will take blood and provide your body with the nutrients it needs while you are inside the capsule. The capsule also provides small electronic pulses to your various muscles to avoid any chance of developing muscle atrophy in your…"

"Enough shop talk. The kid is probably dying to see the game by now," Rob interrupted Judy again.

Judy's face turned slightly red as she leaned out of the capsule and moved to monitor one of the external screens.

"After you log-in you're going to be in… Well, I don't think I want to ruin it for you. Good luck and have fun!" The door to the capsule shut after Rob made some quick commands on the keyboard.

Without the light bleeding in through the door, the capsule was pitch dark and Luke could feel some electronic leads attach to his arms. The monitor directly above him chimed on. It had a black background with white text appearing one letter at a time.

Welcome **Lucas Patterson***.*
Please speak a character name…

Luke thought for a minute. This could be a way to reinvent himself, to be King Arthur, Dragon Slayer or something like Shadow Master. Something that sounded cooler than Lucas Patterson, but after much contemplation, he didn't think he was clever enough to think of anything better than just "Luke."

Processing…
*Character name "***Luke***" accepted.*
Please review your physical appearance before accepting.

A slowly rotating 3D representation of Luke appeared on the screen. It looked like the same six foot overweight college student he saw in the mirror every day, with short shaggy brown hair and rectangle shaped glasses. The image appeared to be an exact model of him, likely derived from the scans he underwent earlier. On the side of the model were many toggles, sliders and customization options. Luke was again hesitating to think of anything other than himself. The only slider he decided to adjust was the one for weight, deciding to make his avatar leaner than his real world body.

That was the quickest and best working diet plan I had ever taken, thought Luke as he hit the option to confirm.

Character's physical appearance confirmed.
Please wait while we initiate the log-in process.
Log-in commencing in 3... 2... 1...

Luke unwillingly shut his eyes from a sudden onset of exhaustion. When he opened his eyes, he was blinking rapidly to clear his vision from the sudden onset of light.

"Hello Traveler."

Luke rubbed his eyes and started searching for the speaker.

"Please relax. The first voyage is often the toughest."

Luke's eyes settled on an old man wearing a long red robe, being propped up by a walking stick. "Where... Where am I?" Luke asked.

"You are in a midway point between your world and mine. This is my study." The man gestured around himself.

Luke was in a small room with books lining most of the walls. There was a table, a few chairs, several candles and various writing implements spread out across the table. When he looked at himself he was wearing a simple white cotton shirt and brown cotton pants.

The jeans and t-shirt he had been wearing were gone.

Luke approached the table and ran his finger across the edge of a book's page.

"Ow!" He pulled his hand back and noticed a small cut that began bleeding. "That hurt... I mean, that actually hurt."

"Of course it hurt. Paper cuts are the worst."

The old man winced at the thought. "No, I mean, I can feel that it hurt. Am I... in the game?" Luke asked with a puzzled expression as he sucked the cut on his finger.

"Most of you travelers call this a game, but this is my world. You are as real here as you are in your world. What would happen in your world if you got a paper cut?"

The old man raised an eyebrow. Luke didn't respond but his expression made the old man feel as if he understood.

"I am here to guide you and answer any questions you may have before you fully transition. Once you are in my world, you can not return here. Are you ready to begin?"

Luke took his finger out of his mouth, checked to ensure the bleeding had stopped, and nodded. The room then melted away and was replaced by an outdoor arena, much like the gladiator arenas of ancient Rome. Sitting on the ground was a dagger, a small sword, a bow, a handful of arrows, a shield and a variety of other basic medieval style weapons.

"Arm yourself quickly," stated the old man as the door on the side of the arena slowly creaked open to reveal a wolf.

"What am I supposed to do?", Luke asked frantically. "I thought I made it obvious with, *'arm yourself quickly'*."

Luke dove for the pile of weapons as he noticed the oversized grin on the old man's face. The wolf let out an ear shattering howl.

Wolf Howl. *Weakened debuff added.*

A floating semi-transparent message box appeared in Luke's vision as he struggled to cover his ears. Luke attempted to click the message's "OK" button, but his hand went through the floating message box.

"You can either focus your vision on the button to confirm it or you can mentally 'click it.' Imagine hitting the button with your mind."

Luke focused on the button and imagined pressing it. As soon as he could focus his thought on hitting it, the button clicked in and the message box disappeared.

"You may want to grab that weapon now. The wolf looks like he's starving."

Luke looked up to see the wolf slowly advancing toward him while bearing his teeth. *He's still far away, I should grab something with the appropriate range to take advantage of the distance.* He grabbed the small bow on the ground and a pair of arrows. His gaze went back to the wolf while he slotted an arrow into the bow. He pulled the string back and released the arrow when he thought he had the best shot at hitting his target.

The snarling wolf appeared ready to dodge or pounce, foam dripping from sharp fangs, and eyes locked on the arrow as Luke released. The arrow traveled about five feet before harmlessly gliding to the ground like a paper airplane. The wolf gazing briefly at it before returning its focus to Luke.

Luke heard the old man laughing as he gritted his teeth and readied another arrow. This time he pulled the string as hard as he could and waited for the approaching wolf to get closer. Again, he released the arrow and, to the surprise of everyone, the arrow struck its desired target in its side. The wolf let out a low whimper when the arrow made contact, and Luke smiled.

*New skill acquired: **Short Bow**, Beginner 0. Basic knowledge on how to use a short bow. Increasing this skill will increase the damage dealt with a short bow. This is a passive skill and requires no activation. Effect: Adds 1+x% short bow damage where x = skill level.*

Congratulations, you have earned your first skill. Skills, spells, and abilities can be used to aid you in your travels. There are both combat and non-combat skills. Skills will level up as you use them from level 0 to 9. Once a skill reaches level 9 and levels up, it will increase in rank. Currently there are five ranks: Beginner, Intermediate, Advanced, Master and Grand Master.
Note: This is a one time system message.

The new pop-up messages distracted Luke long enough for the wolf to close the distance between them and sink its teeth into his leg.

"Ahh!" he screamed as he was pulled to the ground. Panicking, he grabbed the nearest object he could find and jammed it into the skull of the wolf.

Critical Hit!
Attacking weak spots on enemies will result in a Critical Hit. Critical Hits do increased damage.

Small Forest Wolf *x1 defeated. 50 exp gained.*

"This hurts! I mean really hurts!" Luke was screaming and clutching his bleeding leg.

"Of course it hurts, you were bitten by a wolf. I thought we went over the pain thing?" The old man approached and lifted his walking stick. The stick glowed a subtle white and another pop-up box appeared in Luke's vision.

*Old Man cast **Cure Light Wounds** on you, 100 HP restored.*

"I thought the pain would be dulled or something. I haven't been bitten by a wolf before, but I imagine this is what it would feel like," Luke spat out as he rubbed his leg.

Looking up, he noticed three small semi-transparent bars in the upper left of his vision. The bars were red, blue, and green. He also noticed a small square box under them with an icon of a feeble looking man and a number one. When he focused his vision on the box, a small description of the icon came up.

***Weakened**, 1 stack. You have been weakened and will take 10% additional damage until the status debuff expires. Expires in 6… 5…"*

This debuff could stack? What would happen if a whole wolf pack attacked me and they were all howling? Luke worried to himself as he stood and faced the old man.

"Not the worst I've seen but certainly nowhere near the best. At least you chose a ranged weapon when the wolf was still far away. Shows that you aren't totally useless."

*New title gained: **Not totally useless**. This title gives you +1 agility.*

Congratulations, you have earned your first title. While you can gain as many titles as you wish, you can only have one title equipped at a time and you will only receive benefits from your equipped titled. Note: This is a one time system message.

Luke pushed up his glasses and cleared away all the system messages. "Is there a way for me to check my character? What is agility good for?"

"You simply need to think of your character and your sheet will appear. Since this is your first time looking at it, I will provide some additional details. If you want to see additional information in the future, just focus on a particular section of your sheet and it will reappear." The old man waved his hand indicating Luke should give it a try.

As Luke thought of himself and his character, a large pair of transparent windows appeared. The left showed an outline of a human with small boxes on most of the various body parts, with labels for where various pieces of equipment could be placed, a list of his attributes, and his current status. The right box showed a list of his skills.

Name: *Not totally useless Luke.*
Class: *Beginner (+3 attribute points per level & +1 skill point per level)*
Primary Profession: *None*
Level 1: *Exp :50 Exp to next level: 950 (calculated at 1,000 x current level)*
Hit Points: *50/50 (50 base + 10 per point in Constitution)*
Mana: *50/50 (50 base + 10 per point in Intelligence)*
Mana Regen: *1/sec (.25 per point in Wisdom)*
Stamina: *35/60 (50 + 10 per point in Agility)(Stamina regenerates 5% of max per second while out of combat and 1% of max per second while in combat)*

Attributes Base (Modifier)

Strength: 1

Modifies damage done by melee weapons, strength based skills, your carrying capacity, and the ability to use heavy armor effectively.

Agility: 1 (+1)

Modifies max stamina, damage done by ranged weapons, agility based skills, stealth, travel speed, and the ability to use medium armor effectively.

Intelligence: 1

Modifies max mana, damage done by spells, and spell learning speed.

Wisdom: 1

Modifies mana regeneration and skill learning speed.

Constitution: 1

Modifies max hit points and resistances.

Social: 1

Modifies social abilities and rate of reputation gain.

Luck: 1

Modifies your luck and chance of finding rare or hidden items.

Skills, Spells and Abilities

Short Bow (Beginner 0): *Basic knowledge on how to use a short bow. Increasing this skill will increase the damage dealt with a short bow. This is a passive skill and requires no activation. Effect: Adds $1+x\%$ short bow damage where x = skill level.*

According to the left screen, he was only equipped with a basic shirt and basic pants, offering him no armor value. Luke closed all the windows and faced the old man.

The old man waved his staff around and the arena melted away, being replaced by the old man's study. "Did you enjoy using a bow? Is that how you want to proceed in this world?"

Luke thought hard. On one hand, he rarely played an archer in games but on the other hand, if it meant he could avoid getting bit by wolves, he was in. Luke nodded and a bow with a quiver appeared on the desk. Luke reached out and grabbed the bow. A pop-up of information appeared.

Basic Short Bow (Common). Adds 2-3 blunt damage when used as a melee weapon.

Basic Quiver of Arrows (Common), quantity 25. Adds 2-5 piercing damage when shot from a bow.

"Hmm... I think I will throw you a bone. To be honest, I think you need it," the old man gestured with his free hand.

Quest alert! **New born baby:** *Learn the basics of using a bow. Hit a target 10 times. Reward: Learning should be its own reward, but here is some experience. Exp: 150. Accept / Decline.*

Congratulations, you have earned your first quest. Quests are offers to perform a specific task or set of tasks for a reward. Rewards can be monetary or otherwise.
Note: This is a one time system message.

"Thank you. So, what's next?" Luke looked eagerly at the old man as he accepted the quest he offered him.

"Next you enter my world. Welcome to Endless Fantasy Online."

Luke's vision went dark for a moment until large letters spelling out "Endless Fantasy Online" came into view. A few moments later his vision blurred, and he was in the middle of a city square.

Disoriented he stumbled a bit, knocking over some stacked barrels of hay.

"Hey! Watch where you're walking, kid." A man who, based on his clothing and pitchfork, appeared to be a farmer picked up the hay and threw it in the back of a wagon. Looking around Luke saw a massive medieval city, castle and all. He could feel the cold breeze on his exposed arms, smell a nearby bakery's bread being baked, and hear the flies buzzing around the farmer's wagon.

Pushing up his glasses, he made a firm declaration. *This game is amazing! This really is the future and I can't wait to explore this world!*

CHAPTER TWO

Baby Steps

The Vortex Capsule was powering down as the capsule door opened and light flooded inside. Looking out of the capsule Luke saw Rob and Judy looking expectantly at him.

"It was amazing! It was so lifelike. Maybe sometimes too lifelike…" Luke rubbed his leg where the virtual wolf had bitten him. There was no mark, scar, or wound, but his mind could have sworn there was supposed to be one.

Judy pulled a tablet out of the capsule and began reviewing data. "Your medical output looks great. No lingering effects and…"

"And how was the game? I take pride in my programming. Was the wolf real enough or should I add more foam in their mouths?" Rob quickly interrupted Judy.

"The wolf was plenty real, trust me. I can see why you kept this game under wraps. A breakthrough like this would disrupt the gaming industry. It would probably disrupt all entertainment industries." Luke was speaking fast, stumbling over himself in excitement.

Rob smiled from ear to ear and nodded his thanks.

"Honestly, I just want to know how soon I can go back in?"

Rob's tablet, much like the one Judy stored Luke's vitals on, came out of sleep mode and started beeping. There were warnings and messages filling the tablet's surface. "Hmm... I'm sorry, there's something I have to tend to. If he clears his scans, Judy, let him back in if he wants, but I want a full write up of what happens to him."

"Can't you just monitor me? I mean, you knew about the wolf." It confused Luke. Why did he have to write a report about what he experienced when it appeared they were watching everything?

"We can see what's going on, but that's different from experiencing it firsthand. We can't feel what you feel, smell what you smell or taste what you taste. We aren't gods of the world. Think of us as silent observers. With players actively connected, we can't modify the world or we would run the risk of modifying your brain waves. That's not something the top brass would even let me think about doing so the system is on full lock when even a single player is logged in. It's a safety..." The beeping coming from Rob's tablet increased in volume and frequency. He glanced at it briefly before abruptly leaving the room.

Judy and Luke shrugged and Judy began performing the necessary scans of Luke. Once all her scans came back showing no negative effects, Luke visited a bathroom and then quickly reentered his pod.

He felt the same medical devices attach to him and the monitors turned on. Sleep quickly took him as he read the system message and slightly cringed at his name.

*Welcome **Not totally useless Luke**.*
Preparations complete.
Log-in commencing in 3... 2... 1...

In a few moments Luke was standing back in the medieval city square where he had logged out just a few minutes ago. The farmer's cart was gone and there seemed to be a lot of foot traffic.

Ok. I have a bow, arrows, and a quest to learn how to use them. Looks like I have a plan. I should look for a barracks or some monsters to fight.

Luke walked around for a bit until he found a man who appeared to be a city guard. He was wearing heavy plate armor, holding a spear, and his chest plate had a phoenix crest on it. Luke recognized the crest from all the flags around the city.

"Excuse me. Do you know where I can find a barracks?" Luke asked politely.

The man turned around and inspected Luke thoroughly.

"A barracks? What do you want with the barracks?" The man's voice was rough and aged.

"I'm looking to get some training with my bow. I'm new around here. Aren't you supposed to guide me or something?"

The guard burst out laughing. "Guide you? Why should I waste my time on you?"

Luke was down right puzzled. *Isn't this a game?* he thought. *Non-player characters are supposed to guide the real players. That's always how it's been.*

Luke waited for the guard to stop laughing before he responded. "I'm a..." He paused for a minute to remember what the old man called him. "I'm a traveler."

"I don't care what you are. I'm on duty and you're bothering me." The guard's response was curt.

Luke pushed up his glasses and lowered his ever-reddening face.

"Leave him alone. He's clearly new you blockhead." Luke raised his head to find a man, not much older than himself, wearing mismatching leather armor. He was taller than Luke and sported a buzz cut. "The name's Thomas." He extended his hand toward Luke for a handshake and Luke detected a hint of a southern accent.

The two exchanged pleasantries, and the guard went on his way, happy to have the new traveler off his hands.

"Aren't guards and NPCs supposed to help us? This is still a game isn't it?" Luke asked.

"As you probably know, this game is different from anything you've played before. The NPCs have real personalities, history, feelings, thoughts, dreams, and aspirations. They feel as real as you or I and respond the same way," Thomas explained.

"How is that possible? I know games have come a long way, but that seems a little too far-fetched to be real?"

"I asked Rob once, and he said because they are real. He said the Alpha test of this program involved scanning the minds and personalities of thousands of people and imprinting them on the NPCs. It was a way to both test their hardware and improve on the realism of the Beta."

Luke pondered the ramifications and possibilities of that but his head began to hurt.

"I think I can feel a headache coming on. Would have been nice if they left that guy out of the programming." Thomas laughed and Luke continued. "Do you mind showing me to the barracks?"

Thomas nodded and began walking down the street. He was kind enough to point out some important places in the city such as the inn, general goods store, the bank, and a couple specialty stores before they reached their destination.

"Here we are, the barracks." Thomas pointed to a tall stone building nearby.

The barracks was located toward the city's primary gate and was impressively more crowded than the town square. A hundred or more people were traveling in and out of the gate at any given moment. Some looked like adventurers, while others seemed to be farmers and workers.

New friend request: **Thomas, the bunny killer** *would like to be your friend. Accept / Decline.*

"The bunny killer?" Luke snickered.

"Not totally useless?" Thomas snickered back.

The two of them laughed before Luke accepted the friend request and he and Tom parted ways. Luke continued into the barracks looking for someone who could help him or someone in charge. It didn't take long for him to find a group of guards and someone barking orders at them.

"You maggots! I want you all running double duty. You three on the wall, and you two relieve the men at the gate and the rest of you train. You look like a bunch of worthless, inbred maggots!" The leader was wearing a more intricate set of armor and had a long rapier tucked into his belt.

"YES CAPTAIN HOLTZ!" The men shouted in unison as they ran to their assignments.

Note to self, don't get on this guy's bad side. "Excuse me… Sir?" The man turned on his heel to face Luke. "I'm looking for some… bow training… Can you help?" Luke pushed his glasses up to calm his nerves.

The man opened his arms wide and addressed the new traveler. "Welcome to the City Barracks my boy!" Luke's gaze turned to one of utter confusion. The man chuckled before continuing. "Don't worry, I don't bite. My name is Captain Holtz and I'm here to help."

"I'm sorry… I saw you with your guards a minute ago and…"

"I have to give them a hard time or they won't shape up." He inspected Luke up and down, much the same way the previous guard did. "If I were a betting man, I would say you're a new traveler?" Luke nodded. "I've dealt with a lot of you as of late and have taken a liking to your lot. Most of you travelers take on a lot of tasks that free up the guards to train and stop crime. Thanks to you travelers our crime rates are the lowest they have ever been."

That would make sense. New players would want to go on lots of quests to gain experience and to loot, thought Luke as he introduced himself to the guard captain.

"Bow training you say?" Captain Holtz pointed to an archery range on the other side of the barracks. "You're welcome to use the various targets there. If you manage to hit a bullseye, I'll even grant you a reward."

Quest alert! **Hitting a bullseye:** *Captain Holtz wants you to hit a bullseye and prove you're a marksman. Reward: Variable. Exp: 100. Accept / Decline*

Luke thanked the captain and moved toward the range. When he got there, he watched the other archers practice for a while, trying to pick up on their techniques. He noticed a lot of them, to his surprise, kept both their eyes open and on their target. When Luke was fighting the wolf, he closed an eye thinking it would be the best way to aim.

After a few minutes, he found an open target and decided to test his skills. Pulling an arrow from his quiver he loaded it on his bow, pulled back, kept both eyes on his target, and released. His shot went wide by a foot or so, clanking on the stone wall behind the target, but he was still happy with the result. The target was much farther away than the wolf was and being so close on the first try made him smile.

He repeated the process and released another arrow.

Quest alert! **New born baby:** *1/10*

Luke grinned and reached for another arrow. He continued this activity until he shot his last arrow, only stopping occasionally to allow his stamina to regenerate.

Quest alert! **New born baby:** *9/10*
Skill up: **Short Bow**, *Beginner 1.*

"My skill leveled up already?" Luke muttered to himself.

"Of course your skill leveled up. You've been at this for a while." Captain Holtz approached.

"Beginner one already." He seemed pleased with Luke's progress. "That means you have a while to go, boy. Why don't you collect your arrows and I'll give you some pointers?"

Luke ran and collected his arrows before returning to the captain and dropped them on the ground near his feet. He grabbed one and got ready to take aim.

"You have a lot of the basics down, but you need to raise your pulling arm up more so it's level with your face. Then rest the bow string against your cheek to better anchor yourself. Keep your eyes on your target, breath in, and release when you let your breathe out."

Luke did everything the Captain suggested and his arrow hit the inside edge of the bullseye.

Quest alert! **New born baby:** *10/10. Quest complete! Reward: 150 exp.*

Quest alert! **Hitting a bullseye:** *1/1. Quest complete! Reward:* **Tattered leather Gloves** *(common). Adds +2 to physical resistance.*

Captain Holtz screamed with excitement as he gave Luke a few hearty pats on the back. The captain hit him hard enough that he lost a few hit points and staggered forward. After recovering, they both laughed together.

SYSTEM ALERT!
SYSTEM ALERT!
ALL TRAVELERS PLEASE REPORT TO THE CASTLE.
I REPEAT, ALL TRAVELERS PLEASE REPORT TO THE
CASTLE.

Luke tried clearing the message but every time he closed it, it just reappeared. While he was reviewing the system message, a messenger ran up to Captain Holtz and handed him a scroll sealed with the wax stamp of a phoenix. The captain broke the seal and a look of fear crossed his face.

"Luke. I need to get to the castle immediately." The captain's stern and less friendly voice had returned. Luke was getting worried.

"I just received an alert to go to the castle too. Do you mind showing me the way?"

The pair of men ran as quickly as they could down the city streets toward a towering castle. When they arrived, the captain told Luke to wait out front with the other travelers as he went past the line of guards toward the entrance.

Luke, confused about what to do, started listening to the surrounding conversations.

Someone said, "they killed the king?"

"I heard travelers did it."

"I don't think a traveler could get past the guards and kill the king, could they?"

Citizens started arriving and an ever-growing crowd was now forming. After a few minutes, Captain Holtz reappeared and addressed the crowd.

"Hello Citizens. I have some dire news to break to you and the travelers. I don't have all the information yet, but it appears that King Henry passed away a few moments ago."

The crowd broke out in shouting, fear, and panic. Captain Holtz gave a subtle nod to the guards, and in unison they began to clang their spears against their shields. The loud clanging cut through the noise of the crowd and they began to simmer down.

"I have more news to share with you." He paused to collect himself. "The queen and princess are also missing."

The statement shattered any semblance of order Captain Holtz regained. He repeated the process with the guards to capture the crowd's attention, taking much longer to silence them a second time.

"People! People! Please let me get through my announcements. I'm offering an open quest to anyone willing to accept it. Find and return the queen and princess and we will reward you han..."

Captain Holtz froze mid-sentence, and the world seemed to freeze around him, draining of all color. The travelers were the only ones who maintained their color and movement. A semi-transparent Rob appeared next to the captain and began to address them all.

"Everyone, I have some unfortunate news to share with you." The travelers all looked puzzled, but Rob was able to grab their attention. "There seems to have been a sophisticated attack on our servers. It appears that a hacker group managed to turn off certain safety protocols and procedures using a very sophisticated virus."

"What safety protocols and procedures?" questioned a random traveler that Luke didn't recognize.

"Well... primarily the ones allowing you to... well... log out..."

The travelers looked around at each other, unsure of how to process the information. After a few moments of no one replying, Rob continued.

"Basically, they locked all of your consciousness into Endless Fantasy Online. In other words, we can't log any of you out..."

Luke noticed multiple travelers looking at system screens that he couldn't see. He opened his own system menu by thinking 'settings' and a new system box came up with a variety of options, including one labeled "Log Out". He tried to mentally click it and was only awarded with a system message.

SYSTEM ERROR!!! Some functions are currently unavailable.

Maybe I thought the wrong thing or didn't mentally click it hard enough, Luke thought as he mentally hit the button again.

SYSTEM ERROR!!! Some functions are currently unavailable.

Panic then descended upon the crowd of travelers. Everyone started screaming at once, and several tried charging Rob, but they couldn't move their feet.

"People, please stay calm."

"Stay calm?! You've locked us into a game! My wife is expecting me home tonight!" screamed one of the travelers that was attempting to charge the scientist.

"I understand, I understand. This isn't ideal."

"Ideal? Unlock my feet and I'll show you what's ideal!" shouted another traveler.

"I don't have long to address you. Freezing the world and manipulating the code like this is extremely dangerous for all of you who are currently logged in. We have moved the game's code to a localized server and cut it off from the outside, so whoever is behind this can't do anything else. We have a staff of hundreds working on this and are doing everything…"

"I'm going to murder you and sue Vortex Industries for everything they have. I'm going to own you when this is done!" an angry woman wearing a robe and holding a staff shouted.

Another figure of a man, this one wearing what appeared to be an expensive suit, then materialized next to Rob.

"Hello everyone. I am the corporate attorney for Vortex Industries. I was hoping you would all handle this better, but I'm here to remind you that you all signed extensive legal documents before joining our beta program. In those documents are clauses that give up your rights to any legal action in the event of something like this happening. Vortex Industries will still pay you and we'll take care of your health needs while we work out this issue."

The travelers got louder and louder with shouting and cursing before the attorney spoke again.

"As Rob explained, it is dangerous for us to interact with you like this. For now, we will give you time to absorb this information and contact you again as soon as we deem it safe to do so." With that, the attorney vanished and Rob began to fade. As he faded, the world began to return to color. Luke could see him mouth the words "I'm so sorry."

As the world regained motion and color, Captain Holtz began speaking again, but Luke didn't wait for Captain Holtz to finish his speech. Once the bomb was dropped on the travelers they just added to the chaos and he feared violence would break out. He needed to get out of there. The only issue was that he wasn't sure where to go or what to do next. He wasn't even sure how to feel about the whole situation. He may be on summer break, but he still had his mom to worry about. *They would have to call and tell her about it right? They would have to tell her.* Luke was lost in thought so he didn't notice the older woman until he bumped into her and her papers spilled all over the ground.

"I'm sorry."

The woman looked frustrated but started picking up the fallen papers and he immediately started to help. He reviewed the documents as he collected them and they all appeared to be various wanted posters and quest fliers.

Luke handed over his stack of papers. "What are these?"

"These are for the job board. Anyone can take them and complete them for rewards. Are you interested?"

Luke pondered. *Well, for now I could use a good distraction.* "Sure."

The woman got up and walked with Luke to the main city gate where she began sticking the fliers up on a large wooden board.

It's my college job board all over again. This is what got me into this mess. Reviewing the fliers Luke wasn't sure how to proceed. There were quests for gathering materials outside of town, finding a lost cat, killing a desired amount of a desired monster, and more. "Am I allowed to take more than one?" he inquired.

"Of course you are. The more you want to help, the better. Please keep in mind that you need to complete the request in the desired time limit or you will face the penalty listed," the woman hanging fliers responded in her best customer service voice.

Luke took another look at the requests and finally settled on two. He reached out and pulled them from the board.

Quest alert! **Herbs, herbs, herbs!:** *Gather enough medicinal herbs to make a few healing potions for the local alchemist. The alchemist wants as many herbs as she can get her hands on. Because of her high demand, there is no time limit or penalty. Herbs 0/25. Reward: 5 gold and added reputation with the local alchemist. Exp 50. Quest accepted.*

Quest alert! **Controlling the fox population I:** *The city guards want help controlling the fox population. Eliminate 10 foxes within a week. Failing to complete this quest on time will result in a loss of reputation with the city guard. Reward: 5 gold and added reputation with the city guard. Exp 150. Quest accepted.*

Coral blue flames gathered at the edges of the fliers after the system messages appeared. He flinched and dropped the papers but they burned away and vanished before touching the ground.

The woman covered her mouth in a failing attempt to hide her giggling. "The flame doesn't hurt. It just stops anyone else from taking your quest. For common quests like those we post several a day, but the magical protection system comes in handy for unique quests."

Luke nodded and made a mental note to be careful around this board. It appears that pulling a flier off the wall automatically accepts the quest and starts a fire in his hand. He thanked the women for her help and started toward the town gate.

When he arrived, he greeted the two guards with a wave and proceeded outside.

"Wait!" shouted one of the two guards. "I don't recognize you. So I'll give you the same warning that I give everyone. Be careful outside, and we lock the gates come nightfall. Once the gates are locked they won't be opened again until first light."

"Should I get some camping gear?"

"You don't want to be out there at night. Someone as low level as you won't survive the night out there." the guard cautioned.

Luke thanked the guards, checked his arrow count and headed out. The contrast in environment immediately surprised him. The dark stone town had such a lack of nature compared to outside the gates. The biggest difference he noticed was the change in smell. The city didn't have a bad smell *per se* but the air outside was leaps and bounds better.

Looking around, there appeared to be primarily farmland surrounding the city walls and a handful of barns. There was a packed dirt path heading out of the gate that opened up to be wide enough to fit several wagons side by side. The land was flat and Luke could see a large forest in the distance.

"I should probably head to the forest if I'm looking for herbs" he said aloud as his feet took him in that direction. As he walked, he noticed the road had paths coming off it for each of the farms and several roads leading off in various directions. He also found it odd that none of the farms appeared to have houses. Did all the farmers go into the city to sleep at night?

The road got less and less compact as he got to the forest and became more of a mud path, so Luke walked on the grass next to the road. When he got 20 feet away from the forest, a wooden post with a sign was sticking out of the side of the road. The sign read *"The Howling Forest."*

Luke pushed up his glasses and an involuntary shiver came over his body, a body now covered in goosebumps. *Howling probably means wolves,* was the only thing going through his mind. He looked up and saw that the sun was only reaching its mid-point and it hadn't taken long to get here. He should have most of the afternoon to explore before having to head back.

An issue popped into Luke's mind: he has no idea what a medicinal herb looks like! He bent down and looked at the nearest cluster of leaves, and a system message popped up.

Identification failed. **Herbalism** *skill not high enough.*

He plucked the leaves anyway and pocketed them. He continued to pluck all the various plants he could find as he continued deeper into the forest. His progress into the forest was slow because he stopped for every plant he could find, but he continued this until a new system message appeared.

New skill acquired: **Herbalism***, Beginner 0. This skill allows you to identify various plant life. At higher levels, this skill will allow you to highlight various herbs in the wild for easier collection.*

Quest alert! **Herbs, herbs, herbs!***: 8/25*

Emptying his pockets on the floor he gave all the plants another deep look.

Identification successful. **Basic herb** *(common). Used in crafting weak healing potions.*
Identification successful. **Dandelion** *(common). A common yellow flower.*

Identification failed on the other handful of plants, so he discarded them to make room for herbs in his small pockets. Looking for herbs went quicker now that Luke knew what he was looking for, so he continued deeper into the forest.

Luke's stomach began to rumble, which surprised him. *How am*

I hungry? I'm still in a game and this body is just 1's and 0's inside a computer... He resolved to head back to the city and get some food. Besides, the sun was setting and he wouldn't have much more time to explore anyway. On the way out of the woods he grabbed as many basic herbs as he could find. In the end, he had over twenty and as an added bonus, his herbalism skill leveled up.

He continued to walk in the shadowed forest, watching the light come in between the leafy tops of trees and just taking everything in. There were worse places he could be stuck right now, he thought as he contemplated his current position in life. He was startled out of his thoughts by five bunnies running under his feet and out of the woods.

Target practice. Luke pulled an arrow from his quiver, grabbed his bow and took aim. Following the tips Captain Holtz gave him he anchored himself, took in a breath, and while letting his breath out, he released.

Forest Bunny *x1 defeated. 10 exp gained.*

Yes! A huge grin crossed Luke's face as he stood up to collect his arrow. A sharp pain suddenly shot up his leg. He let out a loud grunt while grinding his teeth and looking down. There was a fox attached to his right ankle, and several more headed his way. He panicked and started bashing the fox with the end of his bow.

He gazed to his upper left and watched as his health was slowly being depleted. He was missing at least 10%. In the bottom left of his view he noticed a combat log that made him panic more.

*You surprise attack a **Forest Bunny** for 10 points of damage (5 * 2 surprise).*
Forest Bunny *is defeated.*

*A **Fox** bites you for 6 points of damage.*
*A **Fox** has lodged itself on you. You will continue to take damage*
until it is dislodged.
*You hit a **Fox** for 2 points of damage.*
*You hit a **Fox** for 1 point of damage.*

Luke went to hit the fox again, but another fox lunged at him and began to claw at his chest. His health was now down to 60% and there was still another fox headed his way. Reacting too slowly, he grabbed the tail of the fox on his chest and tossed him away. The fox didn't appear to take any damage and was quickly back on his feet.

The fox went back on the offense, leaving no room for Luke to recover. He raised his bow to guard against the lunging fox, but the third fox took that opportunity to attack Luke's back. Luke let out another scream of pain and involuntarily dropped his guard. Luke looked forward, knowing a fox was descending upon him.

"Ahhhh!" A large blade, double the size of most swords Luke previously saw in video games, struck down the fox and split it in two. The figure holding the large blade swung around and used his momentum to drive his sword down into the body of the fox clamping onto Luke's ankle. "Lay down! Now!" He screamed at Luke at the top of his lungs.

Luke immediately complied and fell flat on his stomach. The fox on his back was still scratching furiously but looked up to hiss at the newcomer to the battle. The man took a baseball-like swing at the Fox, slicing it apart.

Fox x3 defeated. Partial exp rewarded for partial participation with a
non-party member. 25 exp gained.

Quest alert! **Controlling the fox population I:** *3/10.*

You are **Bleeding**. *Bleeding debuff added. You will continue to take damage until you are healed or the bleeding stops naturally.*

Luke looked at his health and he was below half. Every few seconds he saw that his health was reduced by a small amount and that the small square icon below his health, showing a blood drop, would blink.

"You're new and you decided to go into the Howling Forest alone? That's either really brave or really stupid." The man reached a hand down and offered to help Luke up. He took the man's hand and when he was on his feet, he recognized him instantly.

"Thomas? How did you know I was out here?"

Shaking his head, Thomas replied. "I didn't. I was out here doing some quests and heard someone screaming. I guess it was your lucky day."

Luke nodded and winced when the bleeding debuff hit him for another point or two of damage. Thomas pulled something from a small satchel at his waist and handed it to Luke.

Small Bandage *(Common) x3 obtained.*

"Wrap one of those around your ankle to stop the bleeding. You will fail the first few times but it will eventually work and you should gain the first aid skill."

Luke nodded and wrapped the first bandage around his ankle as tight as he could and looked at his work. The bandage quickly became a deep red, and it slipped down his foot, not taking hold. He repeated the process two more times, and on the third attempt he was rewarded with a system message.

*New skill acquired: **First Aid**, Beginner 0. Basic knowledge on how to apply basic first aid and use basic bandages. Increasing this skill will increase your knowledge of first aid techniques and increase the speed at which you can apply this skill.*

"I got the skill. Thanks." Luke pushed his glasses up and glanced at the status bars to confirm the bleeding icon had disappeared.

"No problem. I was new once also, so I get it. Consider it southern hospitality."

"I don't see my health going up now though. My stamina is going up, but my health seems to be sitting around 20%." Luke was gazing at his system screens.

"Your health regens at an insanely slow pace. Imagine if a fox bit you like that in real life. You wouldn't magically have your wounds close up and your blood replenish would you? This game is a lot like real life when it comes to these types of things. I would toss you a healing potion, but they aren't cheap and I'm not rich. Everything involving magic in this game is expensive, and healing potions take mana to craft."

"You have done plenty. Thank you." Luke hesitated before continuing. "You wouldn't want to group up, would you? At least until we head back for the day?"

Thomas considered Luke's proposal for a long moment and finally responded. "Ok, but only till we get back. No offense but I'm still much higher level than you and the monsters I'm going to be fighting aren't as friendly as these foxes were. Understand?"

Luke nodded and smiled.

Thomas, the bunny killer *has invited you to join his party. Accept / Decline*

Luke hit accept and under his status bars appeared three new status bars. They were smaller than his own and the label at the top of them read Thomas, the bunny killer Lv 5. *It looks like I can see my other party member's status and level when we party up*, he thought as the two continued around the outskirts of the forest looking for enemies to fight.

"Are we looking for anything in particular?" Luke asked while keeping an eye out for herbs or threats.

"I have several quests for a variety of monsters, but with you in your current condition, we'll stick to the foxes. They are still easy prey for me and you can provide some ranged support." Thomas pointed to Luke's bow. "One thing I would highly recommend is delaying your system notifications. If you open your settings, you can set them to build up until either the end of the day or when you choose to see them. It helps not to have large boxes pop-up in your face during a fight. Just trust me on this."

Luke opened his settings and found the area for notifications. He modified them per Thomas's suggestion, closed his menu, and nodded.

"Now let's get some experience and head back before they shut the gates."

CHAPTER THREE

Magic Affinity

The sun was finishing its descent when the pair made it back to town. The guards were making preparations to close the city gates, ushering in the latecomers, and screaming their warnings to NPCs and travelers alike.

Upon entering the city, Luke said his goodbyes and thanks to Thomas. The two of them had killed enough foxes and gathered enough herbs to complete both of Luke's Quests. With that in mind, Luke decided to check his built up system notifications. Luke mentally clicked the blinking icon in his view to pull them up.

Fox x13 defeated. 195 party participation exp gained.
Bunny x4 defeated. 40 party participation exp gained.
Skill up: Short Bow, Beginner 2.
Skill up: Herbalism, Beginner 3.
Quest alert! Controlling the fox population I: 10/10. Quest complete! Rewards: 150 exp. Turn this quest in to the quest giver for any additional rewards.

Quest alert! **Herbs, herbs, herbs!:** *25/25. Quest complete! Rewards delayed until you speak with the quest giver.*
Additional battle notifications are available. Would you like to review? Yes / No

Luke decided against reviewing all the additional battle information, he didn't want a reminder of how much Thomas did and how little he could contribute. Luke landed a few lucky shots during their time together but Thomas did all the heavy lifting. It was clear he had a long way to go before being at Thomas's level.

Luke approached one of the gate guards to turn in his fox quest and the guard instantly had a look of shock and worry on his face.

"Is everything ok?" Luke asked.

"I was about to ask you that question." The guard pointed at Luke's chest, so Luke looked down to review himself.

His shirt was in tatters and he could see scratch marks covering his chest. Looking up at his health, he was only around 25%. *Man, you really heal slow in this game. I hope these scratch marks go away when I heal up,* he thought as he continued down to see that his pant leg was also ripped to shreds.

"I… was hunting foxes for a quest?" Luke said in a questioning tone, hoping that would help explain his current attire.

"Yes, the fox population quest. I see you have completed all the requirements for payment." The guard reached into his satchel and handed over a handful of coins.

The coins resembled an olden days quarter, before the world switched to a fully digital currency system. Luke recognized the appearance from his grandfather's antique coin collection. The only difference is that one side had a phoenix crest on it and the other had a large number one and smaller writing going around the coin's edge in a language he didn't recognize.

"If you don't mind me asking, what's the writing around the outside of the coin?"

"That's magical writing. It's on all Phoenix Kingdom currency. It's imbued with special royal mana that ensures that the coins are valid. Anyone trying to replicate that writing without royal mana would have their mana and HP drained until they… well…" The guards shifted uncomfortably. "Let's say they wouldn't get a second attempt at duplicating it."

Luke nodded, thanked the guard and was on his way after stuffing the coins in the pocket that had less wear and tear.

The alchemist would be his next stop if the shop was still open. Luke's stomach suddenly growled loudly. Luke looked at his stomach as he began to rub it. *I guess food first. Did my digital body even need to eat?* As if the system heard him, he received a system message.

*You are **hungry** and **thirsty**. Hungry debuff added. Thirsty debuff added. You will take a small penalty to your stats and actions until you satisfy your hunger and thirst. This penalty will increase the hungrier and thirstier you get. Warning, this debuff can kill you if not removed.*

Red icons resembling a glass of water and meat on a bone appeared in Luke's status area. Both had a roman numeral one on them, signifying they would increase in intensity if Luke didn't find something to eat and drink soon. *Well, the Alchemy shop is probably closed by now anyway. I might as well go to the inn Thomas showed me and get some grub and sleep.*

After a short walk, Luke was in front of a three-story stone building. Even without the sign in front, reading *The Winged Pig*

Inn, it would be clear to him that this was the inn. Not only was there a massive chimney with plumes of smoke coming from it, this building was one of the few that still had light pouring out of all the windows on the first floor. It was also the rowdiest of all the buildings with several stumbling patrons spilling from its large double doors.

The moment he entered the inn, it assaulted his senses. The large open room, with many thick wooden pillars, was well-lit with hanging chandeliers. It was so loud that Luke could hardly hear himself think. Several people in the room were passed out and more than one pissed themselves drunk. A long counter covered most of the back wall with a large fireplace covering the remainder. Luke could see the kitchen behind the fireplace. The fireplace was likely being used to not only light and heat the space but also to cook food. Staircases donned the other two walls, and the floor was covered in round tables and chairs.

Not knowing anyone he sat at the bar as there were still a few empty stools next to one another and, being a shy person, he didn't want to socialize with strangers. Pushing up his glasses, he weakly raised a hand in an attempt to gain the bartender's attention.

A very tall, muscular, dark-skinned man wearing thick tan colored pants and an apron walked over. He was bald but had a thin grey beard. "What can I get ya kid?"

"How much would a room and some food run me?"

"One night in a basic room will run you 2 gold. It'll be more if you want some extra comforts. I could run you a deal if you rent for multiple nights but I require payment upfront. Food and drink varies depending on what'cha want." The man had a friendly but stern voice which helped put Luke at ease.

"I'll take a basic room please and whatever a gold or two in food is." *I should save a gold or two to buy some new clothes and some healing items,* he thought as he put three gold on the table.

The man behind the counter scooped the gold up and walked away. Luke didn't have to wait long for the man to return with a tray. He placed the tray down on the counter in front of Luke and walked away. The tray had what appeared to be a buttered loaf of sourdough bread, a tall glass containing a dark liquid and a copper key with the numbers 2 - 5 carved on it. Luke assumed that meant the second floor, room five but was too shy to call the man back for clarification.

He didn't care too much for the noise or smell, so he took the tray to his room. He chose one of the staircases and ascended to the second floor. Doors lined both sides of the hallway, barely spaced apart and behind him was another staircase leading up to the final floor. Exploring the hallway, he found room number five and his key opened the door.

Inside the small room was just enough space to fit what he assumed was his bed. The bed was comprised of a wood rectangle nailed to the floor creating a roughly 3ft wide by 6ft long space that was filled with hay and a blanket loosely thrown over it. The blanket was on its last leg as it had more patched areas than the original material and there was no stuffing left inside it.

The bed was against the back wall underneath the only window in the room. The bed was only about a foot from the door, just enough space to allow the door to swing inward. There wasn't enough space on either side of the bed to even fit Luke's fingers, which made him wonder why they bothered adding sides to the bed when they could have just used the walls of the room.

He contemplated for a minute if he should upgrade his room or at least go downstairs to eat as there wasn't a table to place the tray on. In the end he decided not to go downstairs and entered the cramped space, closing the door behind himself.

Placing the tray on the limited floor space, he locked the door and sat cross-legged next to the tray. He ate half of the loaf of sourdough and drank the whole glass of, what he now knew to be, ale. *I bet if I drank enough of this I would get plastered. I can already feel the one tall glass. Interesting that they would program that in.*

Thinking about programming brought his current situation back to the forefront of his mind again, leaving him in sorrow. He laid on, what he was deeming, the bed and started pondering his predicament. *What if they can't figure this out... What if I'm stuck in here forever... What would my Mom think... Would she be ok without me...* His exhaustion from a full day of physical activity won over, beating the sorrow and he fell into unconsciousness.

The sun was beaming onto Luke's face as he opened his eyes. Any relaxation a night's sleep brought him slowly drained out when he heard the faint squeaking sounds coming from the foot of his bed. When he sat up to peek down, he saw a pair of mice finishing the sourdough bread he left on the floor. Jumping to his feet he stomped around the mice to scare them off and they quickly scurried into a hole in the wall.

The bed did no wonders for Luke's back and he proceeded to stretch in an attempt to get his blood flowing. The effort was in vain as his back pain started to flare up.

Looking around the room he made sure not to leave any of his meager belongings behind as he grabbed the platter of half-eaten mouse bread and proceeded downstairs to return it to the kitchen. He was kind enough to lock the room back up for the inn's staff before heading for the stairs.

Coming down the stairs, the scene was almost the stark opposite of last night. There were less than six people in the wide open area and some of those were staff still cleaning up from the previous night's festivities. Luke approached the bar and set down the platter before turning around and bumping into the bartender from last night.

"How'd ya sleep?"

Luke pushed up his glasses before he answered. "All right I guess."

"It's ok. I know those simple rooms aren't great for anything other than saving a few gold." With that, the man walked past Luke to get behind the bar, giving him a friendly slap on his back.

Luke smiled and left, the pain in his back flaring up again. *I wonder if they have massages in this world,* he thought to himself as he vowed to earn more gold to rent a better bed.

To get to the alchemist's shop, he had to pass by the open market square where he stopped and got some fruit for breakfast. He approached a stall that had various fruits in baskets and hanging from various wooden posts.

"Wow, what happened to you kid?" asked the burly woman running the stand.

It puzzled Luke at first but then remembered his shirt was hanging on by threads and his pants weren't in much better shape. "I was out fighting yesterday and I guess I need to pick up some new clothes."

"I wasn't talking about your clothes, sweetheart." The woman moved a handful of apples off a silver platter and held it up to Luke as a mirror. When he looked at it, he realized what the women was referring to.

Even though his hair was on the short side, it now was messier than he had ever seen it with straw generously mixed in. He had large purple bags under his puffy bloodshot eyes and stubble covering his lower face. If his skin was any lighter, he was concerned he would have to fend off travelers trying to slay the zombie he was looking more and more like. He doubled down on his vow, making a bed his number one priority in this world.

"Sorry, I had a rough night."

He ended up purchasing three apples from the woman for two gold before heading to the alchemist shop. On his way he picked most of the straw from his hair in an attempt to look even slightly better.

The alchemist's shop was a small two-story cottage in the business district. There were a few stone steps that led to a small landing and the front door. The outside walls were almost completely covered in vines with spots of white plaster poking through. A wooden sign hung from a black iron pole near the front door that read "Rose Alchemy".

When he opened the door, he immediately smiled, the inside of the shop smelled like walking through a field of flowers. Compared to the dung smelling city, Luke wished he could spend his entire day here. The shop contained rows of cluttered shelves both on the walls and covering the floor. There was a counter on one side with a door behind it leading to what he assumed was a storage room.

"Hello?" There was no response, so he increased his volume. "Helloooo." After a moment he shouted. "Is anyone here?" A sound like glass breaking came from the room behind the counter door and he could hear a woman shouting angrily before the door slammed open.

He was confused at first because he didn't see anyone on the other side of the door, but he heard footsteps behind the counter. A woman's head peeked above the counter's edge as she climbed a small staircase and stood at the counter's center.

The woman couldn't have been over three feet tall. She was slender and had short frizzled emerald green hair that matched her eyes. She was wearing a white long-sleeved shirt, brown work pants, and a large leather apron. The apron had various tool ends sticking out of its several rows of pockets and her forehead sported a pair of thick goggles. She also had something Luke hadn't seen before, long pointed ears.

"What the heck do you want?" The woman barked.

Luke was so shocked by the appearance of this woman he stumbled out a response. "Umm… I brought you herbs."

"I'm a gnome jack-ass, you can stop staring now."

Embarrassed, Luke averted his gaze and started emptying his pockets onto the counter. After a few moments of not getting a response he pushed up his glasses and built up the courage to look up again. The woman was inspecting the herbs and didn't seem all that pleased.

"You brought some extra herbs but they aren't in great condition. Have you had these in your pocket all night? It looks like you laid on them. They've lost half of their durability."

"I'm sorry. I'm still new to this world and didn't realize I was hurting them." He shuffled uncomfortably.

The woman looked up at Luke. She used both her hands to place her goggles over her eyes and she gave him a good look up and down.

"Hmm… a traveler… yes… yes… level one… and herbalism beginner three… interesting…" She opened the register at the end of the counter and handed five gold over. She also took out the extra herbs and handed them back. Luke took the gold but shook his head to the herbs.

"Since they didn't have full durability, why don't you keep the extra herbs as a gift. Also, sorry for staring, I haven't met a gnome before." He didn't think the herbs would last much longer in his pockets anyway. Better to give them to her in hopes it would smooth things over a bit if he let her keep them.

She moved her lips towards one side of her face in thought

before she relaxed. She lowered her shoulders and let out a sigh. "I'm sorry. I've been working all day on some new formulas and nothing's worked out for me. I may have taken some anger out on you. Let me make it up to you." She clapped her hands together and then stretched her arms out, palms up, toward him. Her hands began to glow green and Luke's body soon followed.

Looking at this status he had two icons he didn't recognize, one was red and the other green.

Nature's Regrowth. You will recover 10 HP every 5 seconds for the next 30 seconds.

Poor Sleep. You have slept in a poor quality bed. You will take a small penalty to your appearance, interactions with others, stats, and actions for the next 1 hour and 24 minutes.

Luke noticed that he still wasn't at full health from a full night's sleep. The nature's regrowth buff would get him to full quickly, and the poor sleep debuff explained a lot of what happened this morning.

"Thank you, I'm Luke." The woman introduced herself as Rose and bowed. Since things were looking up, he asked a favor. "Any chance you could teach me the nature's regrowth spell? It would really come in handy."

She took another look at him but a much harder look than the first time. "What are your affinities?" Luke shrugged and after letting out an exaggerated sigh, she continued. "Everyone has two spell affinities. They determine what spells and abilities you can learn. There are neutral spells and abilities that don't require affinities, like using that bow on your back. But you can only learn spells from your specific affinities." Luke continued to give her a confused stare before she sighed and continued. "Come with me." She walked down the small steps attached to her counter and went through the door into her back room.

Her back room was a workshop with large cauldrons, books, plants, and vials everywhere. It was a cross between a mad scientist's lab and a witch's hut. Rose climbed onto a small metal platform and pulled on a rope. A large bag of sand started descending from the ceiling as the metal platform started rising. She hopped off the platform when it reached a few rows high.

Rose was hunched over a crate tossing things out until she declared. "Aha! I knew it was in here." She pulled out a large crystal ball that had a swirling vortex inside of it. "This is an affinity globe. It's used to test and check one's affinities." She placed the orb down on the shelf and explained that all Luke had to do was hold it with both of his hands.

He picked the ball up and held it, waiting for a reaction. He was about to open his mouth when he started to feel a tingling sensation in his fingers. The spinning vortex inside turned white and started to warm up. It pushed toward the outside and closer to his hands. Before touching his hands, it quickly retracted and the crystal ball became jet black and cold. A fire started in the middle of the darkness and exploded outward, only to retract in with the darkness. Replacing the fire was a cooling sensation of flowing water and that too exploded outward from the center. Instead of retracting, the water coated half of the inner orb.

"Ahh, your first affinity is water," Rose declared as the orb continued working its magic.

The water stayed to one side as a mini tornado formed and tried to take hold to the other side. Right when Luke was sure the tornado would take hold, a rock formation surrounded it and snuffed it out. The rocks continued to spread until they covered the inside of the crystal ball. Water rapidly began to flow through the cracks in the rocks before calming and creating a peaceful scene of flowing water through earth.

Congratulations, you have unlocked the **Magic Affinity** *system. You can now learn spells of your unlocked affinities. There are six affinities, but everyone is born with only two. Learning new affinities or changing your affinities is almost unheard of, and there are only a small number of people who have done so in their lifetime. Note: This is a one time system message.*

Water Affinity *acquired.*
Earth Affinity *acquired.*

"So you're a nature affinity." Rose took the globe back and placed it back in its crate.

"Nature affinity?" He inquired.

"Yes. Someone with earth and water affinities is called a nature affinity. Water and air is called snow, fire and earth is volcanic and fire plus air is a lightning affinity. There's also light and dark affinities, but those are more standalone. Each affinity spell has its strengths and weaknesses but, unless you go down a mage path, you shouldn't worry too much about that. Just use your noggin and it's pretty straightforward. Water puts out fire, but air freezes water. It's all a balancing act."

"Does this mean you can teach me nature's regrowth?" He spoke with hope.

Rose smirked. "It means you can learn nature's regrowth but I can't teach you." Luke started to respond, but she raised a finger in defiance. "I'm not a mage and don't have the teaching skills needed to teach you a spell. I can, however, provide you a spell scroll to learn the spell, but magic isn't free."

Rose pulled a rolled-up piece of parchment from one of the many pouches on her apron and handed it to Luke.

Quest alert! **Helping the Alchemist:** *Rose the alchemist has taken a shine to you. In exchange for a spell scroll, she would like you to plant a rare flower for her. Moonherb planted 0/1. Reward: Nature's Regrowth spell scroll and added reputation with Rose the alchemist. Exp 300. Accept / Decline*

The scroll showed a crude map of what appeared to be the Howling Forest with an X marking the location to plant the flower. He accepted the small satchel containing a potted flower and gave his thanks. He left and headed for the city's gate.

Before leaving the city, he spent 2 of his remaining 5 gold on a shirt and a pair of pants. He tried purchasing health potions and armor, but they were all well out of his price range. *I just have to keep moving forward for now. I can't do anything to get out of this game so I might as well enjoy it.* If Luke was honest with himself, he was truly enjoying his time in Endless Fantasy Online, even if he couldn't leave.

He smiled and left the city on his next adventure.

CHAPTER FOUR

You Are Dead

Critical Hit! **Fox** *takes 10 points of damage.*
Fox *defeated. 15 exp gained.*
Skill up: **Short Bow**, *Beginner 3.*

Luke had been advancing into the Howling Forest for over an hour now, taking things slowly to prevent what happened last time and gather herbs for Rose. He didn't think a traveler would randomly come to save him for a second time. He also turned on battle notifications again but made them appear only in his log. Having them popup in his face was still too distracting but this way he could monitor how much damage he was dealing and how much the creatures could take before being defeated. He estimated that a fox had somewhere between ten and fifteen hit points, but a bunny only had between three and six. He made mental notes of all this for future battles.

Checking over his map it appeared the quest destination was just ahead to the right. After going around a dense patch of trees he saw what had to be the spot. There was a circular patch of grass surrounded by foliage but no trees. Since there were no trees, it allowed for sunlight or moonlight to reach the spot.

Luke pulled the potted plant out of the satchel and began to replant it in the ground. He used one end of his short bow to dig up the earth and packed the plant down tightly.

Herbalism check, successful.
Quest alert! **Helping the Alchemist:** *Moonherb planted 1/1. Quest complete! Rewards: 300 exp. Other rewards delayed until you speak with the quest giver.*

Congratulations, **Level Up!** *You have been awarded 3 attribute points and 1 skill point, based on your class. Be careful with your decisions as they can not be undone.*

When he leveled up, his health and stamina both maxed out and a wave of euphoria washed over him as he heard a trumpet's fanfair play in his ears. Pulling up his character sheet and giving it some thought, he added two points in agility to increase his damage and one in constitution because having more health never hurt anyone. He didn't spend his ability point because he wanted to wait until he got his new spell. He then reviewed his sheet to look at the progress he had made.

Name: *Not totally useless Luke.*
Class: *Beginner*
Primary Profession: *None*
Level 2: *Exp 150 Exp to next level: 1850*
Hit Points: *60/60*
Mana: *50/50*

Mana Regen: 1/sec
Stamina: 80/80
Physical Resistance: +2
Elemental Resistance: Water +10, Earth +10

Attributes Base (Modifier)
Strength: 1
Agility: 3 (+1)
Intelligence: 1
Wisdom: 1
Constitution: 2
Social: 1
Luck: 1

Skills, Spells and Abilities

Short Bow (Beginner 3): Basic knowledge on how to use a short bow. Increasing this skill will increase the damage dealt with a short bow. This is a passive skill and requires no activation. Effect: Adds 1+x% short bow damage where x = skill level.

Herbalism (Beginner 5): This skill allows you to identify various plant life.

First Aid (Beginner 0): Basic knowledge on how to apply basic first aid and use basic bandages. Increasing this skill will increase your knowledge of first aid techniques and increase the speed at which you can apply this skill.

"Not so bad if you ask me," he muttered aloud as he packed up his belongings for the trek back.

"Not bad at all," came a deep voice from the woods.

Luke frantically searched the dense trees for the source of the voice but didn't see anyone. He reached for his bow just as a dagger sunk into the ground at his feet.

"Let's not try something stupid now," said the same voice, but this time Luke could see the man coming out of the tree line. The man was wearing all black leather and a crimson red cloak with a hood pulled over his face, concealing it in shadows. The only other identifying mark was the red outline of a dagger on his breast piece.

"Ya, nothing stupid." Another man in matching attire came out of the trees to Luke's right, followed by another on his left.

"Nice to meet you guys, but I really need to get going to town." Luke attempted to act brave.

The men closed in on Luke, leaving no space for him to run.

"We'll be taking your gold, weapons, armor, and anything else you happen to have on you." The man pulled a pair of daggers and his motions were quickly copied by the other two men.

Luke emptied his pockets of his three gold and collected plants, and tossed his bow to the ground.

Pointing a dagger at Luke's hands the main thug continued, "The leather armor too."

Pulling off his only piece of armor and tossing it to the ground, Luke backed up a bit while the two other men came forward and started stuffing Luke's possessions into a bag. In the meantime, the main thug started digging out the Moonherb.

"Hey! Leave the plant alone." Luke shouted in protest.

The man threw one of his daggers at Luke and it sunk into his gut. His shirt quickly became blood stained, and he fell to his knees. The man got up and stood over him. "That plant is worth decent gold. I'm going to dig it out and sell it and there's nothing a noob like you can do about it."

Filled with anger and fueled by adrenaline, Luke went for the dagger in his gut in order to make a last ditch effort to kill the man who stood in front of him. At least that's what he wanted to do. As soon as he grabbed the dagger, pain wracked his body, and he collapsed before he could pull the blade out more than a few centimeters.

The man bent down and placed his face next to Luke's ear. "Your death was courtesy of the Crimson Shadow Guild." He snickered as he pulled his second dagger across Luke's throat.

Luke's vision went dark and a system message came into view.

*You have **died**. Respawning at last known home point.*

It was hard to tell how much time passed in complete darkness. It couldn't have been more than a couple of minutes. Then Luke reappeared next the same fountain where he first entered this world.

*You have **died**. Death is a part of life. When you die, you lose all experience toward your next level. You will also drop everything that was not soul-bound to you at the time of your death. After dying you will respawn at your last known home point with the recently deceased debuff.*
Note: This is a one time system message.

***Recently Deceased** I debuff added. You will suffer a 50% penalty to all exp gained for the next two hours.*

Luke rifled through his pockets, confirming all of his coins and plants were gone. He then opened up his character sheet and confirmed that he had lost exp and was now at zero of two thousand needed for the next level. He checked his skills, and was thrilled to see that his skill point was still available to use.

At least I came back with clothes on, he thought timidly. After looking at himself he noticed that he had on the same simple white cotton shirt and brown cotton pants he started with, minus the leather armor he got as a quest reward. His armor and other items were all stolen by the Crimson Shadow guild.

Luke looked to the sky and noticed the sun was beginning to set. He didn't have enough time to finish another quest and no money to do anything. He then decided to return to Rose's and complete the one quest he still had.

Luke entered Rose's shop to find it empty. The back workshop door was open so he peeked in and saw Rose. She had several plants in front of her and was cutting branches off them. After cutting a branch off one plant, she would place it against the trunk of a miniature tree. Covering the spot with her hand caused green and blue light to emanate from the spot her hands covered. When she pulled her hands away, the branch would grow and weave itself around the trunk. Small flower buds then started sprouting from the newly placed branch.

"That's amazing!" Luke couldn't contain his excitement over the small display of magic.

Rose looked up and pulled her goggles back to her forehead. After recognizing her visitor, she walked over and climbed to her regular spot on the store's counter. "You're back so soon. I didn't expect you until tomorrow at the earliest." She inspected him before continuing. "It appears you completed my quest, and a deal is a deal." She pulled another small scroll from one of her apron pockets and handed it to him.

Nature's Regrowth Spell Scroll (Rare) x1 obtained. Requirements: Earth Affinity

Luke looked at the scroll for a while before responding to Rose.

Pushing up his glasses he asked, "How much does something like this sell for?"

Perplexed, Rose responded. "Sell for? Didn't you want that for adventuring?"

"I did…" Luke's hands clenched into fists. "But that was before I was murdered and had all of my belongings stolen." He suddenly remembered that they also took the Moonherb he planted. He put the spell scroll back on the table and pushed it toward Rose. "I'm sorry. The people who killed me ended up taking the Moonherb. I don't actually deserve this."

Rose displayed a warm expression and took Luke's hand in her own. "An adventurer's life can be hard. As an immortal, you will probably die a lot in your journeys. That is something you will have to cope with. Non-travelers who choose an adventurer's life aren't as lucky." She looked at Luke but he felt as if she was looking past him, as if her mind was recalling something. Her eyes started to well up before she let go of Luke's hand and wiped her face.

*100 **Reputation Gained** with **Rose the Alchemist**.*
*New Status: **Liked**.*

Reputation can be gained or lost by performing specific actions, completing quests, or speaking with various factions and NPCs. Reputation starts at Neutral but can be gained to a status of Family or lost to a status of Blood Feud. Positive and negative reputation comes with additional boons or detriments depending on your level of reputation and will affect your social interactions with anyone in that given faction.
Note: This is a one time system message.

He smiled at the system prompt and cursed the Crimson

Shadow for killing him and, inadvertently, hurting this kind woman. *Woman?* He thought. She was technically just an NPC with a real person's personality imprinted on her. Nothing more than 1s and 0s in a computer game. *Aren't I just 1s and 0s though? With my mind imprinted on this character?* He shook the thoughts from his head. Contemplating this was like contemplating the meaning of life and he wasn't a scholar by any stretch of the imagination.

"How do you feel about herbalism?" Rose inquired as she went behind the store's counter to grab something.

"It's fun, I guess. I saw what you did with those plants in the back and that looked neat."

Rose returned to the counter carrying a large thick book. She was definitely struggling to carry the book up the stairs but the look she gave him said "Help me and you'll lose a finger." She threw the book down and a bloom of dust flew around the room. "This is a basic herbalist's book. It should teach you everything you need to know to take care of the plants in my greenhouse." She raised one eyebrow.

"You want me to take care of your greenhouse?"

Her face went warm again. "I can offer you a fair wage, lots of herbalism experience and a bedroll to sleep on if you need a place to sleep. I'm offering you a chance to learn before you venture out on your own again. Keep you from dying and all that." She smiled.

"This seems kind of sudden." Rose had a hurt expression on her face. "I didn't mean it like that." He quickly recovered. "I just mean... why are you helping me? Aren't there a ton of people who come through your shop that would be more qualified?"

Rose gazed through him for a moment before her attention went to him again. "You remind me a lot of someone I knew a long time ago. Someone I was close with. I can offer you one more thing." She took one of his hands in between both of hers and there was a quick flash of white light.

*Rose the Alchemist is offering to teach you the **Herbalist** profession. **Herbalists** gain +2 Intelligence and + 1 Wisdom while they have Herbalist set as their primary profession. Herbs and plants will also emit a glow that brightens the closer you are, making them easier to find. Accept / Decline*

Professions offer a different style of gameplay. Choosing your first profession will mark it as your primary profession. You will gain faster exp for activities related to your profession, but be careful before accepting any profession. You can only have one primary profession and will be unable to change your primary profession or learn a secondary profession until level 10. You can then change your professions every 10 levels after level 10. Note: This is a one time system message.

Luke had no reason to leave the city, and he definitely didn't want to run into the Crimson Shadow again. This sounded like a great offer to him, so he waved away the system message and hit the accept button on Rose's offer.

The next couple of days went by fast. After he accepted his new profession, Rose showed him to the small greenhouse behind her shop. She gave him a bedroll to put on the floor inside. It wasn't that bad, and it didn't give him any debuffs when he woke up in the morning.

Rose would meet with him every morning to show him a variety of plants and how to take care of them. She was even kind enough to give him the Nature's Regrowth spell that he returned to her. After tending to the plants, he would join Rose in her shop and handle the register while reading books on various plants, growth techniques, and even alchemy.

All this learning resulted in huge gains for his character. He learned several skills like alchemy, gained points in herbalism, and even gained a few points in intelligence after he finished reading several books. It surprised him to gain attribute points from reading, but Rose explained that he could gain attribute points from all sorts of activities. For example, if he made enough wise decisions he could gain a point in wisdom, or if he ran a few marathons, he had a chance of gaining a couple points in agility or strength.

Another great advantage was that Rose would have him go out and buy reagents for her at various shops. Not only was he quickly learning the city's layout, but he would also get quest prompts to fetch her the items and gain small amounts of exp upon his return.

The city was also changing. Every time he went on a shopping run he noticed fewer guards around town, and that a lot of the players spent most of their time at the local bars or doing small quests around town to earn enough money for drinks but rarely did they ever leave the city. A wave of depression seemed to hit them all. Luke would be in the same boat if it wasn't for Rose keeping him occupied.

Returning to the shop, Luke put his backpack full of Rose's reagents on the counter and began to unpack them. "Hey Rose." She raised her head from her current experiment and looked at Luke. "Do you know why there seems to be fewer guards in the city?"

Rose went back to her experiment while answering him. "Ofcourse. Didn't you listen to Guard Captain Holtz the other day? He's sending all spare men outside the city to search for the Queen and Princess. Apparently no one has completed his quest for information."

Luke scratched his head and tried to remember something about the Queen and Princess. With a Eureka moment he remembered. *The King had passed away a few days ago! Captain Holtz was telling everyone about it before Rob interrupted with that lawyer to tell us we couldn't log out. That must be hard for Rose and the other citizens to cope with.*

"Hey Rose. Are you ok with all that? I mean, he was your king right?"

She looked up and gave him a warming smile that he was growing fond of. "Yes, my boy. King Henry was a good king and his passing saddens me but as long as we find the Queen and Princess, I think the whole Phoenix Kingdom will be fine." She paused for a moment before continuing. "Ask me again if they don't find them," she concluded with a cautious smile.

The bell above the door rang as the next customer entered and Luke returned to customer service mode. "Welcome to Rose Alchemy. Is there anything I can help you find?"

The woman walking in was wearing pieced together armor. Her gloves, hood and leg guards appeared to be leather. Her chest piece was definitely chain mail and her boots appeared to be generic work boots. The most massive feature was a shield strapped to her back. A major grin of excitement at every little thing in the shop, and her armor choice, told him right away that she was a traveler. All of the NPCs he met who wore armor had matching sets. To be honest, he understood why. She looked downright ridiculous.

"Do you have any health potions?" the woman questioned.

Luke pointed to a bookshelf near the counter that had boxes full of various quality health potions. She perused them for a short while before pulling out two lower quality health potions and handed them to Luke. They were stored in two small red vials, about the size of his index finger, with cork stoppers in them.

Low Quality Health Potion (Uncommon) x2 obtained. Restores 25 hit points when the contents are drunk. The whole contents must be drunk for the effect to take place. Health potions can not be shared.

"Sure, that will be thirty gold."

The woman's jaw dropped. "Thirty! Don't you think that's kinda expensive? Would you take twenty?"

He smiled as this had become one of his favorite parts of the job, bartering. Rose had spent a full day explaining her pricing to him and how much she would accept for all her items. She left the rest to him and trusted he wouldn't give away her shop. After the first couple successful bartering attempts with various NPCs and travelers he gained the bartering skill, which gave him a small bonus to all bartering attempts.

"Sorry, we simply can't accept twenty." He knew Rose would take as low as fifteen gold per potion of this quality, but he thought he owed it to her to get as close to retail price as he could. "We have more than that invested in them. I could go as low as twenty-seven gold for the pair."

"Hmm… I can only spare twenty-five. Mind meeting me in the middle?" she quickly rebutted.

He grabbed his chin and attempted to seem like he was thinking hard on her counter offer. He nodded and a system pop-up rewarding him a skill point in bartering appeared. Smiling, he took the woman's money, added it to the register and handed her the potions.

"If you don't mind me asking, what level are you?" He inquired to the mystery women.

"I'm a level three shielder." She responded with pride. "The name's Penelope, but everyone calls me Penny." She extended her hand in greeting.

"The name's Luke, level two beginner."

Her eyes went wide. "Wait a minute. You're a traveler?" He nodded in response. "How the heck are you working at an NPC shop?"

Luke explained his brief time in Endless Fantasy Online. His starting quests, meeting Rose, unlocking his elemental affinities and finally being murdered and offered a job.

"The Crimson Shadow are the worst!" She shouted.

"You know them?" He questioned.

"They're a guild of Player Killers. The sickos actually get pleasure from killing other travelers. I would be level four if it wasn't for them. They killed me right before hitting level three and I lost a whole level's worth of experience."

"What did you do in response?" Luke was curious if he could turn off some feature that allowed other players to attack him. Maybe a menu option he didn't see.

"Nothing really. Nothing I could do. I tried reporting the crime to a guard, but he laughed at me. Said I couldn't have been murdered because I was standing in front of him. *How could I be standing in front of him if I was dead?* he kept repeating to me." Luke chuckled a bit at the mocking baby voice she used when saying the guard's line. "I ended up joining a guild of my own though. A bunch of us get together and adventure outside of town. The Crimson Shadow seem to only go after lone players."

"A guild?"

"Yeah, Travelers 4 Hire or T4H for short. We're currently working on saving up gold for a guild building."

"Hay beds in the inn giving you back pain?" He giggled briefly at the thought.

She looked at him with a serious look in her eyes, signifying she knew exactly what he was talking about. They held their gazes for a few moments before they both broke out laughing.

"You know, we're recruiting nice people to join. No requirements at the moment, other than not being a jerk."

Luke contemplated her offer for a moment but he didn't want to leave Rose. "I'm sorry. I just got this position with the shop owner and I really…"

"Nonsense, boy!" Rose came from the back room and up her regular stairs to the counter. "You've been cooped up here for almost a week now. I know an adventurer when I see one. Of course you do owe me, so I expect you to still help take care of the plants from time to time and run the shop when I need to take care of errands."

He allowed a grin to cross his face before responding. "You got yourself a deal. As long as I can still sleep on your greenhouse floor." He visibly shuddered when thinking about returning to the straw beds at the inn.

"You can go around back and let yourself into the greenhouse. Just don't come in the shop and wake me up if you get in late." She gave him a serious look.

He nodded and faced Penny. "I guess I'm gonna meet with your guild, Travelers 4 Hire."

CHAPTER FIVE

Travelers 4 Hire

Penny took Luke to a large warehouse toward the bad part of town. He was getting concerned that he was being lured into a trap until they opened the large double doors to reveal a well lit room with many people going about their business. Everyone was smiling and seemed to be having a good time. It reminded him a lot of The Winged Pig Inn because of all the tables and chairs that were set up.

"Guild Master Shrapnel!" Penny shouted across the room as she waved her arm in the air. She quickly pulled on Luke's shirt, dragging him toward the man in question. "Guild Master Shrapnel, I have a potential new recruit for you." Penny told Shrapnel everything about how she met Luke and what happened to him. At the mention of the Crimson Shadow, Shrapnel balled his hands into fists and his expression changed to one of anger.

"Listen. If you are against the Crimson Shadow, I would be happy to give you a probationary spot," Shrapnel stated while gesturing his hands at Luke.

"Probationary?"

"As a guild in the Phoenix Kingdom, we are only allowed a specific number of members based on our standing with the Kingdom. I don't know if you know this yet, but reputation is hard to come by in this game." Luke knew that. After working for Rose for almost a week and completing a laundry list of quests for her, he still hadn't advanced from the liked status into friends.

Luke pushed up his glasses and responded. "Sooo, what do I have to do?"

"Join one of our parties and complete a couple of quests. I'll ask your party leader in a couple days how you are doing and we'll see where we are at that point. Sound fair?" Luke nodded in response and a pop-up appeared.

*New guild request: **Guild Master Shrapnel** of the **Travelers 4 Hire (T4H)** guild would like you to join on a probationary period. Accept / Decline.*

Joining a guild is a great way to mingle with fellow travelers and complete quests that are above and beyond your solo experience. Warning! You can only be part of one guild at a time and while part of a guild, a portion of all your exp, quest rewards and reputation will go to the guild. You didn't think everything in life was free did you? Note: This is a one time system message.

"Wait, I have to give up part of all my future experience, gold and reputation?" He was hesitant in hitting the accept button. Maybe this still was a trap.

"Don't worry. While you are on your probationary period, we collect nothing. If our guild likes you and you decide to stick around, I will give you a standard new guild member contract. We will only take one percent of all your gains to start unless you want to contribute more. It's to help the guild gain good reputation and earn some money to buy a guild house in the city. We're renting this warehouse at a high daily rate and we really want to buy a headquarters."

"What about the experience?"

"Guilds can level up in Endless Fantasy Online. The higher tier our guild gets to, the more perks all the members share. Currently all members get a small percentage to HP regeneration."

HP was hard to gain back when lost in this game. Luke had a spell to take care of that now, but to offer that to the whole guild would be a big boon. He wondered what other benefits came to the guild and thought the offer was pretty good. Plus, he could always leave if he didn't like things.

He hit the accept button and a sound of fanfare trumpeted in his ear. A new guild screen came into his vision with a list of known members, levels, classes and statuses. The screen also showed the current guild level, which was two, and the current boons, small HP regeneration. There was alo a message board of people talking about forming parties, asking for quest help and general chatter. Luke's current status in the guild was listed as probationary so when he tried adding a message to the message board, he got an error stating it was for full members only.

"This is kinda neat. I'm glad to find some players who are doing more than drinking their days away in sorrow about our current status of being stuck in the game." Penny, Shrapnel and most of the surrounding people within earshot all sighed in near unison.

"We don't really talk about that around the guild. Kinda a debbie-downer thing to say. We are all just trying to forget about it for now and make the best of our situation," Penny blurted to break the mood that was settling over the room.

"I'm sorry. I didn't mean anything by it."

Shrapnel and Penny shook their heads and suggested to Luke that he forget about it.

"Penny, would you mind taking Luke out on your team today? You're the one who brought him to the guild in the first place and I know you're looking for a fourth anyway. Kinda works out nicely."

Penny nodded and sent Luke a party invite that he quickly accepted. Penny laughed out loud when she read Luke's title. Then the two of them headed for the city gate while they waited for their other party members to join them. Looking over his party list, Luke noticed two other people. There was someone named Backstabber Backstab and Nanoc, the Shirtless. They were both level three.

"I see that you're still a beginner but what's your primary focus? How do you fit in the team?" Penny inquired.

"I'm ranged with some support, I guess."

"Do you know about choosing a class yet?" Luke shook his head and Penny continued. "When you hit level three, the system will offer you a list of classes to choose from. They are all basic, but they advance into higher tiers as you level up your skills and meet certain requirements. They base the list of classes on your current skills and character statistics."

He was happy to know that he wouldn't be a beginner much longer, and excited to see what the game would offer him. He didn't have to wait long as the other two party members had just arrived. Backstabber Backstab was a slender, somewhat shorter male. He wore all dark leather armor with all sorts of short blades strapped to his sides, legs, chest, back and every other spot he could see. Nanoc, the shirtless, was the polar opposite. He was wearing fur shorts and boots but nothing else. He had long black hair and he wore a strap across his front that tied into a massive two-handed axe on his back. The axe blade was bigger than Luke's head and he had no idea how the shirtless man could wield it.

"Ok everyone." Penny clapped her hands to get everyone's attention. She introduced Luke and let the two others know that he would accompany them as they went outside of town for the day. "Before we go, let's all quest up." They moved to the board that hosted all the requests and the three of them all grabbed the same three quests as if moving on muscle memory.

"Luke, come grab these three. There's one for killing wolves and foxes and another for bringing back their pelts." He followed his party leader's command, and the three headed out into the wilderness.

The party moved at a much quicker pace than Luke was used to. Luckily he had high enough agility that his stamina recovered quick enough for him to keep up. But on more than one occasion he had to go into his pack and get water. At such a quick pace, they got deep into the howling forest in record time, but their pace soon slowed as they got deeper into the forest and started hunting their intended targets.

"Everyone pay attention," Penny whispered as she hunched down and gestured for the party to follow. "There is a pack of wolves straight ahead. I count at least four of them. Backstab, do you think you can reach them with a throwing dagger at this distance?" Backstab nodded his affirmation. "Good. Luke, do you think you could target one as well?" Luke slowly pulled his bow off his back and nocked an arrow. "Ok. Luke, you aim for the one on the right and Backstab go for the left. If you can't get a kill shot on them, try to slow them down. When the other two rush us, Nanoc and I will hold them at bay while you two finish off your targets. When you finish them, join us in taking the other two out. We'll keep them off you until then. Got it everyone?" Everyone nodded and got into position.

Luke looked at Backstab who had several long, thin blades in both of his hands. Backstab was looking back at Luke and nodded for him to start. Poking out from cover, Luke shot an arrow that hit the wolf in its lower stomach. Immediately the remaining wolves turned and started bolting toward him. Before the wolf on the left could get far, several knives flew at an incredible speed toward it. Being caught unaware, the wolf tried to dodge them, but could only avoid one of the blades.

One of the remaining wolves was about to reach Luke when Penny let out a loud shout while banging her sword on her shield. She was definitely using an ability, because he noticed a red glow emanating from her shield and the wolf instantly switched its trajectory toward her. "Hurry up and finish your wolf off. These things are level four and we'll need your help!"

Pulling another arrow, Luke took aim at the wolf that was still coming toward him, albeit at a much slower pace. He aimed for its head but it was still quick enough to move out of the way. Daring to glance over he noticed Backstab had finished his intended target and was moving in to help Nanoc while the large man blocked claws and fangs with his axe head. Another shot landed true, and the wolf fell to the ground.

"I got him!" he shouted with excitement.

"That's great. Ya know, anytime you wanna help me would be even better." Penny had succeeded at pushing back the wolf, but a misplaced foot left an opening the wolf capitalized on. The large, clawed paw swiped and ripped into her leg, forcing her to her knees. She let out a grunt of pain while pulling her shield in to block the next attempt at her life.

After readying another arrow, he hesitated. Luke didn't want to accidentally strike Penny or his other comrades who were fighting behind her. His moment of hesitation cost her another swipe to her shoulder. Penny grunted with pain as Luke released the arrow. It landed in the back of the wolf's head, scoring a critical hit.

The wolf attacking Nanoc lunged for him, and instead of blocking the wolf's attack he dropped his axe while sidestepping it. As the wolf flew past him, he wrapped his arms around it, immobilizing it. "Backstab," exclaimed Backstab as he appeared in the air above the pair of combatants, using his momentum to drive a dagger into the wolf's spine.

Forest Wolf x4 defeated. 300 party participation exp gained.
Quest alert! **Controlling the Wolf population I:** *4/10.*

"Penny, are you ok?" The woman was holding herself up with her shield and was panting heavily. They wolved had torn up her right leg and her shoulder. She couldn't have been feeling all that much better after taking the full force of that last swing. She reached her hand out to stop the panicking Luke. Then she took a potion she bought from Luke out of her bag, getting ready to drink it.

"Wait!" he shouted a little too abruptly, causing Penny to almost drop her potion onto the ground. He ran closer to her and lifted his palm for her to see. His palm lit up green briefly, becoming warm, and Penny's body followed suit.

Skill up: **Nature's Regrowth**, *Beginner 1.*

"What are you… Ohh? That is incredibly useful." She said as she let out some of her built up tension.

"What did he do?" Backstab questioned.

"Wow! Look at her status bar dude. She's got a leaf icon and her health is steadily going up," added Nanoc.

"I can't believe you can heal. I can't believe you can use magic!" Penny was giddy and starting to get back on her feet.

"It's really not much. It's the only spell I know, and it has a long cooldown period before I can cast it again. It also used up more than a third of my mana." He was waving his hands around defensively to stave off his embarrassment.

"Luke, I don't think you get it. I've been beta testing for almost a month and I have only met about six people, seven including you, who can cast spells. And of those seven, you are the second one to have a healing spell. Magic is really rare in this game, and it's hard to unlock. You have to open something called an affinity channel and then find someone either talented enough to teach you a spell or save enough money to buy a spell scroll. How the hell did you learn that?!"

He thought back to his mentor Rose and how much she was really helping him. If that was the only way to learn magic, she basically gave him a small fortune because he reminded her of someone? He had some questions for her the next time they crossed paths.

"A kind NPC helped me unlock my affinities. After completing a unique quest, they rewarded me with the spell scroll."

All of their eyes were wide with astonishment and a hint of jealousy. "When Shrapnel finds out, he's going to beg you to stay in the guild. You would make the third or fourth person in the guild who can use spells."

He blushed a bit and pushed up his glasses before the group grabbed all their gear and began skinning the animals. Since he didn't bring a skinning knife with him, Luke offered to carry some pelts in his pack. He wanted to help contribute when he found an opportunity to. They obliged and gave him one of the pelts. Penny and Nanoc carried the rest as they had higher strength levels.

After packing away the pelts they continued into the forest and found another pack of wolves, this time five in total. "Ok team. Same game-plan. I need you two to take out two from afar. Nanoc, you hold one of them and I'll taunt the remaining two. As soon as you two finish your ranged targets, I want you both to finish the one on Nanoc so the three of you can surprise attack the rest of them from behind." They all nodded with understanding. "Hey Luke, after taking your first target out, cast your healing spell on me before helping those two. It should be more than enough to keep me standing until you're all able to assist."

Backstab was the first to unleash his attack this time. Five daggers went flying from his hand, three hit their mark, one went wide and the other landed in the side of another wolf. As soon as the wolves took off toward him, Luke took aim with his arrow but before he released it the wolf in the pack's front let out a loud howl. This caused a system message to pop-up, causing him to miss his shot.

Wolf Howl. Weakened debuff added.

Pulling his hands away from his ears, he launched another attack at the wolf closest to Backstab. The impact caused the wolf to veer off course and collide with a tree. The wolves stopped and took in the party. One wolf in the rear howled.

Wolf Howl. Weakened debuff II added.

"We have to stop them from howling! We're going to take too much bonus damage!" Penny shouted over the piercing howling noise.

After casting nature's regrowth on Penny, Luke took a few more shots at the wolf pack, but both arrows missed as the wolves approached the party with caution.

"I don't think we took these by surprise Penny. I think it's time for me to get angry!" Nanoc let out a manly roar of rage and his skin took on a reddish tint. Roaring again he charged into the pack, activating another ability that swung his axe with two hands outward in a cleaving motion. The attack created a large cut in three of the five wolves and blood began to stain their coats.

As the wolves were getting ready to counter attack, Penny started her taunt ability by bashing her sword against her shield rapidly. The three injured wolves took off in her direction while the undamaged wolf sprung on Backstab. Acting quickly and sticking to the plan, Luke finished off the initially damaged wolf with a few shots in quick succession.

*Skill up: **Short Bow**, Beginner 4.*

Turning to help Backstab, he ran in and swung his bow at the wolf to distract it. The wolf clamped its teeth around the bow. "Backstab," cried Backstab, letting out what Luke now understood to be his trademark phrase as he plunged a dagger into the backside of the turned wolf. Pulling his bow from the wolf's mouth as it yelped from a backstab, Luke finished it with a point blank arrow shot to the temple. Checking Backstab quickly he noticed he had a few new claw marks in his armor but didn't seem to be worse for wear, causing him to turn his attention to his other two party members.

Penny and Nanoc weren't faring too well as the wolves were quickly overpowering the two melee fighters. Backstab quickly activated an ability that gave him an incredible speed boost. Rushing in, he leaped into the air, arcing over one of the wolves. As he passed over the wolf he released several throwing daggers he had pulled from his chest strap. Following up his attack, Luke released two arrows. The first missed a wolf going for Nanoc and the other landed in the wolf that Backstab helped weaken, killing it.

Luke checked his party status in the side of his vision and saw that both Penny and Nanoc were in the low 20% of their max health. With nature's regrowth off cooldown, he cast it again on Penny and jumped in to aid Nanoc. After casting the spell and readying another arrow, another wolf's howl came out.

Wolf Howl. Weakened debuff III added.
Area Event Triggered! **Alpha Wolf!** *The continued howls of a wolf pack have summoned their Alpha for aid. Kill the Alpha Wolf for a reward.*

A hulking wolf the size of a horse sporting gray fur and red stripes down its back appeared in the tree line.

"Everyone get ready. Try to finish off the lesser wolves before that thing makes it to…" Penny began to lay out an attack plan until the massive alpha wolf leaped at them. The wolf cleared almost half the distance in a single leap, only adding to the growing dread everyone was feeling. "Never mind. I'll hold off the little ones, everyone take that thing down!" Penny triggered her taunt ability again as she shouted out her latest command.

Luke shot an arrow at the alpha but it didn't penetrate its thicker fur. Backstab also attempted a ranged attack but the wolf just shrugged them off as it continued its sprint. Nanoc cleaved the remaining two wolves, killing one and distracting the other long enough for Penny to drive her sword upwards into its chest.

Backstab activated his speed ability again and dashed almost imperceptibly toward the alpha. Suddenly he vanished, reappearing with daggers in his hands in the air above the wolf. "Backst-" He was cut off as the wolf abruptly stopped, leaned back and jumped upwards toward him with his mouth open.

The alpha wrapped his teeth around the thin man and began to shake his mouth rapidly, treating the rogue as a chew toy. Activating nature's regrowth again on Penny, Luke took several shots at the wolf but none found purchase. Running low on arrows, he ran to the side of the battlefield to collect some of his arrows that missed while Nanoc and Penny charged the beast.

While collecting his fallen arrows, he noticed a familiar plant growing on the side of a tree.

Identification successful. **Parashroom** *(uncommon). An uncommon mushroom that is known to have paralytic effects when eaten. It is a common ingredient in several alchemy recipes.*

This could work, he thought as he carefully gathered some of the orange and yellow mushrooms alongside his arrows.

Looking back, he saw Penny shielding Nanoc as he attempted to pry the wolf's mouth open in an effort to free their trapped comrade. Meanwhile, Backstab was attempting to stab the wolf repetitively with his daggers while he was being shaken about.

"Get his mouth open. I have an idea." Luke took an arrow and cut the caps off a handful of parashrooms. Taking the caps, he drove his arrow head into them so they were lodged enough not to come off during flight. He took aim at the alpha's mouth and waited. Nanoc used his rage ability again and his large red tinted hands began prying the creature's mouth open. Backstab lifelessly fell to the ground, leaving the alpha's mouth wide open.

"If you're gonna do something, do it already!" Shouted Nanoc as an arrow flew by his side and into the mouth of the wolf. The wolf yelped and started thrashing wildly, forcing Nanoc to let go. The alpha's thrashing continued, and he sent both Penny and Nanoc soaring.

The alpha turned to Luke and revealed his nearly foot long fangs in defiance. The wolf leaped from a standstill toward Luke, leaving impressions in the ground. Thinking quickly, Luke launched several arrows toward the beast but they were all ineffective. The wolf charged directly into Luke, forcing him off the ground and into his mouth. Luke felt an incredible amount of pain and his health bar plummeted to 20%.

The wolf continued its charge into a tree, Luke still in his mouth, and the tree broke in two. He was now down to 10% and dropping quickly. He was resigned to his fate and shut his eyes, waiting for the inevitable death screen to appear.

After a few moments of not seeing the system message alerting him of his failure, he opened his eyes. The wolf still had a loose grip on him but it wasn't moving. He was just standing there and breathing lightly. It took a moment for it to dawn on him: the wolf was paralyzed!

"NOW! I don't know how long this will last!" Luke screamed for his party to advance on the creature.

"Die you bastard!" shouted Nanoc as he took off at a full sprint toward the creature, his axe being dragged behind him. Using his sprinting momentum he swung his axe up in a large cleaving uppercut, throwing a cloud of dirt into the air as the blade tore through the ground. The blade shot up with all of Nanoc's raging ferocity and the attack separated the alpha's head from its body. The alpha's body fell limp as its head rolled to Nanoc's feet.

Several system messages flooded Luke's vision, but he waved them away. His health was below 10% and he needed to cast nature's regrowth on himself. Before he finished casting the spell, he gazed at his party menu to see if Backstab needed it more. Backstab's status bars had all turned a dark gray, signifying that he was dead and being sent to respawn. He finished casting the heal on himself and repeated the process on the others when the spell was off cooldown. With the party out of danger, he pulled up his system messages.

*Area Event Complete: **Alpha Wolf!** Alpha Wolf slain 1/1. Since you are the first party of travelers to complete this quest, you have been awarded the title WolfsBane. You have become a bane to the local wolf population. While this title is equipped you will gain +1 in Intelligence, +1 in Wisdom and are immune to the ability Wolf Howl. You have also gained +2 attribute points and 500 exp.*

__Forest Wolf__ x5 defeated. 375 exp gained.

*Quest alert! **Controlling the Wolf population I:** 10/10. Quest complete! Rewards: 250 exp. Turn this quest in to the quest giver for any additional rewards.*

*Congratulations, **Level Up!** You have been awarded 3 attribute points and 1 skill point, based on your class. Be careful with your decisions as they can not be undone.*

*Congratulations on hitting level 3! You have been awarded a basic class. Please select from the available options based on your recorded play style: **Alchemist, Apprentice Mage, Archer, Earth Mage, Herbalist, Merchant, Ranger,** or **Water Mage.***

There were buttons to hit for more information, but he waved the screens away, deciding to help the team skin the wolves and leave his class choice for later. Only Nanoc could carry the massive gray pelt left behind from the alpha wolf, and Penny was stuck carrying back all of Backstab's possessions. This left Luke tp carry the bulk of the pelts back to town.

Starting their trek back to town, he began sweating heavily from the extra weight in his pack. To distract himself, he brought the class options back up and explored them.

Right off the bat, he eliminated merchant from the list. Running a shop was fun but not as fun as being able to explore the wilderness with a group. He made a commitment to solidify membership with Travelers 4 Hire when he saw Shrapnel next. Not knowing which option to look at first, he pulled them up in order.

Alchemist: The alchemist brews potions and poisons to aid his allies or defeat his foes. They strive for creating new things and finding new mixtures to maximize their potential in whatever path they choose. Automatically receive: +1 Intelligence, Book of Basic Potions, Book of Basic Poisons. New Attributes per Level: +1 Intelligence, +3 Attribute Points. Note: If alchemist is your current primary profession, you will be allowed to choose another at your leisure.

Apprentice Mage: Learning to walk the path of a Mage is hard but rewarding. As you unlock your magical ability, you learn to unlock the power of your mind, and a powerful mind conquers all. Automatically receive: +1 Intelligence, +1 Wisdom, choice of the following spells: Water Jet, Earth Toss. New Attributes per Level: +2 Intelligence, +1 Wisdom, +1 Attribute Points.

Archer: Killing your foe from afar is your specialty. A good archer can end a fight before it begins. Defeat your enemies before they have time to know what hit them. *Automatically receive:* +1 Agility, +1 Constitution, Aimed Shot. *New Attributes per Level:* +2 Agility, +2 Attribute Points.

Earth Mage: *As an earth affinity mage, you specialize in harnessing your earth affinity magic at the cost of your other affinity. No one will be your equal when it comes to earth magic. Automatically receive: +1 Intelligence, +1 Wisdom, Earth Toss, Stoneskin. New Attributes per Level: +2 Intelligence, +1 Wisdom, +1 Attribute.*

Herbalist: *All life stems from… a stem. Plants are the center of life, and as an herbalist you are at the center of plants. Learn about a variety of plant life and how it interacts with the world. Herbalists strive to make amazing discoveries in their field. Automatically receive: +1 Intelligence, Book of Basic Herbs, Herb Bag (soulbound), Growth. New Attributes per Level: +1 Intelligence, +3 Attribute Points. Note: If herbalist is your current primary profession, you will be allowed to choose another at your leisure.*

Ranger: *Learn to utilize magic to enhance your skills with a bow. Rangers are less proficient with their bow than Archers, but offer more utility through use of their magic. Automatically receive: +1 Agility, +1 Intelligence, Elemental Shot. New Attributes per Level: +1 Agility, 1+ Intelligence, +2 Attribute Points.*

Water Mage: *As a water affinity mage, you specialize in harnessing your water affinity magic at the cost of your other affinity. No one will be your equal when it comes to water magic. Automatically receive: +1 Intelligence, +1 Wisdom, Water Jet, Cleanse. New Attributes per Level: +2 Intelligence, +1 Wisdom, +1 Attribute.*

The choices were staggering, and by the time he could read all the additional information they could see the city in the distance and it appeared to be in trouble. Large plumes of thick, dark smoke were bellowing into the air, and there appeared to be large crowds running from the city gates.

The group looked at one another. Their new home was in trouble. Without uttering a word, the three were in silent agreement. It was time to defend their home.

CHAPTER SIX

The Crimson Shadow

When the party arrived at the front gates, they gazed in horror. The gate guards were absent, but the street was littered with bodies.

"What the hell is going on?" Patty looked shocked and had a hint of fear in her voice. A large explosion came from the other side of town and they could see another building going up in flames.

Looking around, Luke saw several families lying dead. Mothers were holding their children as they tried and failed to flee the city. Panic hit Luke when his mind thought of Rose.

"Rose!" He looked at his friends with dread. "I have to make it to the alchemist's shop. I have to check on Rose." His eyes were pleading for them to join him.

Penny looked at him hard and contemplated whether they should head back to the guild or help Luke. "Luke…" She hesitated. "We'll join you but we have to head for the guild after."

Luke was grateful to them for agreeing to help. While he was also concerned about the guild, they would respawn if they got caught up in all this death but if anything happened to Rose, she'd be gone forever. Luke didn't want to lose his friend and rushed his party down the street.

When the group reached the turn that took them to the merchant's row, they stopped. In front of them were two figures in dark leather attacking some locals. Before confirming with his party on how to proceed, Luke had swung his bow off his back and released an arrow. To his surprise, his party didn't hesitate either and following his arrow was Penny and Nanoc charging the dark armored assailants with their weapons drawn.

The arrow struck one man in the back and he let out a scream. "Son of a..." The man was turning around, but they cut his response off. Nanoc brought his axe down and across the chest of the man, almost splitting him in two.

The man's partner responded quickly and took a leap backwards. Penny slammed her sword on her shield and activated her taunt. The man blindly walked forward against his will and began attacking her. Distracted by the taunt, the man could not dodge the flurry of arrows Luke released on him. After the third arrow hit its mark, the man dropped to the ground lifeless.

*Traveler **HotZone** (Red) defeated. 200 exp added.*
*Traveler **Boomer** (Red) defeated. 150 exp added.*

Killing other travelers not marked as Red, attacking NPCs unprovoked, breaking the law and other illegal activities will mark you Red. Other travelers and NPCs will see this status on you and will be allowed to attack you on site without penalty until this status goes away. The Red status will cause town guards to attack you on site.
Note: This is a one time system message.

Luke rushed over and cast nature's regrowth on the merchant with a slash in his chest. "Stay with us." The man's cut started to stitch back together. Reality hit Luke hard as he looked up at the battlefield. Luke just killed a man. The man was young, younger than Luke but all life had drained from his face. His eyes were white and blood stained his armor.

Did I do that? Did I... did I kill someone? Luke shuttered at the thought of being a murderer. The man's body slowly began to vanish, leaving behind its armor, weapons and bags. The equipment dropped from the body in the same layout it had been in, creating a pseudo-outline of a person. It resembled a crime scene outline but filled in with equipment.

Luke stared at the spot where the man used to be. He felt a hand on his shoulder and looked up. Penny was staring down at him with a concerned look on her face. "Luke... We have to keep moving." She paused for a moment before continuing. "Isn't Rose's shop up ahead?"

Luke pushed his glasses up and, for the first time, noticed the tears streaming from his eyes. He enjoyed being part of a party and taking out wolves. It was a game after all but this was different. He wasn't sure how to cope with this, but he knew one thing: he didn't want anything bad to happen to Rose. Rose took him in, cared for him and gave him a home when he wasn't sure about his future. He wanted to make sure she was safe and would bottle up his emotions until then.

"Rose!" he shouted as he burst through the front door. "Rose!" he repeated with growing concern. He ran into the back office but it was empty. Running out back to check the greenhouse, he noticed blood on the doorknob. The greenhouse was also empty, and he wasn't sure how to feel. Does this mean she was safe or should he be concerned?

Nanoc and Penny came into the shop and found Luke putting vials into his bag. He noticed the two enter and tossed them some health potions. "Let's take these potions and head to the guild house. Let's find out what happened to Shrapnel and the others."

Luke started walking past them for the door but Penny stopped him. "Luke? Is Rose ok?"

He looked back with watery eyes. "I don't know... no one's here and I can't just sit around and wait for her. Can we... can we just go, please?" She nodded and followed him outside.

Running for the guild house, the team stopped several times to pass out health potions to NPCs and travelers alike. They tried to get information from people, but no one really knew what was going on. Everyone could just agree that the city was under attack by masked men and they seemed to kill everyone on sight.

The group made it to their guild home without any more encounters and were happy to see it still in one piece. When they entered, the building appeared to be abandoned. None of the guild members were there and items laid scattered everywhere.

"This makes no sense." Nanoc commented.

"Wait! Can't you post in the guild message board? I don't have access as a probationary member." Added Luke.

Penny was quick to answer. "We can't. I tried and the whole message board is blacked out with a message saying something about an area event quest going on and communications being blocked."

"Well... where do we go from here?" Luke inquired.

Penny scratched the back of her head before snapping her fingers together. "Backstab!" Luke could tell she was pulling menus up and scrolling through options because her hands and eyes were zooming around in front of her. "My party sense ability shows him heading for the castle. I bet we'll find more guild members over there." Both men nodded and ran back outside in the castle's direction.

As they got closer, they saw a large number of travelers and NPCs being rounded up in front of the castle. The group kept their distance but stayed close enough to listen.

"Hurry up." said a man, dressed the same way as the two they had slain. He was pushing a group of NPCs along with the edge of his blade. One of the NPCs, a frail looking older gentleman, stumbled and fell to the ground. "I said hurry!" the man repeated as he moved the tip of his blade toward the man's face. "Get up and move or you're just dead weight." A few other NPCs helped the man to his feet, and they were back en route to the castle.

*New skill acquired: **Sneak**, Beginner 0. While others try to be honest and fair, you sneak around in the dark, looking for opportunities to strike. What are you really doing hiding in those bushes? Cost: 1 stamina per second. Effect: +x% chance to sneak and +1x% chance to perform a sneak attack when attacking while hidden, where x = skill level.*

"They're heading for the castle. We should circle around and get a better vantage point," Penny whispered as she pointed down an alley. Proceeding down the alley they started looking for a building that had windows facing the castle. They quickly found one and slowly entered the unlocked door. Luke pointed to the staircase and Penny nodded. The group moved upstairs and entered the room that should contain the windows facing the castle's courtyard.

It was a small bedroom and, like the rest of the home, was empty of occupants. The group moved to either side of the window and peeked out. The castle's courtyard was packed with travelers and NPCs. Surrounding the crowd were more of the dark armored people garnishing their blades. In front of the castle was a hastily erected stage with a man walking up to it.

"People, people." The man was raising his hands, trying to settle the crowd down. He was wearing what appeared to be a thick black robe with a hooded cloak. "I know you're all concerned with what's going on but I'm here to answer all your questions." A man in the crowd tried speaking up but was quickly silenced with a sword hilt to the back of his head. With a sinister voice, he continued. "Now there, I don't like interruptions. I am Shadow Incarnate, and I am your new king."

The dark armored people among the crowd started cheering uncontrollably while the rest of the crowd appeared to just look confused. A guard approached the stage and spoke. "You... you are not our king! Our king died and we serve the royal family!" The crowd looked uncomfortable and unsure who to side with.

Shadow Incarnate started smiling and dark shadows filled his eyes as they became matte black. Dark clouds formed above and darkness fell upon them. He lifted his arm and faced his palm out toward the guard. A large black fireball formed in the open palm and with a forward thrust of of his hand it shot toward the guard at an alarming speed. The fireball connected with the guard's metal chest plate and instantly spread across his entire body. The man let out shouts of pain as the fireball consumed his flesh, but it appeared to be doing no damage to his equipment. When the fire finally put itself out, all that was left of the guard was his equipment and bones.

"Now rise, child of shadows." The man raised both his arms up slowly and the skeleton of the guard's bones started clacking. The guard slowly stood back up as a newly raised skeleton, with dark flames for eyes behind his helmet. The crowd started shouting in terror but the dark armored men prevented them from going anywhere.

"That's not right," whispered Nanoc as his grip tightened on his axe.

"Now you know what your king is capable of and what happens to those who disobey." He paused to let his threat sink in. "Join me, join your new king, join the Crimson Shadow!" Applause and shouts of encouragement again rained from the dark armored members of the crowd. Nothing but fear was shown on the faces of everyone else in the crowd.

"The Crimson Shadow! Is this guy a traveler?" Luke questioned aloud.

"No way. The beta only started a month ago. I was in the second round of participants and I've only been in the game for a little over 3 weeks. There's no way he gained that much power in a month. That's got to be a master level skill. I know travelers are part of the Crimson Shadow but there's no way this guy's a traveler." Penny responded but hesitated. "We… we need to go down there. It's one thing being trapped in a game, but I can't be trapped in a game where that man rules over me."

"If a high level guard can't do anything, what are we supposed to do?" Luke rebutted.

"I agree with Luke. As much as I want to shed some blood with my axe, I don't want that blood to be mine," Nanoc chimed in.

"I'm going down." Penny had a serious look on her face. "If we don't stand now then when? We're immortal, remember? Even if he kills us, we'll just come back to fight him again." She smiled but Luke could tell it was a fake smile. Penny was just as scared as he was.

The two men agreed to her plan, and they headed downstairs. They left through the back door, trying to stay as silent as possible. "Should we just attack or is there more to your plan?" Luke nocked an arrow, awaiting her reply.

"I think the focus is to take out as many of the Crimson Shadow as we can, so the NPCs can get away. Their safety is our number one priority. Remember, they don't respawn."

"I get to take out Crimson Shadow members? And it's not even my birthday," Luke teased playfully. When he got a nod from Penny, he released his arrow and it flew directly into the back of a Crimson Shadow member.

Sneak Attack!
Attacking while not being seen has the chance of scoring a Sneak Attack. Sneak Attacks do significantly increased damage.

"Ahhh!" the man screamed as he dropped his blade and reached toward his back looking for the intruder. Penny and Nanoc began their charge.

When they reached the crowd, they collided with a row of ready Crimson Shadow members. Penny quickly activated her taunt and Nanoc's skin went red with rage. Distracted by her taunt, an armor bound thug's back was torn open by Nanoc's large axe. Unfortunately, there were still six other people raining down attacks on her shield, and she was quickly getting overrun. Right before a man could stab her in the side, an arrow struck him with such force that he stumbled back. She didn't bother looking over her shoulder as she knew it was Luke covering her flank.

Luke cast nature's regrowth on her, but a quick review of his party screen showed nothing promising. Even with his heal, Penny was well below half health and Nanoc wasn't too far behind.

Five or six more thugs started charging Penny but were interrupted when a few travelers jumped on them. "We got your back!" screamed Guild Master Shrapnel as he threw a small red fireball from his hands.

NPCs started taking off in all directions once the chaos broke out. Luke and his team continued their onslaught, but he started noticing something. Every target they did significant damage to started getting back up and their wounds seemed to be healing themselves. The man whose back was sliced open by Nanoc was charging him again only moments later. The slice on his back had strange black semi-translucent tentacles coming from it and they were pulling the wound back together. By the time the man reached Nanoc again his wound was fully closed, and the tentacles vanished.

Looking around, Luke saw Shadow Incarnate smiling with his fully black eyes glowing. "Hey guys," he panted as he released another arrow and noticed his stamina bar was down to 20%. "I think that the main guy is healing everyone."

"Yeah." Penny raised her shield to block several strikes, but a dagger still broke through her defences and sliced along her side. "Ahh! Yeah, I noticed! Not much we can really do. He's beyond us."

Luke didn't accept that and ran forward. He dodged a few strikes as he got closer to the main crowd. When he thought he was close enough, he took a shot at Shadow Incarnate. The arrow flew true but stopped mid-air when it was a foot from its target. Black ripples glimmered around Shadow Incarnate as a transparent shield came into view. The arrow ignited in black flames and turned to dust.

"You dare take a shot at me. AT ME! Your new king!" Shadow Incarnate raised his hand and a familiar black fireball formed in the man's palm. He shot the fireball at Luke and Luke took off running.

His running was in vain as the fireball quickly gained ground on him. When it was about to connect, a white and red column of light shot down from the sky, piercing and dispersing the dark clouds above. The fireball faded from existence as a man appeared clad in full plate armor and wielding a golden bastard sword in one hand and a large golden shield with a phoenix insignia on it in the other. The insignia was engulfed in flames and the phoenix appeared to be living.

The column of light faded as the man stepped forward. "Your rule ends here Shadow!" The man raised his shield and the flaming phoenix shot forward.

"Shadow Shield!" A jet-black wall formed in front of Shadow Incarnate and the phoenix collided with it. The phoenix wasn't stopping, and the wall began to form cracks. The wall broke moments later, and the phoenix went straight through him, splitting him in two. As the top of his body started falling to the ground, both halves became completely black and flattened like a sheet of paper. The man's shadow on the ground became a full-color clone of him and raised up. The clone began to fill out and turn 3d as it took the place of the shadow that was just torn in half.

"The same tricks as always Shadow, but this time you fell for my trap." The heavenly man's bastard sword erupted in white and red flames. "Holy Fire Slash!" He took a large, deliberate swing with his sword and as it swung through the air, a visible line of pure burning energy shot out of it, directly toward the stage. When the line of energy hit the stage, it exploded, and smoke surrounded the area.

Luke's mouth was agape. He may have only been playing for a couple of weeks, but the level of power these two exhibited was beyond anything he thought was possible. Part of him was scared at the sheer force of the battle, but a part of him was buzzing with adrenaline. *Could I become that strong?*

The heavenly man took one massive wave of his shield, treating it like a giant fan, and the smoke cleared. There was a large crater where the stage once stood and the rest of the battle had gone silent. A horde of town guards swarmed in and quickly surrounded the remaining Crimson Shadow members. As the guards went to put cuffs on the men, their shadows came off the ground and flowed over them like water. When they were completely covered, their shadows pulled them down into the ground and all signs off them were gone.

"Search the city!" screamed Captain Holtz to his men. "If you find any of them, I want them alive!"

Luke released a breath he didn't realize he was holding as his party ran over to him. He spoke before they got the chance. "Are you guys all right?" Penny and Nanoc gave thumbs up toward him as he cast nature's regrowth on a very wounded Penny.

"King Henry." Captain Holtz had approached while the party came together and knelt before the heavenly man. The three travelers turned and began awkwardly following Captain Holtz's motions.

The king raised one eyebrow at the bunch of travelers. "Rise Rupert, and rise travelers. We can save the formalities for later." Everyone got back on their feet and waited attentively for what the king had to say. "Send a squad to guard the gates out of town. If any of the Crimson Shadow didn't make it out with that shadow escape spell, I don't want them making it out on foot." The captain ran off and began barking orders at guards passing by.

The party began to take their leave before the king stopped them. "Wait a moment you three." They all turned and for the first time got a good look at the mountain of a man. He was easily seven feet tall and chiseled with muscle. He had a long brown beard, and hair was flowing from the front opening in his helmet. Even if he didn't display such awe-invoking power during the previous fight, it was obvious that he was a warrior king. "I saw what you three did. I have a lot going on right now, but I expect to see you three at the castle in the morning. I want to speak with you."

Quest alert! **An Audience with the King:** *King Henry wants you to meet with him in the morning. It wouldn't be wise to refuse a king. Reward: Unknown. Exp: Unknown. Accept / Decline.*

The party all accepted the quest, bowed and left the king to search for Backstab. They quickly reunited with him because of Penny's party sense, and they shared both handshakes and laughs. Backstab also confirmed that they gave him the Audience with the King quest, likely because he was a member of their party.

The group split up for the night and headed off to bed. They had a long day and real darkness would soon be upon them. Before leaving, they handed out most of the health potions they took from Rose's shop and Luke headed back there for the night. He was still worried about Rose's whereabouts and he hadn't seen her in the crowd of people outside the castle during the battle.

When he reached her shop, he tried the door and to his surprise it was locked again. He proceeded inside but after searching the house, found no one present. *Where could she be... Maybe she's out healing others?* Luke tried not to worry too much about it and went to bed. He hoped to be woken up by Rose making noise in her workshop.

When he woke up, it was already late morning. He must have been more tired than he thought. He shot up and began his normal morning routine. He tended to Rose's garden and headed into the shop. It was still vacant, so he tidied up a bit. The place was a mess from the day before when he stormed in and ransacked it for healing potions.

After about thirty minutes a loud knocking came at the door.

"Sorry, we're closed for the day." The knocking persisted until he couldn't ignore it.

"Luke, open up. It's Penny and the rest of the party."

Opening the door, his vision took in a freshly bathed and dolled up version of his party. Everyone but Nanoc was wearing matching white robes, and they had polished their equipment. Nanoc was wearing long white pants instead of his normal fur shorts.

"Umm… you guys look nice…" Luke muttered.

"No shit Luke. We're on our way to meet the king, remember? Hurry up and put this robe on." He obliged and quickly ran to the bathroom, or the room you would call a bathroom. The room was comprised of a hole in the ground and had a few pails of water for cleaning. He put some water in his messy hair and slicked it back as best he could before rejoining the others.

When they reached the castle, Captain Holtz was waiting for them and rushed them inside.

"Shouldn't you take our weapons or something?" Penny threw Luke a hard elbow to his side, implying he should shut up.

"Normally we would, but, not to sound hurtful, at your current levels you couldn't collectively hurt the King if you tried," responded the Captain mirthfully.

"I thought the King was dead?" Penny elbowed Luke even harder. Enough so that he took 5% damage and let out a low grunt of pain.

"The King will explain everything." The captain gave them a warm smile as they proceeded through several hallways leading to a large set of double doors. "When we go in, walk with me to the throne and kneel. If you are wondering what to do, just look at me and do what I say and you'll be fine."

The captain pushed open the twenty-foot doors and walked inside. The room was large and open with marble columns on both sides of a long red carpet. The rug ran from the double doors to a small set of stairs. The stairs lead up to a platform where three large, cushioned seats and one simple wooden seat were positioned. Two of the cushioned seats were together in front and the remaining two seats, one on each side, were positioned a little farther back. The king sat in one of the regal-looking chairs with an older woman next to him. The cushioned seat to the queen's side housed a young girl. The plain chair to the King's side was the only empty chair.

When the group reached the king, they all knelt and waited for permission to stand.

"Rise loyal subjects, so we may speak face to face." The King began speaking and the group all rose. Captain Holtz walked up the steps to sit beside the king in the simple wooden seat. "I wish to reward you for your bravery and valor yesterday. Stepping up to face an enemy that was clearly stronger than yourselves to help aid my citizens… It was incredible and far beyond what I thought travelers were capable of. Forgive me for saying this, but most travelers seem to only care about themselves."

The king paused, waiting for a response, but everyone was too nervous to speak. Hating the silence, Penny stepped forward and elected to speak for the group. "Thank you for your kind words, your majesty. We travelers," she pointed to herself and her party, "come from a different world. In that world many people are just out to get ahead." The king didn't look completely satisfied with that answer and gave her a look that told her to continue. She started and stopped several times, not sure how to proceed.

Luke pushed his glasses up and took a step forward. "We didn't want to see people die. As travelers, we have the ability to resp… come back to life when we die. Your people don't."

"But why? That still doesn't answer my overall question of why. Why make that sacrifice. Does it not hurt to die?" The king pushed for answers.

Luke shook his head aggressively. "No, it hurts. It hurts a lot. I never want to go through that kind of pain again. It's just..." He thought of Rose and the kindness she showed him. She gave him a reason to keep going when he wanted to throw in the towel and give up like a lot of the travelers in town. A warm, genuine smile crossed his face before he continued. "Your people are special. One of them took me in when I had nothing. She treated me like family and lifted me up when I was spiraling down. I wouldn't be here today if it wasn't for her and if I have to die a thousand more times to save a person like that, traveler or not, I will."

Social +1.

King Henry kept his eyes locked with Luke's for a long moment before his expressions changed. A smile crossed his face before he spoke. "I'm so glad to hear that."

Quest Alert! **An Audience with the King:** *Meet with the king 1/1. Quest complete! Reward: Rare Class Item Box, 200 reputation with the Phoenix Kingdom. Exp: 1,000.*

New Status: **Liked.**

Gaining or losing reputation with the kingdom as a whole will positively or negatively affect your social interactions with the kingdom and its subjects as a whole. Individual benefits or detriments from reputation changes with individuals will still apply, regardless of overall kingdom reputation.
Note: This is a one time system message.

A small square box appeared in front of each traveler, floating in mid-air. Luke reached out to his and grabbed it with both hands.

Rare Class Item Box (*Rare*) *x1 obtained. When opened, this box will award you one rare item associated with your current class. ERROR: Class not chosen. The Beginner Class can not open class item boxes.*

"I hope that shows you how grateful I am for your assistance." He hesitated for a second but pushed on. "I would actually like your help again." The king continued to explain that his death was all a ruse. The day they announced the king's death, the castle was indeed attacked, but the king was able to stop the intruders after a lengthy battle. The king wasn't sure who was behind it and so he came up with a plan.

The king would fake his death, trusting only his captain with the truth. He went into hiding and had guards searching the surrounding area for any information. In his absence, Shadow Incarnate invaded his city and it forced him out of hiding.

Finishing his story, he continued with his request for help. "With the reappearance of Shadow Incarnate, many things have been set into motion and I fear my city is in great danger. No matter how events unfold, please defend my people with your lives."

The party looked at one another, and this time Luke was the first to respond. "Sir, I mean, your majesty. With all due respect, I'm not sure how much of a help we're all going to be."

Both the King and Queen chuckled before the King spoke up. "If you display half the bravery you did today, our kingdom is in good hands."

Quest alert! **City Defenders:** *King Henry has tasked you with aiding in the defense of his city. It takes a lot to make a warrior king ask for help, try not to disappoint him. Reward: Unknown. Exp: Unknown. Accept / Decline*

Quick glances around revealed not an ounce of hesitation on their faces as they all hit accept.

CHAPTER SEVEN

Class Acquired

"Well, that was fun," Luke added as the group reached the courtyard outside the castle. "I want to help him but I don't think any of us are strong enough." Nanoc raised his hand ready to object but lowered it after realizing Luke was right. "I'm just not sure what we can…" A loud gong sounded in his ears, forcing his eyes shut in pain. When he opened his eyes, he noticed the rest of his group covering their ears as a system alert entered his line of sight.

SYSTEM ALERT! SYSTEM ALERT! UPDATE FROM VORTEX INDUSTRIES!

The message below the alert appeared as a hand-written letter from Rob.

Hello Travelers, it's Rob. Vortex Industries and I wanted to reach out to you all and update you on the current situation. The top brass forgot about the time dilation and wanted to wait a couple more days before sending you any updates, but I thought we should update you as soon as possible.

I'll spare you all the technical jargon, but we haven't been able to recover the hacked data yet and bring you all home. We thought about rewriting the code but to be honest, we're hesitant to do extensive testing while players are logged in. We don't want to mess with your minds and all. Don't fear though, we're still working around the clock to get you guys home! The FBI has even stepped in to lend their assistance. They said the unique virus preventing you guys from logging out has the same coding signature as others they have dealt with. They said it's the signature of some extreme hacking group called the Crimson Shadow? Not sure what that means, but they are trying to track down their leader.

In other news, we're working on getting you all some in-game support. If I can convince my boss, we will open the game to another round of beta testers. Now, before you all start freaking out, they won't be capsule users. The next round of beta testers will all use traditional VR headsets to login and won't be transferring any of their consciousness into the game. I figure more players equals more fun, right? It's about all I can do to help at the moment with the FBI taking over the investigation. You should see some new players, pending approval, in the next week. Well, two weeks for you.

I hope you are all doing well, and at the very least, the traditional VR users will give us a window into the game again. We had to shut off all external connections in fear that the hackers would somehow gain access again. We're no longer able to monitor you, so stay safe.
I guess that's all for now. I'll update you again as soon as I have more information.

Sincerely,

Rob Xanders

P.S. Sorry I couldn't show up in person again. When we stopped the world last time, we started overheating the mainframes housing the game. I guess freezing an entire world for a few minutes takes a lot of computing power. Who would have thought?

It took a moment for all of them to finish reading the message and process its contents. "The Crimson Shadow! Those bastards!" Nanoc roared in anger.

"Now, now. We don't know if it's the same group." Penny attempted to calm him. "I agree that it's a weird coincidence though…"

"And what's this about a time dilation?" Luke inquired.

"Oh, that's an easy one. Didn't you read the user manual?" Penny responded.

"I wasn't given a user manual. I got trapped during my first log-in session." Luke replied.

"Ahh, that explains why you know so little. Endless Fantasy Online runs at double the speed of Earth. For every two days we spend in here, only one passes back home. The manual said they did it so people could spend more time engaged for less of a time commitment in real life. Think if you only had a week off from work, you could spend a whole two weeks vacationing in the Vortex Capsule," Penny explained.

"That's both amazing and scary. We've been stuck in the game for a little over two weeks but that means it's only been about a week in the real world?" Penny confirmed with a nod and Luke continued. "Looks like we'll have more players soon too. Wonder if that's a good thing or a bad thing."

Nanoc spoke up. "More players will make the game more

interesting, but it also means we'll have more competition for hunting grounds, loot and the sort. It's probably best we level up as quickly as we can, that way we're not fighting people for monster spawns."

Everyone agreed that they would grab as many quests as they could find tomorrow and spend the whole day hunting. They would have gone out today, but it was already past lunchtime and the gates would only be open for a few more hours. As they parted ways, with plans to meet first thing the next day, Luke headed for Rose's shop.

When he arrived, he searched the shop for what felt like the hundredth time for any clues leading to Rose's whereabouts. He even searched her upstairs living quarters. There was no mess and there weren't any signs of a struggle or break-in either. It didn't appear that any of her personal effects were missing. He locked the upstairs door again before heading back downstairs to the workshop in order to think.

With Rose gone, someone will have to tend to her crops and run the shop. But that would probably cut into my leveling time. Could I hire someone? He wasn't sure what to do and for now posted a sign outside that the store would only be open first thing in the morning and late at night. That would allow him enough time to tend to the plants, serve some customers, and spend the day adventuring. He could open the shop back up before sleeping each night. That thought reminded him of his sleeping arrangements.

The main shop area had a small storage closet that didn't hold a lot of inventory. They mainly used it to store crates of empty bottles and pots for plants. He went about clearing the space out and moving the boxes into the backroom. If Rose wasn't going to show up anytime soon, he could use the space more than her.

Before he could get to work, he needed to prepare. He stopped at the bank and emptied his account. Fifty gold would be enough money to make change for the customers, but it would be tough to pay his other expenses. He considered how much he could afford to spend as he headed to the carpenter to commission some furniture.

"Umm… Hello?" Luke called out to the man working outside the carpenter's shop.

A short round man, who was putting the finishing touches on a chair, looked in his direction. "How can I help you, son?"

The man had a thick accent that Luke didn't recognize and was having trouble understanding. "Uhh, I came to buy a simple bed, a chair and a desk. Nothing fancy, just something serviceable and cheap."

"Cheap implies poor workmanship. Dwarfs don't do poor workmanship." The man approached Luke.

"I didn't mean to imply anything. I just don't have a lot of spare coins at the moment. All of your wares look excellent and top-notch." he backpedaled.

The dwarf gave him a stink eye.

"How much for these pieces?" Look pointed to an ornate chair and desk.

"Hrmpf." The dwarf grunted and put his hammer and chisel down. "Follow me." Luke was lead inside the cluttered shop and told to wait while the dwarf grabbed a couple of pieces of furniture from the back of the shop.

When he returned, he had a small desk over one shoulder and a stool in the other. Both pieces looked well made but simple. There weren't any carvings, symbols, designs or woodworking techniques present. They looked like something Luke would have come up with back home if he was pressed to build his own furniture, only sturdier and professionally built.

"Those are perfect," Luke gestured at the furniture.

"I have a bed in the back that matches, but you must buy your own mattress. Since this is my new apprentice's work, I won't charge you much. How does… 25 gold sound?"

Having already insulted the dwarf, he decided against bartering and accepted the deal. "That sounds like a great deal. Do you know the shop 'Rose Alchemy'? Would you mind bringing the furniture there?"

"Yeah, I know the place. I have some deliveries to make later in the day. I can bring them by then." the dwarf said as he was cleaning filth off his hands with a rag.

Luke handed over half the contents of his coin purse and spent another ten gold on his way back to the shop on a mattress and pillow. He paid extra for a feather mattress because just the thought of sleeping on straw again made his back hurt. Returning to the shop, he deposited the rest of his gold into the register and began moving crates into the back room. By the time he had the place cleared out, the carpenter had delivered his furniture and Luke arranged it to his liking.

It was now dark outside, and he was exhausted from a day of lifting heavy boxes and running around. He grabbed a few pieces of fruit and lay in bed, taking in his hard work and new room. When his eyes passed his desk, he saw the class item box the King awarded him and he shot up to a sitting position in his bed. *I'm an idiot! I need to choose my class!*

He opened his menu and reviewed his choices again. He eliminated them in his head until it left him with archer, apprentice mage and ranger. *Archer would make me a ranged killing machine, but I would be a one-trick pony. If I became a mage, I could learn a ton of spells but I would have to give up my bow.* He continued thinking through his options until his choice became clear.

As he hit the Ranger class with anticipation, the system presented him with multiple system messages.

Ranger Class acquired. You have been awarded +1 agility, +1 intelligence and an Elemental Shot skill.
New skill acquired: *Water Shot* (Beginner 0): Infuses your arrow with water. When shot it will fire off like a water jet and do increased water affinity damage. Cost: 25 + x mana. Effect: Increases arrow travel rate by 10% and adds 1x water damage where x = skill level. Range: Touch arrow.

Luke reviewed the new skill in awe. *This skill is amazing! It's a huge drain on my mana, but adding 10 damage to my attack almost triples my current damage output!* Leaping from bed, he walked over to his desk and grabbed the class box.

Rare Class Item Box (Rare). When opened, this box will award you one rare item associated with your current class. Current class: Ranger. Open? Yes No

Luke hit yes, and the box popped open with a burst of white light. Sitting on his small desk was what appeared to be a ram's horn. The horn was slightly larger than his hand and was tinted green at the horn's large circular base. He picked the horn up for closer examination.

Identification failed. OVERRIDE: Quest reward.
Beast Summoning Shofar (Rare). Blowing into the shofar will summon a random animal companion of at least rare level rarity. The summoned companion will automatically become bound to the summoner.

Contemplating whether or not he should add taking care of an animal to his growing list of responsibilities, he set the horn back on the desk. Growing up, Luke wasn't allowed to have a cat or dog because his mother was allergic to them. Even if she wasn't, he was always working to help pay bills and never had time to take care of a pet. *This could be my only chance at owning a pet,* he thought as he picked the item back up. Shrugging his shoulders, he put the item up to his mouth and blew into it.

The shofar produced a deep, consistent bass sound. When he was done blowing, he pulled his mouth away and cracks started forming up the shofar's base as it began to burn hot in his hand. He released his grip on the horn but it stayed floating in midair. A small orb of white light came into existence at the item's center and it began to expand. It expanded until it was the size of a basketball and then slowly descended, touching down on the wood floor.

A roulette-like wheel appeared above the orb. The wheel had ten wedges on it and an arrow at the top, pointed to one wedge. Each wedge was outlined in silver except for two that were gold. As he examined the wedges, he noticed that each contained a pure black silhouette of something he couldn't make out. After a few seconds, the wheel started spinning as though an invisible hand had just launched it into motion. Ticking sounds kept ringing out every time the arrow passed over a new choice until the wheel started to slow.

Tick. Tick. Tick.. Tick… Tick…… Tick……… Ding!

The wheel stopped on one of the golden choices and then it began to melt. The molten wheel oozed into the white orb of light, mixing in with it and turning it gold. After the orb was completely gold, it began to take the shape of the silhouette that was inside the spinning wheel's selection. When it was complete, rays of golden light shot out of its center before fading and revealing a small gray wolf pup.

Animal companion acquired: **Baby Alpha Wolf** *(Epic). The beast will follow your commands to the best of its ability but will not follow commands that brings itself harm for no reason.*

New skill acquired: **Resurrect Companion**, *Class Skill. Resurrects your animal companion if they have unfortunately died. Allowing your animal companion to die will negatively affect your relationship, and they may choose to break their bond with you. Cost: 100% max mana. Effect: Channel this spell for 10 seconds to resurrect your animal companion at full health. Cooldown: 24 hours. Range: Self.*

New skill acquired: **Beast Mastery**, *Beginner 0. You have bonded with a beast and taken a baby step in befriending the animal kingdom. Improving this skill will increase your bond with your animal companion and increase their proficiency in battle. This skill also scales based on your social attribute. Effect: +1% animal companion's attributes.*

Luke was happy that he got something of such high rarity and that he acquired new skills, but he had a sour expression on his face. *Why did it have to be a wolf? Is the game purposefully mocking me?* he thought as he sat cross-legged on the floor.

"Hi there little guy. What's your name?" He reached his hand out in his best attempt to appear non-threatening. When his hand touched the baby alpha wolf, a prompt came up.

Please name your new animal companion.

"Oh, you don't have a name yet." The animal licked his outstretched hand before crawling into Luke's lap and staring up at him. He began to slowly pet the beast, and the wolf began to push its head against Luke's hand. As he was petting him, he noticed that the wolf had sporadic sky blue spots in its fur. They were almost unnoticeable unless you were up close or knew to look for them.

"Hmm... I suppose you don't want the name Wolfy or Spots? Heck, I don't want you to have those names. Hmm.." The wolf leaped out of his lap and bent over, sticking its butt in the air before starting to growl at Luke's half-eaten apple on the floor.

"Are you hunting an apple?" He started laughing and grabbed the round green prey. Biting off a piece, he placed it on the floor in front of the unnamed pup. Luke watched to see how the wolf would respond. It approached the piece of apple with caution but began sniffing it when he got near. When the wolf determined it wasn't a threat, he put the whole thing in his mouth and started chomping.

Luke smiled and put another bite on the floor. "I think I got a good name for you little guy." Luke entered the name Ringo into the prompt before confirming his choice.

*1,000 **Reputation Gained** with **Ringo***.
New Status: ***Best Friends***.

Ringo looked up at Luke and barked his approval before letting out a long yawn. Luke stood, picked up Ringo and moved to his bed. While he was getting comfortable again, Ringo walked toward Luke and lay directly on his chest.

Before drifting off to sleep Luke pulled up his character sheet and noticed he had a lot of unallocated skill and attribute points. Still unsure what skills were the best, he saved his skill points and assigned his attributes points. When he was done he reviewed his character sheet for the first time in a while.

Name: Luke, Wolfsbane.
Class: Ranger
Primary Profession: Herbalist
Animal Companion: Ringo (Alpha Wolf Pup)
Level 3: Exp 1380 Exp to next level: 1620
Hit Points: 70/70
Mana: 110/110
Mana Regen: 1.75/sec
Stamina: 90/90
Physical Resistance: +0
Elemental Resistance: Water +10, Earth +10

Attributes Base (Modifier)
Strength: 1
Agility: 5
Intelligence: 4 (+3)
Wisdom: 2 (+2)
Constitution: 3
Social: 4
Luck: 1

Skills, Spells and Abilities

Short Bow (Beginner 4): Basic knowledge on how to use a short bow. Increasing this skill will increase the damage dealt with a short bow. This is a passive skill and requires no activation. Effect: Adds $1+x$% short bow damage where x = skill level.

Herbalism (Beginner 8): This skill allows you to identify various plant life.

First Aid (Beginner 0): Basic knowledge on how to apply basic first aid and use basic bandages. Increasing this skill will increase your knowledge of first aid techniques and increase the speed at which you can apply this skill.

Nature's Regrowth (Beginner 2): Harness the power of nature to speed up the natural healing and growth speed of the target. Cost: 3x mana. Effect: Heal for 1x every 5 seconds for 15 seconds where x = skill level. Cooldown: 60 seconds. Range: 10 feet.

Alchemy (Beginner 1): Knowledge of basic reagent combinations. Increasing this skill will increase your knowledge of alchemy and increase your chances of combining new reagents successfully. Effect: Add x% chance that a new combination will be successful where x = skill level.

Bartering (Beginner 2): Trading is a craft, and you have taken the first steps in learning that craft. You will receive small bonuses when attempting to barter. Effect: +x% bartering results where x = skill level.

Sneak (Beginner 0): While others try to be honest and fair, you sneak around in the dark, looking for opportunities to strike. What are you really doing hiding in those bushes? Cost: 1 stamina per second. Effect: +x% chance to sneak and +1x% chance to perform a sneak attack when attacking while hidden, where x = skill level.

Water Shot (Beginner 0): Infuses your arrow with water. When shot it will fire off like a water jet and do increased water affinity damage. Cost: 25 + x mana. Effect: Increases arrow travel rate by 10% and adds 1x water damage where x = skill level. Cooldown: 60 seconds. Range: Touch arrow.

Resurrect Companion (Class Skill): Resurrects your animal companion if they have unfortunately died. Allowing your animal companion to die will negatively affect your relationship and they may choose to break their bond with you. Cost: 100% max mana. Effect: Channel this spell for 10 seconds to resurrect your animal companion at full health. Cooldown: 24 hours. Range: Self.

Beast Mastery (Beginner 0): You have bonded with a beast and taken a baby step in befriending the animal kingdom. Improving this skill will increase your bond with your animal companion and increase their proficiency in battle. This skill also scales based on your social attribute. Effect: +2% animal companion's attributes.

He put a few of his points into social to help him run the shop and to help Ringo survive. He was rewarded when he noticed beast mastery now gave an extra percentage to Ringo's stats. He split the rest of his points into agility and intelligence as those were the main attributes for his ranger class.

As his new found excitement started to falter, his previous exhaustion crept back. Soon after reviewing his character sheet, he blew out the few candles near his bed and fell asleep.

Luke awoke to a scratching noise the next morning. When he rubbed his eyes awake, he saw Ringo scratching his claws against one of the bedposts. He must have been doing it for some time as the bed post had dozens of new indentations.

"Hey! Stop that." Ringo leaped back and lay on his stomach, pointing his head down in shame. "At least I didn't buy nice furniture," he mumbled under his breath before getting out of bed.

He got dressed and headed for the greenhouse, Ringo following closely behind him. When he opened the back door, Ringo ran out and quickly relieved himself. Luke gathered some herbs that were stored in the greenhouse and watered the remaining plants. He gave Ringo his fair share of water in a saucer when filling the watering can. Returning to the shop he noticed the sun was still down and went to work on his alchemy for a bit before heading off and meeting the others.

The sun soon began to rise, so he gathered the things he needed for the day, eager to try his new spells. Before opening the door, he looked back at Ringo following him. Luke contemplated what to do with his furry companion. He was supposed to bond with the animal and use it in battle but he hesitated at the thought of bringing a baby wolf along while hunting more of its kind.

"Ringo." The young cub looked up and cocked its head to the side. "You don't understand what I'm saying do you…" Ringo's head cocked the other direction. "I think you should stay here. It's not safe for you yet." He began backing up toward the door while stretching his arms out to perform a staying motion. He tossed out some apple slices on the floor and opened the door behind him. He opened it just wide enough for him to slither through, shutting it behind him. He heard light scratching and whimpering sounds from behind the door. It hurt him to leave his new pal behind, but ultimately it was for the best.

The shop wasn't far from the city gate, and he quickly spotted his party looking over the job board. Running up to them he waved and gave a warm good morning to the group.

"So what quests are we doing today?" He inquired.

"I think we should grab the same three for now. Controlling fox and wolf populations and the pelts quest. Killing while advancing in the forest should take us most of the day and give us enough time to make it back," Penny commented.

"Ok." Luke looked all around the board before spotting the fliers that hosted the quests he needed and ripping them down. "If it's ok with you guys, I need to gather a bunch of herbs as we go."

"As long as you don't slow us down, I don't care how you spend your time in between fights," Backtab commented.

"My agility is high enough that I can catch up to…" the growing sound of barking in the distance interrupted him. Looking around, he spotted the now familiar gray site of Ringo charging toward him. When Ringo got to him he leaped up but since Luke wasn't expecting it, Ringo fell backwards after bouncing off his knees. "Ringo! Are you ok?" Leaning down, Luke scooped the rambunctious animal into an arm.

"Oh... my... god... HE IS ADORABLE!" Penny bumped Luke and forced Ringo into her arms. "You are the cutest thing I have ever seen! I could just eat you up!"

"Umm... please don't?" He responded dryly.

Nanoc and Backstab just watched in confusion as Penny acted like most adults do around young babies. She made goo-goo noises and spoke in a baby voice.

"That kind of looks like a..." Backstab's vision went distant, signifying he was looking at a game screen that no one else could see. "That is an alpha wolf! That thing's dad, or brother, or cousin, or whatever just killed me!" He was pointing an accusatory finger at Ringo while grabbing a dagger in his other hand.

"I think Backstab is just wondering what you're doing with a wolf alpha cub?" Nanoc joined the conversation to try and defuse things.

"He's my animal companion." Luke tried brushing past the threats to Ringo's life. "I got him from the King's quest reward after I picked my class."

"You picked your class?" Penny finally looked up from her new best friend.

"Yeah. I went with Ranger. It's a mixture of magic and bow skills. I even got a cool new attack spell I want to try out."

"Wait, you choose ranger and got a familiar from the King's box? Now I feel like I got cheated by only getting a life stealing axe." Nanoc lifted his axe in display.

"I wonder if he's a ranger only reward? I would love a cute little thing like this. Makes me kinda miss my cat. You know something Luke?" Penny waited for an answer.

117

"What?" he quickly replied.

"I'm petting this little guy's belly and I'm noticing he's missing certain... how do you say... parts that would make him a... him." Penny did air-quotes with her free hand.

"Huh?" Luke's eyes went wide when he looked at Ringo's private parts. Ringo was actually a female baby alpha wolf. "Ringo, you're a girl! Now I kinda feel bad for never checking." He scratched the back of his head in embarrassment.

"You got an awesome pet wolf from a glowing box that a mystical warrior king gave you and you didn't bother to check between its legs?" Backstab mocked.

The group all looked at one another before bursting into laughter.

"That reminds me Luke. We have something for you: welcome to the guild." Penny set her backpack down, which Luke just noticed was more full than normal.

"Is it a guild invite?" Luke chuckled.

"Well, that too." Penny fiddled with some invisible menus and a system notice came into view while Penny continued rummaging through her bag.

*New guild request: Guild Officer **Penny** of the **Travelers 4 Hire** (**T4H**) guild would like you to become a fully fledged member. Current contribution settings for members are 1% exp and 5% gold. Note: The guild will also share a small percentage of any reputation you gain or lose, so be careful with your actions. Accept / Decline.*

Happy to finally get the invite he knew was coming, he hit accept. When he did, the message disappeared to reveal Penny holding gray furs laid out across her forearms. "What's this?" She bobbed her head and stretched her arms out more showing she wanted him to take what she was presenting.

Fur Armor (uncommon) x1 obtained. Adds +5 physical resistance.
Fur Leggings (uncommon) x1 obtained. Adds + 4 physical resistance.
Fur Gloves (uncommon) x1 obtained. Adds +3 physical resistance.
Fur Boots (uncommon) x1 obtained. Adds +3 physical resistance.

Running his hands across the fur he saw specks of red among the gray. "This… this is from the alpha, isn't it?"

"We thought you could use some armor since you didn't have any and you pretty much kept us all alive." Penny commented.

"Plus, it's really manly looking!" Nanoc added.

"Don't move around too much or I'll think you're a wolf and backstab you!" Backstab gave Luke an evil grin.

"Sorry we didn't have enough for the helm but…" Penny stopped speaking when she saw tears rolling down Luke's face. "You're one of us now, Travelers 4 Hire. Besides, we saw how much that one attack took out of you. Without armor, you'd be dying all over the place."

Luke wiped his face with his forearm and pushed up his glasses. He choked out the words "Thank you" before grabbing Ringo, deciding she was now tagging along, and the party proceeded out of the city.

CHAPTER EIGHT

The Den

The trip to the Howling Forest took much longer than usual. Luke had to continually run after Ringo when she would get off the path to explore something. If it moved, she wanted to know about it. They stopped for every ladybug, butterfly, or noise. It didn't seem to bother anyone as much as it bothered Luke.

"Ringo! Stop, please just stop." Luke pleaded with his companion as it ran after a butterfly floating just off the path. Luke ran over, picked Ringo up and decided it was best to carry her the rest of the way.

"Way to show her who's boss." Nanoc joked and Backstab chuckled but Luke didn't seem amused.

"Shut up," Penny commanded.

She bent low and pointed toward a clearing up ahead. There were several foxes carrying rabbits in their mouths and they were all heading in the same direction. She put a finger to her lips and started to whisper.

"It appears they are heading back to their den. If we follow them, we could find it and possibly get an area quest to clear it out. Luke, make sure Ringo stays quiet. The foxes get more jumpy the closer they get to their den.

He nodded as he positioned his large bag to hang from his side, placing Ringo in it. He cinched the top of the bag so that Ringo could only get her head out. "Stay in there and don't make a sound. If you do, I'll give you some apple slices." At the mention of apple slices she closed her mouth and Luke could have sworn he saw her nod her head.

The party waited for the foxes to be out of sight before leaving their spot in pursuit. They followed the well-beaten path until they spotted several small holes on the side of a small hill. The foxes were carrying food in and out of the hill. Penny raised a fist into the air to signal the group to stop their pursuit and gestured at a cluster of nearby trees. Hiding behind the trees, Penny started planning.

"Ok Luke, I need you to shoot some arrows into the next couple of foxes who enter or leave the den. Nanoc and Backstab, you two circle around and get on top of the hill. Neither of you wear heavy armor, so you can move more quietly than the rest of us. I will wait with Luke for the foxes to charge him. Let a couple of them leave the den so they can come after us but then leap down and surround the. Everyone good with that?" The group all nodded. "And Luke, you also need to pay attention to our HP. We have potions but I think I speak for everyone when I say we would rather not drink our gold away." Backtab nodded extra fast at that before sneaking off with Nanoc.

Unable to use his bow with Ringo bouncing at his side, Luke set Ringo down. "Stay hidden and quiet Ringo. And don't go far from me." The wolf cub ran behind the closest tree and poked his head around it and looked back in Luke's direction. Luke smiled and turned back to the upcoming fight. Penny and he waited until they could see Nanoc and Backstab crawling on their stomachs up the hill. When they were in a good position, Penny gave Luke the signal to open fire.

Luke released his first arrow, and it hit its mark, piercing the side of a fox. The creature took one more shaky step forward before falling over on its side and curling up. Instantly, the remaining foxes all stopped moving in unison. Rather than charging at the pair as expected, they quickly ran into their den.

Nanoc and Backstab shrugged their shoulders and gave Penny a look that said, "What now?" Turning around, she signaled Luke to follow her as she cautiously approached the den. He nocked another arrow and told Ringo to stay put before he followed Penny.

When they got to the den they tried peeking inside one opening but it was too dark to see anything past the first few feet. They could hear the fox running in the distance and it sounded like the noise was reverberating deeper, as if the fox was descending somehow. Luke poked his head in so that he could hear better.

*Congratulations! You are the first to discover this dungeon, **The Den**. Because you are the first to discover the dungeon, your party has been granted exclusive access for the first 24 hours. You will also be granted bonus experience and loot for the first 24 hours while inside The Den. Note: All dungeons grant a bonus reward item if you are the first party to clear it. Happy hunting and good luck. Time remaining 23 hours and 59 minutes.*

Luke pulled his head out and saw that his party's eyes were all distant. "I assume you all are reading the system message?" he asked.

"A dungeon! This is huge! I haven't heard of a single group

finding a dungeon before. We could be the first group to ever defeat a dungeon. Think of all the treasure and gold that might be down there." Backstab's eyes lit up with excitement. Backstab started drooling and rubbing his hands together. Luke was surprised he didn't have dollar signs floating above his head.

"I don't know guys… It seems pretty dark and narrow in there," Penny stated.

"I agree! I don't think I'll have enough room to swing my axe in that hole," Commented Nanoc.

Backstab saw his opportunity fading and started to panic. "Wait, wait. Let's not get hasty here. I have a skill called minor dark vision. Let me go in a little way and see if it opens up at least." Penny started rubbing her chin in thought. "I mean, unless you're scared or something?" Penny's cheeks filled with pink.

"I'm not scared of anything. Go on in then." She gestured her arm toward the hole in the manner a game show host would show off a prize. "After you."

Backstab had a wicked grin on his face before he started crawling into the opening. He quickly disappeared into darkness and the group was unable to follow his movements. A few moments later, his head popped back out. "There's light in here, well, sorta. Come on!" he said excitedly before disappearing back into the dungeon.

They all looked at each other and shrugged. What did they have to lose? So they all quickly crawled in after him.

Luke hesitated and called over Ringo. "Hey girl." She ran over and he began petting her, testing out different spots to see her response. She seemed to like under the chin the best because her foot began to kick vigorously when he scratched her there. "Hah, you like that girl." Ringo let out a low groan of pleasure in response. "We're going to head into this dungeon and I'm not sure how safe it is for you but… I don't really want to leave you out here alone…" Ringo barked and began moving toward the opening of the dungeon. "Well… I guess you're coming then…" Luke still wasn't sure about bringing her along but didn't have a better alternative, so he didn't fight her enthusiasm.

After crawling through the narrow space for a minute he saw the feet of his comrades gathered near a blueish light at the end of the tunnel. The hole opened up into a much larger cavern. The rocky walls of the room had blue crystals jutting out of them in what appeared to be a random fashion. The entire room was illuminated by the blue glow of the crystals.

Luke noticed Ringo was on his back while Penny was scratching her tummy. "Traitor," he mumbled loud enough to be heard.

"Sorry, I LOOOVE dogs." She responded.

Luke smiled in return and waved away the comment. "I'm just messing with you. Actually, I'm glad someone in the group knows how to take care of her. I've never had a pet before."

"Gawk. Can we drop the cutesy talk and do this dungeon? I need loot!" Backstab cut into their conversation. Nanoc shook his head in disapproval of Backstab's words. The group quickly located a wide staircase that descended steeply.

"This must be where all the foxes went. Ladies first." Penny mocked Backstab by reaching her arms outward and presenting the staircase. "You first, you little girl."

"Normally that would hurt me… but there's loot down there so I don't care," said Backstab. He proceeded down the stairs with the party in tow. Luke scooped Ringo up and put her in his side bag, instructing her to stay quiet.

The staircase was spiral in shape and the group seemed to descend faster than expected. Along the walls of the staircase, connected to the ground were small holes with remnants of rabbit bodies near them. "I think that's where all the foxes went." Luke mumbled.

Just when they thought the staircase would go on forever, the staircase opened up into a small room. The room was shaped out of the surrounding rock but there was a stone wall with a plain wooden door on one side. Hanging on the wall were two lit torches.

"Should we knock?" Nanoc asked genuinely.

Penny shook her head before speaking. "Let's have our resident rogue check it out. I knew there was a reason we put up with you."

Holding his chest in mock pain, Backstab said "That really hurts. I think I just took 50 points of damage from a broken heart." Penny exhaled from her nose loudly and Backstab proceeded to the door. He grabbed a dagger in one hand and lifted his other hand in the air to chest level as he closed his eyes. He pointed his fingers upward and his whole hand began to glow dark purple briefly before fading.

"What skill is that?" Luke asked.

"Detect traps. Basically, I pull ambient mana from the surrounding area into my open hand and then flow the information that mana contained into my eyes. I get a bonus to finding any hidden traps, and it highlights any obvious traps for me. At least that's what the skill description says. This is the first time I've ever used it." He looked around the door for a while before bending down and slashing the air with his dagger. "There was a tripwire here. My skill says it was tied to a blade trap."

"Nice find," Penny complimented. "I knew you weren't useless."

Backstab ignored her words and slowly turned the doorknob. He pushed the door slightly ajar with the smallest amount of strength and peeked inside.

"It looks well lit inside. I don't see anything from this angle but the torches are against the wall so they cast all the shadows in the opposite direction. There easily could be enemies inside."

Nanoc pulled his axe off his back and rolled his shoulders to loosen his arms up. Penny drew her sword and tightened the strap holding her shield to her arm. Luke put Ringo down, grabbed his bow from his back and nocked an arrow toward the door, ready to pull back when the door was opened.

"How about a little shock and awe?" Penny grinned while looking at Nanoc.

Nanoc gave a wicked-looking smile of glee before approaching the door. Lifting a large, muscular leg tinged red with rage, he gave the door one massive kick and splinters went flying inward in all directions. Dust clouds bloomed up from most surfaces and obscured their vision. Luke pulled back on the bow string, ready to shoot the first thing that moved.

The dust clouds slowly began to disperse as a spear flew out of the dust, pulling a dust trail along with it. The spear landed in Nanoc's shoulder and he staggered backward, letting out a grunt of pain. The spear's trail left a temporary hole in the dust cloud that gave Luke an opening to release his arrow at the green-looking monster at the other end of the room.

"Enough of this!" Penny rapidly fanned her shield and dispersed the remaining dust.

The room appeared to be a cross-shaped entry room with some tables and chairs in various spots. On the opposite side of the room was another door and four short green humanoid creatures. They were standing battle ready, one with an arrow in its leg. They had pointed ears, extra long witch-like noses, large guts, sharp claws and long, sharp teeth that didn't seem to fit their mouths. Their teeth were spilling out between their lips, even when their mouths were closed. They didn't have any equipment other than a few spears and they wore only loin cloths. The goblins started shouting something unintelligible as they charged the party, their spears pointing out.

"ARRRRR!" Nanoc roared loudly and Luke could feel small traces of power in his words. He grabbed his axe low with both hands. He lifted his hands in the air until the axe was behind him. "TOMAHAWK!" He brought his hands down with all his power, releasing the axe as he did. Spinning like a vertical helicopter blade, the axe soared through the air and seemed to pick up speed as it raced toward the goblins.

They tried to jump to the side but time wasn't on their side. The axe slammed into the chest of one goblin, and the momentum carried the monster in the air all the way to the opposing wall. The axe still had enough power left over after hitting the goblin to drive itself into the wall, leaving the body hanging from the axe.

The sheer strength demonstrated by his teammate left Luke amazed. Not wanting to be shown up, he decided to test out his new skill. Mentally activating water shot felt completely different from nature's regrowth. Instead of his body and hand warming up, he felt cool water flow through the arm that held the arrow. It flowed down from his shoulder to his hand and when it reached the tips of his fingers, it lingered briefly as the arrow gained a small blue aura.

When he released the arrow it started off like normal, but when it was about two feet away from Luke, it shot off like a geyser, instantly gaining speed. A goblin was getting up from dodging Nanoc's attack and was knocked back to the ground when it took the speedy arrow to its chest. Luke looked up and noticed he was missing about a quarter of his mana, but the goblin seemed to be down for the count.

Penny raised her shield and ran at the goblins, an unarmed

Nanoc in tow. The remaining two goblins had recovered by now and thrust their spears towards Penny's exposed side. Penny parried one goblin and the other could not finish its advancement. Backstab had circled around the group during the confusion of Nanoc's attack and drove two daggers into the goblin's back. "Backstab."

The remaining goblin wasn't giving up on its attacks and charged Backstab, the least threatening looking of the three. "Crap, crap, crap." Backstab's daggers were lodged in the back of the goblin, and he was having a difficult time of pulling them out. By the time he could reach for another dagger, a spear head was lodged into his gut. The goblin smiled, revealing misaligned and decaying teeth. The goblin's smile quickly faded as he looked down and saw a sword stained with green blood coming out of his chest.

"Backstab," Penny said with a nod to her teammate.

The goblin's body went lifeless after a moment and it fell to the ground as Penny pulled her blade out of its back. Acting quickly, Luke ran closer to Backstab and cast nature's regrowth on him, watching his mana bar drop by nearly half. He recast the spell on Nanoc when the skill was off cooldown to bring the rest of his party to full health.

The group rested to allow their stamina and mana to regen, so he pulled up his notifications. Before entering the dungeon, he switched his battle related notifications back to only show up when prompted, and changed them to only show a condensed version. He still hadn't found a setting with his notifications that he liked enough to make his permanent configuration.

*Skill up: **Short Bow**, Beginner 5.*
***Goblin Scout** x4 defeated. 123 party participation exp gained (100 base + 25% discovery bonus - 1% guild contribution).*

Luke made a mental note of the system math behind the experience gain. The game system rounded up with decimals, taking two exp for guild contribution instead of one. He also noted that the positive effects seem to happen first before the negative ones.

"What the hell was that?" Penny sounded angry as she looked at Nanoc and Luke. The pair looked at each other and then back at Penny before giving her 'no idea what your talking about' expressions. "Those skills. Why were you hiding them, and what else are you two hiding?"

"I don't know about Nanoc but I just got my skill from becoming a Ranger. I really didn't think I was hiding it." Luke was being defensive.

"I got mine from practicing axe throwing with the guards," Nanoc added.

Penny scoffed. "You have to let me know your capabilities so I can plan our encounters. It worked out this time but we may not be so lucky next time. These are goblins. They aren't geniuses but they are capable of formulating plans and working as a team. This is a new kind of enemy for us, a more intelligent enemy. I need to know everything you guys can do if you want me to keep you alive." They both apologized and promised to let her know about their abilities in the future.

"Hey guys, looks like we finally got some loot!" Backstab called the party over and pointed at the pouch tied to one of the goblin's waists. Opening the bag revealed a handful of gold coins that he gave out to the group.

Gold Coins x3 *obtained.*

"Not a bad haul and a good experience. Let's push on, but

everyone be on the lookout. Those spears did real damage." Penny cautioned the team and pointed at the next door.

Backstab approached and after a few moments, gave the go ahead. The door let out a large creak as he attempted to silently open it. Letting out a few choice words, he continued to open the door and look around. There appeared to be no one in the next room and he relayed that to his team. Penny gave him the go ahead to enter the next room.

The door let out another loud creak as they opened it to reveal a circular room. There didn't appear to be anyone in the room and there was nowhere for someone to hide, so the group decided to enter. There were lit torches around the room and a variety of open and closed crates scattered about. In the middle of the room was a large hole with a rope ladder hanging down.

Luke checked the hole and saw the flickering of torchlight at the bottom. Checking the crates, he found mining tools in some and raw ore in others. This appeared to be the entrance to a mining site. There were even buckets attached to a crude pulley system for getting ore out of the hole.

"The group we just encountered must be the advance defense party. Most are probably down there. I was wondering why they didn't get reinforcements. I mean, we weren't exactly quiet during the fight." Luke looked directly at Nanoc when he said the last statement. He turned a little red and not from his rage ability.

Backstab walked up to the ladder and promptly jumped off the edge. The others ran over and looked down. Backstab was holding on to either side of the ladder, sliding down at a fast pace. Before hitting the bottom, he tightened his grip and came to a stop. He dropped the last few feet into a roll, spring-boarding forward into the shadows and vanishing from sight.

"All clear," he shouted up to the party.

"Show off," muttered Penny as she proceeded down the ladder at a normal pace. The rest of the party were quick to follow her down.

The group could hear the banging of pickaxes against stone as they approached the opening in the room. When they peeked inside they saw a massive chamber lit by glowing crystals. They were at the top of the chamber but it appeared to go down for hundreds of feet, disappearing into fog. There was a snaking path leading deeper into the chamber and goblins hung from ropes in various spots as they bashed rocks with pickaxes.

Looking around Luke saw an ornate set of doors about two stories down on the opposite side of the chamber. The path leading to it appeared to connect to the snaking path in front of them. He pointed the doors out to everyone, and they planned to try and sneak there.

Clinging to the wall in fear of the sheer drop, the party began another descent. Nanoc seemed to fear the edge the most and was progressing at a speed that was slower than a crawl. He had his back to the edge and his body pressed firmly against the rock wall.

"Hey Nanoc. Do you happen to be afraid of heights?" Backstab said in a mocking tone. Nanoc gave him a choice hand gesture before quickly moving his hand back against the wall.

An arrow landed in the wall next to Penny, who was leading the charge, and her head turned to find the offender. One of the hanging goblins, about thirty feet up and to her right, was shooting arrows at her. Other goblins quickly joined in and the party was now facing six goblins freely firing at them.

"Get behind me! Luke, Backstab, do your thing!" Penny slammed her shield into the soft dirt path, creating a wall of metal between the arrows and her group.

Luke and Backstab were forced behind the shield wall by the

numerous counterattacks that met their every attempt to take a shot. Nanoc refused to move away from the wall and was taking serious damage. Luckily Luke was close enough to cast nature's regrowth and the barbarians' health started refilling.

"Not really sure what we do here. I can't get a shot off." Luke complained.

"Most of them are too far away for me to even hit." Backstab added.

Luke tried again to lean out from the side of the shield to shoot an arrow and was struck in his arm as a result of his efforts. He waited for the cooldown of his healing spell to be up and quickly cast it on himself.

"I'm open to ideas here." Luke attempted to hide the growing panic in his voice. Looking at his party's status bars, he noticed Nanoc was below half and Penny's small amounts of damage from using her shield wall were starting to add up. She was close to half as well. The group was taking damage faster than Luke could heal and if something didn't change quickly, they were facing a full party wipe.

A high-pitched howling started coming from Luke. Backstab and Penny looked at him and spotted Ringo attempting to howl. She took a deep breath and released another high-pitched howl. Luke had to blink several times because he was seeing the sound waves of her howl rippling outward from her.

Your animal companion **Ringo** *used* **Confusing Howl.** *Confusing Howl adds the confusion debuff to all enemies who hear it, unless they are able to resist.*

"I'll explain later but we need to attack!" Luke was speaking as quickly as he could before jumping out from Penny's protection.

He released as many arrows as he could, as quickly as he could. By the time one arrow left his quiver he was already reaching for the next one and preparing to release it, aim be damned. Most of his shots were missing their targets, but he was shooting so many that he was still hitting most of the goblins.

Backstab was slower to react but quickly joined Luke by throwing knives at the closer targets. The goblins were all holding the sides of their heads in pain. They tried several times to retaliate, but their aim was way off. The nearest shot was aimed at Nanoc and landed in the stone wall about seven feet from him.

A few moments of this went by until all the goblins were floating lifeless from their ropes.

*New skill acquired: **Rapid Fire**, Beginner 0. Most people take careful aim at their targets to ensure they hit, but not you. You just keep shooting until something sticks. Cost: 2 stamina per second. Effect: Increase arrow firing rate by $x + 2\%$ and decrease your aim by $x + 5\%$ while channeling the spell where x = skill level.*

***Goblin Scout** x6 defeated. 185 party participation exp gained (150 base + 25% discovery bonus - 1% guild contribution).*

"I got a new skill. It's called rapid fire and for a constant stamina drain it will increase my firing rate but reduce my accuracy by a fair amount. Also, it appears little Ringo was holding out on us. He used something called Confusing Howl that added a confusing debuff to the goblins." Luke was patting Ringo on the head.

"That's great Luke but haven't you reviewed Ringo's abilities yet?" Penny questioned. When she got nothing but a dumbfounded look in response, she continued. "Ringo has a character sheet just like yours. Well, it's a dumbed down version since he's a companion but it should still list his skills."

"How do you know that? Was that in the user manual?" Luke was really starting to hate the fact that he wasn't given a user manual.

"Not exactly. They mentioned something along those lines but a pet store owner told me." Luke nodded at Penny's response but pushed for more information. "I was really missing my cat the other day, so I went to a pet shop and spoke with the owner. He mentioned that the pets you get in the shop are just vanity pets. They are real, require food, and attention but they aren't like animal companions. He said those are on a whole different level from pets and can be used in battle. He explained that they were a lot like adventurers or travelers and had a limited character sheet of their own." she paused. "You know, you should really get out more and spend less time in your garden."

Luke's eyes went wide. How could he be so stupid and not explore the city more? Sure he knew where the local shops in his area were but the city was huge and if he explored it more, he would know a lot more about this game's mechanics. "Thank you Penny. I really do need to get out more." She agreed to show Luke to the pet shop when they got back to town so he could speak to the owner and get advice on how to take care of Ringo properly.

"Well, this sucks." The group, excluding Nanoc, all looked at Backstab. "I can't get the loot." The group all shared a laugh at Backstab's feigned annoyance.

Continuing down the path, they began to hear pounding-metal noises. A few more meters down they saw a large outcrop in the wall. The pounding-metal sound was coming from that room and had gotten so loud that the group could easily sneak up on the opening without being detected. The room was a makeshift forge and metal processing area. There was a pair of muscular goblins pounding on anvils while a handful of others were processing metal in a large cauldron. The blacksmith goblins were easily a foot taller than the ones they had fought up to this point. The walls were lined with various weapons and makeshift armor, all goblin sized.

"Damn. Those smiths are level six and have a ton of HP." Penny cursed as quietly as she could.

"How do you keep doing that?" Luke asked.

"Doing what?" She replied.

"Seeing the enemies level and stats," he responded.

"It's a skill called inspect. Focus your sight hard on the enemy and try to determine their strength. Keep focusing until you get the skill. It's one of the first ones I acquired," she commented.

Luke bore his eyes onto the enemy, looking him up and down and trying to gauge his strength. He continued to look and began squinting his eyes so his vision would focus only on the creature.

New skill acquired: **Inspect**, *Beginner 0. Knowledge is half the battle. By focusing on your opponents, you can now glean basic knowledge of them. Leveling up this skill will grant you more information and allow you to inspect a wider range of enemy levels. Effect: Gain basic knowledge of enemies up to double your level.*

Inspect *Successful!*

Name: *Goblin Smith*
Level: *6*
HP/MP/Stamina: *500/0/100*
Status: *Hostile*

"That seems incredibly useful." Penny nodded at him and surveyed the room.

"I count four of the helper looking goblins and the two smiths. I think our best bet is to take the helpers out first. They should drop pretty fast. Nanoc and I can hold the smiths off until you two can join us. Agreed?" Penny proposed.

"I have an issue." All attention moved to Luke. "I only have a handful of arrows left."

"I'm also really low on throwing daggers..." Backstab added.

"Luke, we're gonna have to hope there are arrows in those piles of weapons. Unless you're still holding out, I don't recall you having any melee weapons or skills." He shook his head to confirm. "Tssk. I didn't think so. Hmm... Backstab, you go into melee with those four and Luke will give you cover fire. Use your arrows wisely! When those four go down, search quickly for arrows in the area but if you can't find any, then grab a random weapon and join us. As always, watch our health the best you can."

She held up her hand and counted down with her fingers. Three, two. On one, she and Nanoc ran into the outcrop. Nanoc was smiling as he now had an open space that didn't face a sheer drop. He activated his tomahawk ability and threw his blade at one of the smiths. It connected but, unlike before, the smith didn't go flying back. Instead, the axe landed in his upper chest and stayed firmly planted.

Luke ran out and took aim at one of the confused workers. To ensure a kill, he activated water shot and released. The arrow struck the worker in the middle of the worker's chest and it fell backwards from the arrow's momentum.

The remaining workers charged the travelers, grabbing weapons from racks as they ran. Backstab engaged the three workers with his dual daggers as Penny and Nanoc were occupying the blacksmiths. The workers swung swords at Backstab but, to Luke's amazement, he was gracefully weaving in between their attacks. He wasn't able to dodge them all outright, but he could dodge the attacks enough to only take glancing blows.

Luke readied another arrow and released at one worker. The worker saw him take aim and was able to dodge the arrow. Dodging caused an opening that Backstab took full advantage of.

"Double strike." Backstab's body had an aura of purple for a brief moment as he launched his attack on the off balance worker. His arms moved so quickly that they almost became a blur before he leaped out of the way of another attack. A moment later, four large lacerations appeared on the goblin's body and blood spurted from them. The goblin became covered in its own blood and it fell to the ground lifeless.

Luke shot another arrow that caught a worker in the leg and it fell to one knee. The last unharmed worker stood in between his injured ally and Backstab, holding his sword out. Backstab backed up a few feet and began a full sprint toward him. The goblin raised his sword but as Backstab was about to reach him, he leaped into the air, arcing over the defensive worker. In midair, he threw both his daggers at the wounded goblin, finishing it.

The remaining goblin let out a laugh, noticing Backstab was out of weapons and charged him. Backstab waved goodbye to the goblin who now displayed a confused look on its face as an arrow drove into its skull.

"Nice shot." Backstab commented.

Luke nodded and turned his attention to the blacksmiths. His comrades weren't faring as well as he had hoped. Penny's shield had large pieces missing from it and Nanoc was on full defense, barely able to keep up with the hammer and sword wielding smith. Both of them were missing half of their hit points with sweat and blood flowing off their bodies.

Luke quickly cast Nature's Regrowth on Nanoc and followed up with a Water Shot toward the smith he was fighting. The smith saw the attack coming and smashed the arrow out of the air with his hammer. *Well, that's new.* Luke reached for another arrow, grasping at thin air. Looking at his quiver he realized he was out of arrows. He also only had enough mana left for one more healing spell. Remembering the plan, he ran to scavenge through the weapons in hopes he would find some arrows.

"Switch!" Penny screamed as she took a large leap backwards and away from the smith. The smith performed a leaping thrust at her but Backstab had appeared to fill the hole in combat that Penny just created. He parried the thrust by driving his daggers down in an X formation. The smith's sword was driven into the ground, but he followed up with his hammer in an uppercut motion. Backstab was caught off balance and had no time to bring his daggers up to block. Unable to avoid the blow, he rolled his shoulder forward in an attempt to mitigate the damage.

A crunching sound of bones breaking could be heard as Backstab went soaring backwards. The smith pulled his blade from the ground in pursuit but an empty bottle smashed into the back of his head.

Penny was wiping her mouth, having just drank a potion and regenerated some of her lost health. The smith turned to continue pursuing the downed rogue but Penny quickly activated her taunt and the two were back in the throes of battle.

Are there seriously no arrows? Luke was rummaging through crates of weapons, not finding what he was hoping to. He ran to the downed workers, pulling arrows from them. The arrow he shot with water shot was broken, but he still could salvage two of the other arrows. He quickly grabbed them along with a fallen sword and ran to Backstab.

"You alright?" Luke asked.

Backstab sat up but he had clearly broken the bones in his collar and shoulder. He grunted in pain but couldn't hold back the tears streaming from his eyes. He fumbled while grabbing for a potion in his pouch so Luke grabbed it for him. Helping him drink it, Luke saw his health bar regenerate, but it stopped at 75%.

"Your health isn't going up all the way?" Luke questioned.

Backstab gritted his teeth and was short with his response. "Potions heal damage, not breaks."

Looking over the battle again he could tell Nanoc was getting exhausted and was taking more and more glancing blows from the smith. Large welts were forming all over his body and his health was already below half again. Penny had recovered with her potion but was unable to attack.

"We need to focus on one enemy together. I think I have a plan." Stated Luke.

"I thought I smelled burning, must have been you thinking," joked Backstab.

"You have a shattered collarbone and you're still making jokes?" Backstab gave him a shaky grin.

Penny blocked another overhead smash from the smith that sent another large piece of her shield flying across the room. Her tower shield, normally the same size as her, now more closely resembled a small circle shield. When the smith went in for another attack, an arrow came soaring at him from the side. The smith had a shit-eating grin on his face as he parried Penny's attack with his sword while simultaneously knocking the arrow away with his hammer.

Raising his hammer hand to deliver another overhead attack, his face scrunched up with pain. Behind him was Luke taking wide diagonal swipes with a short sword. The smith gave him a confused look, thinking *wasn't that the ranger?* He swung around and cleaved with his sword, cutting across Luke's stomach and deflecting onto

Penny's shield hard enough to force her to the ground. The smith pulled his sword back and thrust it at Luke.

Instead of jumping out of the way, Luke attempted to block the blow with his own blade. The smith's strength was much greater than Luke's and the parry forced Luke's own sword to drive into his side. The smith smiled and Luke responded with a shit-eating grin of his own before uttering a single word. "Backstab."

One of the fallen goblin's blades drove through the smith. Penny followed up Backstab's attack and drove her blade down from overhead. The blade sunk down into the neck of the smith and poked out his waist. Backstab and Luke collapsed to the ground from a mixture of pain and exhaustion while Penny stood, panting heavily.

Luke saw that Nanoc's health was dipping into critical levels and tossed him a heal before forcing himself to his feet. Even though he was in extreme pain, he couldn't help but smile. He wasn't sure if it was adrenaline or insanity, but he sure was loving this game.

Penny quickly joined Nanoc's fight and served as a distraction for Nanoc to unleash a flurry of revenge strikes on the smith. The smith tripped over himself trying to block in two directions at once and a hammer blow meant for Nanoc's head instead led to the barbarian catching the hammer and ripping it from the smith's hand.

Luke joined the fight by launching his remaining two arrows and hitting his mark both times. Without his hammer, the smith could not withstand the attacks from all sides and was quickly overpowered. The fight ended when Nanoc split the goblin's skull with his massive axe as the smith went to block one of Penny's thrusts.

Goblin Worker x4 *defeated. 123 party participation exp gained (100 base + 25% discovery bonus - 1% guild contribution).*
Goblin Smith x2 *defeated. 618 party participation exp gained (500 base + 25% discovery bonus - 1% guild contribution).*

The team rested and waited for Luke's mana to recover. They let him heal them all to full instead of wasting potions. To his surprise, nature's regrowth set and healed the bones in Backstab's shoulder and neck. It took an extra cast to fully heal him, but it was well worth the price to get their rogue back on his feet. When the team was finished resting, Luke pulled up the rest of his notifications. He ended up gaining a rank in nature's regrowth, short bows and water shot.

"I know that fight was intense, but you can't ignore gains like that." Penny commented.

"Sure, if you don't mind shattering your bones," Backstab muttered.

The group searched the room but the only thing of value they could find was a quiver of arrows buried in a crate. Penny replaced her shattered shield with the biggest shield she could find. It wasn't anywhere close to the shield she had, but it was still much larger than the shard of metal that was left of her original tower shield.

They started heading the rest of the way down the chasm and stopped in front of the ornate doors. Everyone pulled out their weapons as Penny pushed them. The doors opened inward to pure darkness. Torches slowly began to light, illuminating their next challenge.

CHAPTER NINE

Boss Fight

They slowly entered the room, keeping their guard up as much as possible. The room had marble columns set in a large circle with torches lighting up a round stone pattern on the middle of the floor. Beyond the columns in all directions was darkness. When they reached the center of the room, the doors shut behind them and the rest of the room lit up. Opposite the double entry doors was a small raised platform.

Standing on the platform was a massive goblin, easily eight feet tall and covered in muscles. He had a giant single bladed bone axe in one hand and a massive circular shield in the other. He was wearing only a loincloth and a metal helmet with eyes glowing red behind the visor.

A chime sounded and in the upper center of Luke's vision appeared the name Xirx, the Goblin Warlord Lv 10. Underneath the new name appeared a long rectangular box outlined in gold with dragons on either side. The bar filled up from empty to full twice, first with a red color and then with green.

"Oh, my god. How am I supposed to tank that?" Penny said with a tinge of fear bleeding into her voice.

Xirx bent his knees and leaped into the air toward them. The group scattered and when Xirx landed, the stone cracked and broke into rubble under his feet. The air pressure from his landing pushed the group even further away. Xirx opened his mouth and let out a massive roar that was so fierce it took one percent off everyone's health.

"Tomahawk!" Nanoc threw his axe at the beast but it turned and knocked the axe away with its shield.

Luke ran behind a column and set Ringo down. "Stay here!" Bolting out from cover, Luke shot a pair of arrows as he ran in a circle around the room. Both arrows landed in the beast's massive body but its health indicator only showed a small dip.

The creature's attention went to Luke but before it could decide on who to attack, Penny began taunting it. "I'll keep its attention the best I can. Luke, focus on healing me when you're able to and the rest of you kill this thing!" Penny shouted orders, regaining her battle composure.

Xirx took some slow swings at Penny that she was able to deflect or dodge without taking too much damage. Backstab ran up behind Xirx and jumped up, daggers in hand. "Double strike." Four long cuts appeared on the beast's back before it swung its shield arm back at him. Thinking quickly, Backstab crossed his arms and braced for the impact. The shield hit him dead center and sent him flying towards a column.

Before hitting the column, Nanoc leaped into the air and caught the projectile rogue. The two fell to the ground and slid for a few feet before stopping. "Let's not do that again." Nanoc got up and began to turn red. "Ahhhh!" Running forward he bent down to grab his axe off the floor without losing stride. He began to spin his body as he approached screaming "Whirlwind!" His axe cut deep into the side of Xirx and green blood started dripping down the boss monster's leg.

Ripping his axe out of Xirx he went in for another strike but its massive shield blocked it. Luke launched two consecutive water shots at Xirx's shield arm. Both hit their mark, and the creature let out a shout of pain. Glancing up, he saw that half of the green health bar was already gone. "We're doing it guys! Let's keep it up." Luke shouted words of encouragement to his team.

The shout distracted Penny just long enough for Xirx's kick to land against her. She went flying back and slammed against the wall. The impact forced the air out of her lungs and she fell to the ground. She began taking large gulps of air and her HP took a 60% hit. Green energy flowed over her and her wounds started healing.

Backstab ran up to the beast as it reeled back and swung a cleaving slash at the fast moving rogue. Backstab took a small jump into the air and landed on the large bone axe's blade. Using the enemy's axe as a springboard he shot forward driving dual daggers into its chest. Quickly pulling his legs underneath him he kicked off the creature and performed a back flip to get out of the monster's reach.

"He may hit like a train, but he's slower than my wood panel station wagon," Backstab commented.

"Shield toss!" A spinning shield slammed into Xirx's back before flying back to Penny. She caught the shield and slid it back onto her arm. "Look! One of its health bars is gone. We're halfway..." before Penny could finish talking Xirx slammed the hilt of his weapon into the ground and he began to emit a dim red light.

The light was getting brighter and brighter as it began to pulse. The group began to wipe sweat from their brows as the temperature in the room started to spike. Taking advantage of the lull in combat, Nanoc charged the boss monster. He took two large cleaves with his axe that dropped another 10% from Xirx's health.

The others quickly joined the assault. Penny was taking large swipes with her sword as Backstab danced around the enemy with his daggers, opening dozens of shallow cuts. Luke wasn't lax either, peeking out from behind a column. He was launching arrows as quickly as his hands would allow, activating his rapid fire ability.

Xirx's health quickly dropped to 5% from the full force of the party. Things were looking up before he let out a howl of pain and anger. A small orb containing fire appeared in front of Xirx, floating in the air. A white hot flash blinded the group as the orb exploded. Fire cascaded outward, coating the entire room in flames.

Luke blinked rapidly to clear his vision. When color and shapes started reappearing, he saw a vision of horror. Xirx was pulling his axe from the ground, surrounded by his fallen teammates. Backstab's leather armor was half melted to his skin, and he laid face down and motionless. Nanoc the shirtless barbarian's skin was deep fried as he twitched. Penny was the only one who didn't look like death incarnate. Her metal armor protected her from the initial blast. Luke could see that her metal armor had super-heated, and an icon of fire appeared under her name in his vision. Another icon, resembling a white explosion, was under all of his teammate's names. He focused on the icons to make the system give him more information.

Stunned. *While stunned, you can not move or take any actions, including activating abilities until the stun is removed or expires naturally. Time remaining: 28 seconds.*

Overheated, *2 stacks. You have become overheated. You will continue to take fire damage for the duration of this debuff or until*

*you correct your body temperature. Effect: 10 fire damage every 5
seconds. Time remaining: 28 seconds.*

Luke began to panic and started flailing about. *Wait... I can
move?* Double checking his own status he saw no active debuffs and
his health was only at half. He instantly knew he was burned, even
before touching the left side of his face to confirm, but his right side
felt fine. It appeared the column in front of him absorbed most of
the blast on his right side. That must have been one of the boss's
game mechanics. We were supposed to hide behind the columns!

His attention was brought back to Xirx when he heard the stone
crumbling from Xirx pulling his axe out of the ground. Xirx looked
around at the carnage and began strolling toward Penny. He raised
his axe high above his head to perform a killing blow. As his axe
reached the peak of its ascension, a water coated arrow pierced his
arm.

Xirx looked over to see Luke let out a grunt of pain. Holding his
bow in his damaged left arm was causing Luke agony. Fearing
thatPenny would soon die, he acted quickly and shot her a heal.
Healing Penny and landing an arrow was enough to draw the
monster's attention. Lowering its massive muscular arm, Xirx took
hulking steps toward the damaged ranger.

Completely out of stamina and with only a sliver of mana, Luke
dropped his bow, panting in exhaustion. Xirx raised his axe in a
familiar killing blow motion above him. Luke looked up and saw
just how close they were to defeating this beast. Xirx only had 2%
of his health remaining. Through gritted teeth he uttered his last
words, "Screw You."

A gray blur suddenly crossed Luke's vision as Ringo wrapped
his fanged mouth around the arm of her master's enemy. Green
blood gushed from the open wound and Xirx let out a scream of

pain. Grabbing Ringo with his shield arm he started pulling with all his might, ripping the small furry wolf away. Tossing the wolf across the room, it collided with a column, letting out a loud whimper of pain.

The goblin warlord turned back to his real opponent, an expression of dread stretched across its face with what he saw. Luke was pointing an arrow bursting with water up at him. Ringo provided just enough time for Luke to recover enough stamina to shoot a single shot.

Imbued with water mana, the arrow launched at an increased speed into the beast's chest. Luke grinned as he saw the monster's health reach 0 and its eyes go lifeless. Xirx's corpse fell back and Luke followed suit, collapsing from reaching zero stamina. He laid back, full of pain, panting and happy as a flood of system messages greeted him.

*Congratulations! You have completed **The Den**! For being the first party to complete the dungeon, you have earned a bonus reward. Because your party was lower than the recommended level, you have earned additional rewards. You have been rewarded five skill points, an Uncommon Class Weapon Box, the title Slayers of the Den and 5,000 exp. You will not be able to re-enter a dungeon after completing it for one week. The dungeon, The Den, is now open to all travelers.*

*Title **Slayers of the Den**. People speak of your great deeds as your renown increases. While this title is equipped you will gain a bonus 2% positive reputation whenever you are rewarded reputation and lose 1% less reputation when reputation is taken from you.*

***Xirx, the Goblin Warlord** x1 defeated. 3,093 (2,500 base + 25% discovery bonus - 1% guild contribution).*

148

*Congratulations, **Level Up!** You have been awarded +1 agility, 1+ intelligence, +2 attribute points and 1 skill point, based on your class. Be careful with your decisions as they can not be undone.*

*Congratulations, **Level Up!** You have been awarded +1 agility, 1+ intelligence, +2 attribute points and 1 skill point, based on your class. Be careful with your decisions as they can not be undone.*

*Skill up: **Nature's Regrowth**, Beginner 5.*
*Skill up: **Water Shot**, Beginner 3.*
*Skill up: **Rapid Fire**, Beginner 1.*
*Skill up: **Short Bow**, Beginner 8.*
*Skill up: **Beast Mastery**, Beginner 3.*

At the last notification Luke remembered his animal companion. He could tell before reaching her that Ringo was dead. Penny walked over, fully healed from her own level up, and placed a hand on his shoulder. "What happened?" she asked droopingly.

"She saved us. If it wasn't for her, I wouldn't have been able to finish off the boss and we would all be dead. She… she died a hero." Luke was unsure if it was his growing affection for Ringo that made him so emotional or if his skill ups in beast mastery were affecting him somehow but he didn't care. His friend had died and died protecting him. Ringo wasn't a traveler and wouldn't come back after death.

"Why don't we take her with us? Maybe someone in the city can resurrect her or something," Penny added with a tinge of sorrow in her voice.

Resurrection! Luke mentally kicked himself for not remembering his own skills. He scooped up the lifeless body of Ringo and walked to the center of the room. Sitting cross-legged, he placed his deceased companion in front of him and activated resurrect companion.

Black lines started tracing a large magical circle around Luke. Several shapes and symbols filled the circle before it was completed. His mana bar started draining rapidly as green energy started tracing over the lines and causing them to glow. After a few moments the entire circle was glowing and Ringo's lifeless body faded out of existence. Another, much smaller magic circle appeared a few feet in front of him and glowed green as Luke's circle began to fade and disappear.

He stood and walked over to the newly formed green circle. Barking came from the ground underneath the circle as Ringo floated upwards out of it like a ghost. Ringo ran into Luke's arms and let out whimpers of happiness as she was reunited with her master.

"Are you crying?" Backstab asked Penny.

"It's like a fairy tale or something." She sniffled before continuing. "If you mention this to anyone I'll make sure you get the aggro of all future monsters." Backstab's eyes became so large that Nanoc thought they would pop out of his head.

"Never again buddy. I won't let you die again if I can ever prevent it." Luke squeezed Ringo tight.

"Sooo. Not to break up this little love fest but that was awesome! I gained a whole level off that and I'm close to leveling up again," Backstab said with excitement.

Luke looked over his party on the system display and noticed everyone gained at least one level. *That explains why no one is screaming at me for not healing them.* Penny had hit level seven, and both his damage dealing comrades were now level six.

"You big fat cheater!" Backstab was pushing Luke's chest with a finger. "You gained two levels? You must have cheated, there's no other explanation." He pretended to be shocked and hurt. "And you didn't include me in your cheating? I thought we were friends Luke. I thought… I thought we had something special."

"I didn't cheat. I was just level three remember? Frankly, if I didn't gain at least two levels I was never going to catch up to you all," he responded in a joking tone.

The group began to all share a good laugh before breaking apart and looking for loot. Luke was drawn to a glowing outline of a mushroom. *Is this where a mushroom should have grown? I don't get it.* He reached out and, to his surprise, felt a bumpy mushroom cap.

Ghostshroom *(rare) x3 obtained. Undetectable by anyone other than an herbalist, this mushroom is hard to locate and grows only in dark humid environments. Used in alchemy.*

"Hey guys, there's a chest over here." Nanoc called for the team to gather. Luke pocketed the mushrooms and joined his team.

"Ohhh, can I open it? Pleeeeease let me open it." Backstab begged like a child as he rocked back and forth on the balls of his feet. Penny nodded, and the rogue threw the top of the chest open so fast that Luke could have sworn he saw the hinges breaking.

Backstab pulled items out and placed them on the ground for the group to see. There was a sword, some daggers, a book, two orange potions, a wooden wand and a bag of gold. When Backstab placed the bag of gold down, he let out a sound of annoyance as the bag shrunk a little.

"What was that?" Luke asked.

"That was the guild's cut. Whenever someone in the party gets gold, the 5% guild tax automatically kicks in. My poor wallet," Backstab replied.

That explained why I didn't lose any of the gold he gave me earlier.

They tax the first party member that picks it up the whole amount. Luke thought as he reached out and picked up the book for a closer look.

Basic Phoenix Kingdom Book of Lore, Bestiary *(uncommon) x1 obtained. This book contains the basic knowledge and lore of common and uncommon creatures around the Phoenix Kingdom.*

The book was heavy and hundreds of pages long. Opening it Luke saw crude illustrations of creatures with names, habitats, favorite foods and things of the sort. "You guys mind if I take this? I also found some rare mushrooms back there. If it's ok with you guys, I'll take the book, mushrooms and my cut of the gold?"

"Can I smoke the mushrooms?" Backstab asked.

"I think it might kill you but I guess you're welcome to try." Luke smirked.

"Hard pass." Backstab made an 'x' with his arms before grabbing the daggers.

The group continued to divide up the loot until everyone got something. Backstab took the enchanted daggers, Penny took the curved sword and Nanoc took the pair of orange potions which turned out to be strength enhancing. The group also split the gold. Backstab and Penny got fifty while Luke and Nanoc got forty-nine because there was 198 in total and Penny had to buy a new shield. They also agreed to donate the wand to anyone who needed it in the guild.

After looting the room, a panel in the wall behind the stage retracted into the floor to reveal a staircase leading up. Proceeding to the stairs, Luke turned around to take in the scene before him. He had just helped slay a massive boss monster among people he truly considered his friends. He had a pet he cared deeply about and could shoot healing magic from his fingers. Endless Fantasy

Online, trapped or not, was changing him for the better.

Smiling, he proceeded up the stairs and toward the exit, toward his friends.

CHAPTER TEN

Learning More

When the party reached the city, something big seemed to be going on. People were rushing in and out at a frantic pace and guards were rushing crates in all directions. The group approached one guard who was catching his breath to ask him what was going in.

"The King…" Pant. "He's getting ready…" Wheeze. "To visit the Elk Kingdom."

"The Elk Kingdom?" Luke asked.

The guard took a large swig of water from his water skin before continuing. "Yeah. The Elk Kingdom." The party just gave him unknowing looks for a moment, so the guard continued. "Man, you travelers don't know anything. The Elk Kingdom is the realm of the Elven King Lorsan Virfield. He wants them to join the effort against Shadow Incarnate." The guard bowed and excused himself by grabbing another crate and running into the city.

"I knew it!" Backstab snapped his fingers, and the group gave him their full attention. "I knew there had to be some nice elven ladies in this game." The group all frowned and Penny punched

Backstab on the shoulder.

"We should probably report this, and the location of The Den, to Shrapnel," Penny suggested. When she received no objections, they all headed for the guild headquarters.

It took them a while to reach the outskirts of the city where the shady warehouse they called their guild headquarters was located. When they got close, they noticed just as much commotion coming from the guild house as there was at the city gate. People were running around like crazy and horse-drawn carts were being loaded with goods. Penny started looking for Shrapnel and pointed him out to the others when she spotted him.

"Guild Master Shrapnel, what's going on?" she questioned.

"Ahh Penny. I'm glad you and your team are back, lots going on and lots to do." Shrapnel moved back allowing space for a guild member carrying an over-sized crate to squeeze by. "It's great news! The King is headed for a neighboring city."

"We heard. Why is that great news?" She gave Shrapnel a puzzled expression.

"The King is promoting the guilds with the highest reputation to City Guilds! Thanks to our actions during the Crimson Shadow's attack, and someone in our guild clearing the game's first discovered dungeon, we have a ton of reputation with the city. We're being given a guild hall near the castle, with easy access to the city gate." He shouted his next words so everyone could hear him. "No more walking an hour to get outside the city!" Loud cheers could be heard from everyone around.

"Actually, that's kinda why we came. We wanted to report what we found." Penny explained their day: finding the dungeon, the goblins inside, the loot they found, and the massive goblin boss they had to fight.

"Wow! That sounds amazing. I'll get word to the guild

cartographers so they can update everyone with the dungeon's location. I want to get parties out there starting tomorrow! If we can only enter once a week, I want groups to start clearing it immediately. Thanks for the information and great find." The group smiled and nodded. "Sounds like you all had a rough day though. Why don't you all take the rest of the day off? If anyone complains that you didn't help today, I'll remind them of who found their new favorite grind spot." The group's small smiles now turned to huge grins of happiness. They began to leave before Shrapnel called them back. "Wait. I don't know if you noticed, but the guild also leveled up from this. We voted and purchased a passive skill that gives us all 1% more experience. Now none of the guild will miss the 1% we tax."

"You're just full of good news today aren't you?" Backstab commented.

Guild Master Shrapnel laughed and warned them to leave in a hurry or he might change his mind about giving them the day off. After marking the new guild headquarters on their maps, the party ran faster than when the wolves chased them.

After they were a good distance away, Nanoc spoke up. "Same plan tomorrow?" He asked no one in particular.

"No." Penny started to shake her head. "I think the guild master has the right idea. We barely won that fight and it really hurt. I was literally being cooked alive in my armor. If Luke didn't send that last minute heal to me, I would have burned to death. I don't know about you guys, but I'm taking a day or two off to rest and find a skill trainer. It's clear to me that we're not ready to take on challenges like that and I think we can afford a day off."

"A skill trainer?" Luke questioned.

"Yeah. There are skill trainers for all classes. They can help you hone your skills and teach you new ones. I think it's a good idea if we all visit our respective trainers."

"But loooot," Backstab complained.

"Listen." Penny put on a serious tone. "We have to start treating this like our lives now and not just a game. I can't speak for you lot but I don't want to die again. It hurts." No one said anything, but they all began fidgeting as they remembered the last time they all died. "Were locked out of the dungeon for a full week, right? Let's all do some personal training and meet back up in a week. We can try the dungeon again and see how much we progressed."

"A fine idea!" Nanoc belted. "I know where my barbarian trainer is and I have a ton of questions on how I can better use my tomahawk and whirlwind skills."

"What about the new VR players? Won't they catch up to us in level by then?" Luke asked.

"They can get close to us, yes but you're forgetting something. The dungeon is instance based. They won't be able to steal that leveling spot from us. Plus, if we hone our skills we should be able to take on much tougher foes than new players of our same level," she countered.

After talking it over for a while they all agreed on the plan and started going their separate ways. Before Penny could leave, Luke made her show him where the pet store was on his map. Taking care of Ringo was his first priority. They had only been together for a couple of days, but Luke cared deeply for his animal companion. Ringo clearly reciprocated the feelings, considering she gave her life for him.

After a short walk, Luke was in front of a long rectangular building with a large wooden sign hanging out front in the shape of a dog bone. The sign read *Critters and Creatures Pet Haven* and Luke could see light coming from the window so he walked in.

The door swung open past a bell that made a loud chime.

"Hello?" A tall slender man looked toward the door. He was tossing pellets out of a bucket into various open displays containing a variety of small animals. "Welcome to Critters and Creatures Pet Haven. My name is Edmund, how can I assist you today?" The man's nasal voice greeted the newcomer to his shop. The man was wearing nice clothing but had on a thick smock to protect the front of his clothes. His long black hair was tied up in a ponytail and he appeared to have long ears like Rose. Not wanting to get caught starting again, Luke's response came out quickly.

"I'm looking for help taking care of my animal companion. I would like to get her some proper food and maybe some treats or something?" Luke was still unsure on how to take care of a living creature and doubly unsure what translated from his world to this one regarding pet care. *Did they have chew toys?* He thought as Edmund put the bucket down and approached him.

"May I see your companion?" Luke thought nothing of it and pulled Ringo out of her pouch and began petting her in his arms. Edmund took out a monocle from his front pocket and placed it in his right eye as he moved mere inches from Ringo. "Ahhh! She is beautiful. Look at those markings." His monocle began to glow blue faintly. "I see... An epic level alpha wolf... Amazing! Her bond with you is strong too. Color me impressed, young one. Few humans can bond with such a wild creature. Most of you bond with horses or birds, but an epic level wolf? That's very rare."

Luke wasn't used to such praise and began to blush a little. He pushed his glassed up before speaking. "It's really that rare?" he asked.

Edmund switched his gaze to Luke and his monocle began to glow again. "Hmm... I see... things make more sense now... You are both a ranger and a nature affinity magic user. That certainly helps explain things." He put his monocle back in his pocket and began walking toward the back of the store, gesturing Luke to follow.

"I'm sorry but I'm a traveler and don't really know what any of that means regarding Ringo and I," Luke choked out.

Edmund stopped walking, turned his head and raised a single eyebrow. "Ringo? Interesting name." He faced forward again and started walking before continuing. "Having an animal companion is not rare. Many races, including monster races, are known for having animal companions. What makes your case special is the type of animal. Only races who are more in tune with nature can generally bond with more advanced life-forms. The bond you have created with your animal is imbued with nature mana. You literally share your soul with your animal." The man went behind a counter and faced Luke head on.

"Share my soul?" Luke questioned with concern.

"Don't be scared. All it means is that you are bonded on a spiritual level. As your bond increases, so will your feelings toward her, and your connection will begin to unlock a new world of possibilities. As I was saying, this bond must be accepted by the ambient nature mana of the world. Since you have your mana affinities unlocked, I assume you know the possible affinities?" He paused to wait for a response and Luke nodded slowly. "Well, each race has certain predispositions to each affinity. As a human, you are more likely to have dark, light, or fire affinities. Contrasted to that, you are less likely to have an air or water affinity, and it's rare for a human to have an earth affinity. Earth affinities are most common among elves. In fact, almost all elves have earth as one of their affinities. Since you have nature, earth and water affinities, you were able to bond with this beautiful girl of yours."

Luke scratched Ringo's head and her tail began to wag. "I guess that makes sense." He wasn't sure he understood everything, but it helped explain why he felt so close to Ringo in such a short amount of time and why she would give her life for him. "Thanks for the explanation. Would you mind teaching me a little more about taking care of her?"

Edmund clasped his hands together and smiled. "It would be my pleasure."

Luke interrupted. "I'm sorry, I forgot to introduce myself. My name is Luke."

"It would be my pleasure, Luke." he corrected.

Luke and Edmund spent the next few hours going over basic pet care techniques. Luke learned that it was best to let Ringo eat raw meat and to allow her to hunt because it helped raise her stats. He also learned that he would be able to see her stats when she grew out of her cub status. Although raw meat was her preferred food, he could also feed her nutrient pellets. Edmund explained that they were stuffed with nutrients and would help Ringo grow, but to Luke they just looked like typical hard dog food from back home. When all was said and done, Luke ended up purchasing a bag of pellets and a sturdy brush for cleaning Ringo. Edmund then explained to him why brushing her fur out would not only be a nice experience for Ringo but would help raise their bond.

"The key is just spending time with her. Do everything together! And make sure to set time aside each day to do something with just the two of you. Raising your bond will make you both stronger," Edmund finished explaining.

Luke thanked Edmund for all his help and for the information he shared with him before saying his goodbyes. He started heading out of the store before Edmund ran up and stopped him.

"Luke... Let me ask you something. Have you put any thought into what your next class advancement will be?"

Luke thought for a while before he responded. "Not really. I mean, I don't know what my options are until I hit level ten so I don't really know what I will choose until I see my choices."

Edmund grabbed some paper, a quill and an inkwell from under his counter. Dipping the quill into the ink he began to draw a diagram. After a few minutes he turned the paper around and pushed it across the counter to Luke. Luke grabbed the paper and studied it. It looked like a bunch of circles with numbers and lines connecting them. He couldn't make heads or tails of it so he looked up at Edmund and waited for an explanation.

"That is a crude diagram of class advancement." He pointed to the first circle that had a one in it. "Everyone in this world starts at level one as the beginner class." He moved his finger along the line that led to a ring of circles with the number three in them. "When someone hits level three, they are given their choice of basic classes. Their choices are determined by how they lived their lives up to that point. If you worked in a shop, you would be offered various trade classes. If you carry a giant sword around, you could be offered the barbarian or warrior class."

"I'm following you so far. Does that mean this smaller ring of choices is the next class advancement?" Luke pointed at the next ring of circles that all had the number ten in them.

Edmund nodded. "At level ten you are given the choice of a specialization. This is different than your basic class choice and if you look at my diagram," he pointed to the particular section in question, "there are far fewer choices at this stage and they all relate to your base class. For example, since you are a ranger, you will not be given the choice to select a knight or arch-mage specialization because your base class wasn't a warrior or a mage type."

Luke followed the line farther up and saw a single circle with the number fifty in it. "Wait, you don't get any choices farther up?" he questioned.

"Exactly! You can get a lot of choices at your basic class and a handful of choices at your specialization but that's it. When you specialize you make a choice to focus on a particular path of advancement. You'll spend your next forty levels sharpening your skills and becoming the best you can be at what you do. Then," Edmund continued traversing his finger up the diagram, "you will gain advancements at level fifty and one hundred. The gods will review your choices and your life up to that point and reward you with an advancement that fits you. It's said to be extremely rare for two people to share the same advancement. There are similarities but no two people at level fifty or beyond are the same."

The gods he was referring to must be the game system. It looks like they review your play style and award unique new classes based on how you play the game. Luke fell more in love with this game at every turn as it appeared that everyone's playthrough would end up being unique. His happy thoughts soon turned to concern when he realized there seemed to be a cap to his advancement. "So you stop advancing at level 100? I don't see anything in your diagram past that point."

"Of course not. I just don't know of anyone who has reached a high enough level to find out what happens. Even our King is rumored to only be slightly above level one hundred. Most knowledge of advancement beyond that point is all rumor and myths because it becomes insanely hard to advance your level at that point. You're likely to die of old age before finding out if there is anything more," Edmund added in his nasal voice.

Luke looked overwhelmed by the amount of knowledge that was being shared with him. "Let me try to simplify things for you with an example. Let's look at the Phoenix King's choices. When he hit level three as a young boy, he was given a large list of choices for his basic class but he chose to be a warrior. When he hit level ten, he specialized as a holy knight of order. This is a rare specialization that is only offered to royalty who complete a legendary level quest. When he hit level fifty, later in his adult life, the gods awarded him the advancement of angelic knight. And finally, when he hit level one hundred, he became a war angel after proving himself on the battlefield countless times."

"That's... That's amazing! I have to tell my party, no, my whole guild about this. A ton of us are about to hit level ten soon and they should know that their next choice will be their last. Thank you for this information, but I have to go now." Luke tried running out of the building but Edmund shouted for him to stop, and waved him back.

"What is it with you young people? You always want to rush from one thing to the next. Can't you ever just relax for a moment," Edmund complained.

"You've called me young several times now but, and I mean no offense, aren't we the same age?" Luke asked.

Edmund's face went red. "No, no no. I'm almost two hundred years old." Luke's jaw dropped and his eyes went wide with disbelief. "What? You've never met a half-elf before? Our life spans are typically four or five times that of a human."

"Wait a minute, you'll live to four hundred or more?" Edmund nodded in response. "But... wouldn't that mean you could level up past one hundred and would know the secrets of specializations?"

"Ah, good point. But the simple answer is no. It's true that some elves strive to level up, but when you live for five hundred years, leveling up is the last thing on your mind. Most elves, or half-elves in my case, retire or take on personal projects when they are middle-aged. They retire even younger if they have children. My daughter is already forty, but she looks like a twelve-year-old human. This is one reason you don't see a lot of elves or half-elves in human cities. It's hard for humans to accept that someone who looks twelve has more life experience and knowledge than they do," Edmund explained.

Luke considered what he said and how hard it would be for a full-grown person to be in the body of a child, especially when interacting with others. He was all too familiar with how cruel human kids and adults could be. He used to get picked on and beat up as a child for being a bookworm, a nerd, overweight, or a laundry list of other reasons. That would only compound it if he looked twelve for multiple years.

"I'm... I'm sorry for what your daughter must have to go through being here." Luke was genuinely sorry and Edmund could see it in Luke's eyes.

"Thank you. Truly, thank you. But that isn't why I called you back. I wanted to ask if you have given any thought to specializing as a beast tamer?"

"A beast tamer?" Luke looked puzzled.

"Yes, a beast tamer. The specialization focuses on becoming one with your animal companion. You borrow each other's strengths to eliminate your own weaknesses," Edmund said excitedly.

"Hmm." Luke paused to think. He'd never played the tamer, hunter, or pet classes in online games before. It was great that he had Ringo but he wasn't sure he was ready to commit fully with the little wolf. "To be honest, I'm not sure." Edmund's smile vanished and Luke rushed his next words. "That's not to say I wouldn't consider it. I just don't know what's out there."

"Well... It's wise to review your options I suppose." Edmund pulled another piece of paper from the stack and began to write. "Tell you what, why don't you go meet a beast tamer and she can tell you more about the class. It's a rare class and not many people choose it." Before Luke could ask questions, Edmund continued his explanation. "People are too focused on their own power and forget that there is strength in the bonds we make." Edmund rolled up the paper and handed it to Luke.

Quest alert! **Passion of Beasts**: *Edmund, the local owner of Critters and Creatures Pet Haven, has expressed his interest in you becoming a Beast Tamer. Take his letter of recommendation to Ursa the Beast Tamer to learn more about the class specialization. What harm could there be in learning more? Reward: Knowledge of the Beast Tamer specialization and increased reputation with Edmund. Accept / Decline*

Edmund had been so nice to me and took his time to teach and explain things. The least I could do is accept the quest. Luke reached out and grabbed the rolled up letter with a hesitant smile.

"Edmund? Can I just ask why you are showing such an interest in me?" Luke questioned.

"That's a very fair question, Luke. Do you know why most people visit my store?" He gazed at Luke but when he received nothing but a shrug, he continued speaking. "They come to buy a flashy pet. Pets differ from animal companions. There isn't a strong bond right away. You have to work at it much harder and earn it. Most travelers treat their pets as vanity items and usually lose interest after a few days. Do you know how many pet falcons I have had returned just this week?" Again Luke gave him a shrug. "Over twenty. Do you know what all of them ask when they buy the falcon in the first place?" Edmund didn't bother looking at Luke or waiting for an answer, he just continued speaking. "They ask nothing. Not a one has asked me how to take care of their pet." His eyes filled with sadness. "No one cares about these animals anymore. Didn't you notice that no one came in to bother us while we sat and chatted for hours?"

Luke did find that odd. He had been here for at least a few hours and barely anyone even walked by the front windows. "I can't be the only one who..." Edmund gave him a serious stare.

"You are the only traveler to ever ask how to better take care of their animal."

"That can't be the only reason you're being so nice... right?" Luke pushed.

Edmund let out a large sigh. "No, it isn't the only reason. I was a beast tamer in my adventuring days and, to be honest, it's not a rare specialization by choice, it's more of a dying specialization." Luke gave him a deadpan face implying he knew he was being set up. "Don't get me wrong, it's a strong choice. The main problem is the requirements. I don't remember them all, it was too long ago, but I remember the big two were having a strong bond with an animal companion and having nature affinity in magic."

"If that was the case, why aren't there a lot of Elves who choose the specialization?" Luke continued to press for information.

"Most elves, especially ones with nature affinity, choose to be mages or spell arrows. Like I said, everyone, even elves, care about personal strength above all else." Edmund frowned as he gazed around the room at all the caged animals.

Luke remembered an old phrase that had something to do with absolute power or the search for power. He couldn't remember the exact phrase, but Edmund's logic made sense.

"Well Edmund, I'll look into it," Luke stated.

*100 **Reputation Gained** with **Edmund**.*
*New Status: **Liked**.*

A small tint of light returned to Edmund's eyes. "Thank you

Luke. If you decide to become a beast tamer, please come back and see me. I will reward you with something special. Even if you don't become a beast tamer, please visit anyway. I would like to see how you and little Ringo grow."

> *Quest alert!* ***Gift from a Friend****: Edmund would like to reward you if you are so inclined to follow in the path of a Beast Tamer. Return to Edmund with Beast Tamer set as your class for a special reward. Reward: Unknown. Exp: 1,000. Accept / Decline*
> *Note: This is a conditional quest with no time limit. If you choose a different specialization you will automatically fail this quest but see no negative ramifications.*

Luke hit accept and Edmund showed Luke on the map where he could find Ursa, the beast tamer. He encouraged Luke to really consider this as an option and urged him to keep the specialization alive.

Luke headed for the door and hesitated, expecting Edmund to stop him yet again. When he didn't hear the half-elf scream at him to stop, he left the store with much more than he went in for.

CHAPTER ELEVEN

The Raid

Leaving the store, Luke wanted to share this new information with his guild. This, in combination with the dungeon, would put their guild ahead of others. Opening his map, he made his way to the marker Shrapnel added for the new guild headquarters.

It took him almost twenty minutes to get there, still amazed at the vast size of the city. The building was several stories tall with windows evenly spaced every couple of feet. Shrapnel wasn't kidding about the ideal location either. The building had a clear path to the main city gate and was only a few blocks away. It also appeared to be a much nicer building than the warehouse he had first been introduced in. Frankly, this building wasn't falling apart like the old one.

Opening the large wooden door, noise and music assaulted Luke. The grand room was much like their old one. There were scatterings of long tables, benches, and free-flowing booze. The room looked much more organized than the random pattern of furniture they used to have and the quality was top-notch. There were several staircases leading both up and down and behind the bar was a hallway with multiple doors leading off it.

"Hey arrow boy." Luke turned toward the origin of the noise and found Penny approaching with a mug in both hands. She extended one of her arms toward him, offering him a drink. He graciously accepted, sniffed the contents and took a sip.

He coughed loudly and repeatedly, not expecting the drink to be so strong. "Oh my god, what is this?" he inquired.

"It's a dwarven brew and I'm too tipsy to even attempt pronouncing it," She replied slowly. "Care to join us?" Gesturing with her open hand, she pointed to the end of a long table. Sitting and drinking were Backstab, Nanoc and Shrapnel. He nodded, and the two headed to join their guild mates. The group cheered in drunken bliss upon Luke and Penny's arrival.

"Now we can really drink!" Shouted Nanoc as he gestured at the bar for another round.

"Shrapnel, I have something to tell you and the others." Luke started before being interrupted by Backstab.

"No! There will be no shop talk while we drink. Listen Lukey boy, we killed a giant goblin today. Let's just relax and focus on how bad-ass we are, ok?"

"Lukey boy? Oh god, I hope that doesn't stick." He muttered under his breath. "But it's really important that I..."

Nanoc pushed another mug in front of Luke while starting to chug his own. He looked expectantly at his fellow guild mates and they started joining in. Luke looked at Penny, the only reasonable one, and pleaded with his eyes for her to listen. She smiled warmly, lifted her mug high into the air, and started to chug. Luke sighed in defeat and joined them in a futile attempt to outdrink their resident barbarian.

After they had several drinks, they started sharing stories of their lives outside the game. Luke was taken aback. Talking about your out of game life was usually taboo in online games but the group was freely sharing.

"I was a dealer at a casino," Backstab shared in between large gulps of his drink. "Made good tips, but I blew most of it on video games. The press conference for the vortex capsule was too great to pass up." The group nodded, remembering just how great the vortex press conference was.

"I'm in college and work on the side as a waitress to help pay for my tuition." Penny added to the conversation.

"Really? I'm in college too," Luke responded quickly.

"What year? I'm a junior in business school," Penny replied.

"Just a freshman and I'm in engineering."

"Engineering? What are you smart or something?" She teased.

"He has to be smart because he can't get anywhere in life with a face like that," Backstab commented as he threw his arm around Luke and pointed at his head while making a stupid-looking face.

The group burst out laughing. Luke wasn't sure if it was the copious amounts of alcohol he had consumed or the fact that it was the first time he had seen Penny in relatively normal clothes but he noticed she had a nice smile. He realized he had been staring at her face too long when he turned around and saw Backstab. He was raising his eyebrows over and over and muttered slowly, "You dog."

Luke's face turned beet read as the group heard a high-pitched hiccup come from the table. Ringo stared up at the group. She was apparently licking up some spilled ale and Luke couldn't have been happier to have the attention off himself.

Is this my normal now? he thought. In truth, he thought this was even better than all the magic in the game. Sharing a drink and laughs with good friends isn't something he did often, or ever, in the real world. He was ok with this being his new normal.

The door to the guild hall burst open and a guard with the Phoenix Kingdom sigil stamped in his plate armor came rushing in. The guard was covered in green liquid, panting and trying to catch his breath. Luke's group all looked at each other, well aware of what the green liquid was: goblin blood. Shrapnel rushed to the guard's side with a drink.

"Here, drink this." He handed the drink over while helping the guard to a bench.

The guard drank the liquid without hesitation and began to speak. "Ra... Raid. Gob... goblins everywhere... Help..." The guard could barely get the words out before a system prompt appeared in Luke's vision.

Area Event Triggered! **Goblin Raid!** *Goblins are attacking the Phoenix Kingdom. As a city guild of the Phoenix Kingdom, you are obligated to help and cannot refuse this call to action. Stop the goblin raid 0/1. Reward: Increased guild reputation with the Phoenix Kingdom. Exp: 1,500.*

The room erupted in a war cry as members of the guild quickly armed themselves and grouped up. Shrapnel began shouting out orders to parties, assigning them to various spots in the city while tasking the non-combat members with distributing potions and locking up the windows.

When Penny's party reformed, they were told to head for the city gate and hold back the invading force as best they could. Having their orders, they all rushed out and Luke looked at Ringo. She was bent over in a pouncing pose and her tail was wagging like crazy. "I guess you're coming?" Ringo barked. "Let's get going then." Ringo jumped to the floor and ran out the door. "Wait for me!" he shouted to his party as they left him behind.

It didn't take long for Luke to both reach the gate and realize that fighting while under the influence was incredibly difficult. Luke's arrows flew feet wide from their intended targets and he ended up hitting a teammate more than once. Luke was just happy that nature's regrowth didn't force him to aim in order to work.

After dispatching a group of three goblins, Luke inspected the next group charging them.

Inspect *Successful!*
Name: *Simple Goblin Warrior*
Level: *4*
HP/MP/Stamina: *100/0/50*
Status: *Hostile*

"Well at least they're only level four." He intended to mumble but the noise of battle made him shout unintentionally. This caused his head to throb in pain. He looked over and his party was fighting normally. His eyes went wide, the debuff for being drunk had vanished from their status bars.

His party quickly dispatched the next wave and shouted for Luke to add more support. When Backstab turned around, he saw Luke holding his head with both hands and ran toward him. He spoke as softly as he could. "First time drinking in-game?" Luke couldn't hear him so Backstab shouted directly in Luke's ear. "Here, take this!" Luke's head throbbed so hard that he fell to his knees in pain before Backstab took one of his hands and forced him to grip a bottle.

Weak cleansing potion *(uncommon) x1 obtained. This potion cures one minor status ailment.*

Luke drank the potion like someone receiving their first drop of water in a desert.

Drunk *debuff removed.*

Luke got back to his feet and patted the dirt off of his legs. Speaking in a calm monotone voice he asked, "Two things. One, thank you for that. And two," he shouted the next part in anger. "Why would you shout at me like that you jerk!"

Backstab grinned before responding. "Those potions cost twenty gold. I was going to charge you for it but watching you squirm around in pain more than paid the price of admission." Luke gave him a deadpan expression in return before pulling an arrow and pointing it at him. "Oh look at the time." Backstab gazed at his wrist and ran back to the front lines.

"Watches don't even exist yet!" Luke spat out before focusing back on the next wave. Five goblins crashed into Penny as she activated her taunt, shouting and bashing her shield to gain the attention of the enemy. It amazed Luke at how nimble and quick she was without her armor on. With the attack being so sudden, she didn't have time to don her full metal armor and now, instead of taking glancing blows, she was bobbing and weaving out of the way. She wasn't nearly as quick as Backstab or himself but she definitely put some points into her agility.

Releasing a water arrow into one of the attacking goblins, Luke sent his healing magic toward Penny. While the goblins were distracted, Nanoc got behind the remaining four and cut them down with a spinning whirlwind. Just when Luke thought they were getting the upper hand a fifteen foot tall creature wielding a massive tree stump for a club burst through the wall of the city. Luke tried to inspect the creature.

Inspect Failed!
Inspect Failed!
*Successful Intelligence Roll, **Inspect** Partial Success!*

Name: *Hulking Ogre*
Level: *?*
HP/MP/Stamina: *?/?/?*
Status: *Hostile*

Interesting. It looks like I can get some information even if they are too high a level. His thoughts were interrupted when the ogre tossed a piece of debris at a nearby building. The building collapsed under the pressure of the ogre's toss and weight of the debris.

"What do we do?" Luke asked to no one in particular.

"We keep the little ones from getting into the city the best we can! We stick to the plan. I can't even see that thing's level. It would take us out with one swipe. Stay focused on the task at hand and ignore it," Penny shouted as she engaged another group of goblins.

Luke was conflicted. The ogre was destroying whole buildings, and they were going to focus on a couple of measly goblins? He shook the feeling off, ultimately agreeing that there wasn't anything they could do. Distracted by his thoughts and the sight of the ogre, he failed to notice the goblin sneaking up beside him.

*You are **Bleeding**. Bleeding debuff added. You will continue to take damage until you are healed or the bleeding stops naturally.*

The bleeding notification accompanied a large slash across his back. Luke spun around, gripping his bow in both hands like a bat and struck the goblin. The goblin staggered back slightly but pressed its attack. Before it could swing its blade again, Ringo pounced, driving the monster to the ground. She opened her maw and bit down hard on the goblin's neck. Blood squirted in all directions as the sharp fangs of an alpha wolf sunk deep and a sickening crunch could be heard as she snapped the neck of her prey.

Ringo thrashed the tiny goblin around a bit before releasing the body from her maw and turning back to Luke, tail wagging. Stunned a bit by the sudden display of ferocity from his cute companion, his tongue tripped over its next words. "Uhhh... good job, I guess..."

He activated nature's regrowth on himself to stop the bleeding and shot another round of arrows at various targets around the battlefield. This pattern continued as Luke and his party, along with other guild mates, took on waves and waves of low level goblins.

The city guards had some success in their efforts to corral the ogre away from the more populated sections of the city. They seemed to surround it on three sides and used their halberds to nudge it in a direction. They weren't doing any damage to the ogre but were minimizing the collateral damage it could cause.

Without warning, two more ogres pushed through the hole in the wall that the first had created. They were swinging their clubs around wildly, sending several guards and goblins flying with each swing. It appeared they weren't concerned about their little green buddies.

A blur of white raced across the battlefield, zigzagging through the many engagements that were underway. Each time it passed by an encounter, the goblins would fall to the ground. The bodies were riddled with several small, needle-like holes, only noticeable because of the white smoke rising from them. It was only when the blur came to a stop, directly under one of the ogres, that Luke recognized it.

Captain Holtz was hunched beneath one of the hulking beasts, his long thin rapier drawn behind him. "Let the gods of light and fire empower me, so I may strike my foe down. Holy Fire!" The captain was shouting to the heavens and at the end of his speech, his rapier ignited in white flames. The ogre swung wide with its tree trunk club but the captain didn't make a move to dodge or block. Instead, the captain slashed the trunk in two. Each end of the trunk where his blade struck erupted in flames that quickly began to engulf the makeshift club.

The ogre tossed his half of the trunk to the ground and raised both fists above his head. He swung downward with more speed than Luke thought possible. Everyone in the area now stood watching, transfixed.

The captain raised his blade in a line above his head as the ogre's fists crashed into him. The sheer force of the blow caused the ground to crack and break apart, sending a cloud of smoke around the site of impact. Luke wasn't sure how anyone could survive blocking that blow, especially with such a thin blade. Thinking quickly, he pulled an arrow and took aim at the massive enemy.

Before he could release the arrow, he saw the creature's arms being forced back upward as the smoke was clearing. The captain had taken the full force of the attack and was now pushing against the colossal strength of his enemy.

"You are strong, but my resolve is stronger! Gods of light and fire, I beseech you!" The white flames around his blade started to concentrate on the blade's tip. "Fifty strikes of flame!" He grunted as he sent one final push upward, causing the ogre to fall backwards. As the ogre fell, the captain placed one arm behind his back and leaped forward. His sword arm moved so quickly that the surrounding air began to heat, causing the sight of it to become blurry.

After a few moments, the captain jumped backward and sheathed his weapon. The ogre stood still for what felt like an eternity but in reality it couldn't have been more than a few seconds. When the ogre took a hesitant step forward, dozens of small holes began appearing in its chest. The pinholes each had tiny white flames pouring out of them as blood spurted to the ground. The ogre fell forward with a loud crash, cracking the cobblestone as it landed.

The guards shouted in accomplishment and praise at their captain's display of strength. Without warning, the captain had at least two dozen small holes appear on his body, blood dripping from them. They appeared to be the same as the wounds he inflicted to the ogre but with the absence of flames. He let out a grunt of pain as he fell to one knee, clutching his chest.

At the sight of their fallen friend, the ogres ignored the guards attempting to corral them and started heading directly for the captain. The captain tried to stand but fell back to a knee when a new round of pain wracked his body. Luke started to rush toward him but was blocked by several goblins, the break in the battle coming to an abrupt end.

"Luke, I need a heal!" shouted Nanoc as he was fending off a handful of goblins solo. Luke cursed that he couldn't get to the captain and sent a heal at Nanoc before releasing several arrows and joining his party back in battle.

When the ogres reached the captain, they looked at each other and laughed. They pulled back their clubs and began to swing. Thick vines shot out of the ground, gripping one of the ogre's clubs and rooting him in place. The other ogre's club swung at the captain, but before it could connect a large gorilla intercepted the blow and pulled the trunk from the ogre's grip, tossing it across the battlefield.

"I think you've gotten weaker Rupert. I don't remember you struggling with a single ogre before," said a small woman with frizzy green hair. Reaching into her pocket she pulled out a few flasks and leisurely tossed them one-handed at the raging ogre attempting to bust out of his constraints. When the bottles collided with the ogre, they shattered and their contents spilled across its body. Green, blue, and red liquid coated various parts of the creature as they began to melt, freeze, and ignite after a moment of exposure to the air.

The ogre screamed in pain as the short woman pointed a walking staff at it. The staff began to glow blue as a baseball-sized globe of water appeared at the tip of the outreached staff. It shot out with incredible speed and collided with the head of the ogre. The ogre's eyes rolled back into its head and its body went limp.

The other ogre wasn't idle during this time and tried to strike the out-of-place gorilla, but the gorilla easily dodged the blow. On the back of the gorilla was a figure completely wrapped in bandages with a loose-fitting t-shirt and shorts over the top. She, only determinable by certain bulges in her wrappings, launched off the gorilla, heading for a collision course with the ogre in front of her.

She and the gorilla began to glow green as she reeled back her fist. The ogre grinned as the woman approached threateningly. The grin was literally punched off his face. When the woman's fist connected, the ogre's head spun around and they could hear a very audible snap and pop. The ogre's head was now facing its back, and the lower jaw where her fist connected had shattered and been reduced to gore. She landed with an impressive backflip on the ground next to the captain and the short woman.

At the death of the ogres the goblins began to shout in frustration and retreat. If that wasn't signal enough of their victory, someone in the distance shouted, "we won!" Everyone either joined in the uproar of cheering or fell over from exhaustion. Luke took this opportunity to collapse to the ground and read system messages.

Area Event Complete! **Goblin Raid!** *You and your guild have successfully stopped the Goblin Raid. Your guild has been rewarded 100 reputation with the Phoenix Kingdom. You have been awarded 1,500 exp.*

Skill up: **Nature's Regrowth**, *Beginner 6.*
Skill up: **Inspect**, *Beginner 2.*
Skill up: **Water Shot**, *Beginner 4.*
Skill up: **Short Bow**, *Beginner 9.*
Skill up: **Beast Mastery**, *Beginner 4.*

Simple Goblin Warrior *x17 defeated. 510 party participation exp gained.*
Goblin Scout *x4 defeated. 100 party participation exp gained.*

Luke was lying on the ground, panting heavily but smiling from all the gains and the victory. Ringo interrupted his view of the stars when she began to lick his cheek. "Ok buddy, ok." Luke started patting and petting her. "I'm ok bud."

"You look older." A familiar sounded voice said.

Luke shot up to a sitting position and saw that Rose was indeed the one speaking with him. His eyes got slightly watery seeing the woman he grew so fond of alive and well.

"Rose?" She nodded. "I'm so glad you're alive, but where have you been? Wait, did you kill that ogre? What were those potions you used? Have you been back to the shop? Oh no, have you seen your workshop? You've seen the workshop haven't you? You're going to hurt me, aren't you?" Luke started rambling, speaking faster and faster to the point where Rose had to slap him out of it.

"Luke! Calm down, you're going too fast for me to follow. I will explain everything after we get back to my shop... wait, what do you mean have I seen what you did to my workshop?" She raised a single eyebrow questionably.

"Um. I did nothing to your shop." His voice raised several octaves toward the end of his response. Ringo barked, bringing the attention back to her.

"Who's this little fella?" She asked.

"Long story, I guess." He responded as his party came walking up.

"It looks like you have some things to finish up with your guild? I have to speak with Rupert for a bit, but I will meet you back at the shop as soon as I'm done." As soon as Rose finished speaking, she walked toward the recovering guard captain. Luke noticed that she was now putting weight on the staff as she walked off.

"You know that crazy bad-ass plant lady?" Backstab asked.

"Did you see those potions? They melted, burned, and froze all at the same time. What the hell was that?" Nanoc added.

Luke shook his head before speaking. "It's a long story, but she's the one who owns the local Alchemy shop I'm staying at. I had no idea she was a bad-ass though."

Penny helped Luke to his feet, and the group headed for the Guild Hall.

CHAPTER TWELVE

Reunion

Luke followed his party back to the guild hall. Opening the door, the group was assaulted with a wall of noise. People were cheering and shouting about their night full of battle. The city guard had dropped off celebratory casks of ale that were partially to blame.

Luke's party began looking for mugs but he stopped them, getting evil glares in return. He quickly promised that it was only temporary while he explained the information he found out about earlier that day from Edmund. Looking around, he found Shrapnel and told him that he really needed to share some important information with the guild. After some groans, Shrapnel put his mug back on the table and ushered Luke and his party to a room in the back.

The door opened to a meeting hall, with a large oval table in the center and chairs lined up on each side. After taking their seats, Shrapnel shut the door but it only marginally dulled the party waiting for them outside.

"This better be good," Backstab stated in annoyance as he

twirled a dagger between his fingers.

"It is. What I'm about to tell you is extremely important for your character progression and future in the game." Luke tried to stress the importance of his words before he began talking.

The group gave Luke their full attention as he recalled everything Edmund told him about class choices and specialization. He stressed that the choice they make at level ten was their last chance to really determine what they wanted to do. The group was suffering from information overload as they began contemplating their own class decisions internally.

"So level three and then ten are the big choices and everything beyond that is unique and custom for individual players based on their earlier decisions and playstyle?" Penny restated Luke's words not expecting him to answer the open-ended question, but he did.

"Yes. It seems like the game creators wanted everyone to have a unique experience. It also seems like you will keep learning spells and skills past level ten but not if they aren't related to your specialization choice," he answered.

"But doesn't that sound limiting? I was hoping I could do everything," Shrapnel said with confusion and concern.

"Maybe. But it also sounds kinda fun and unique." The group looked at Backstab, wanting him to continue his train of thought. "Think about it. This game is like a lot of other online RPGs. You pick a role and you're stuck with it. The way you're explaining it, Luke, is that we pick a role but depending on how we play that role, the game will reward us with unique skills, abilities and classes that enhance our unique style of playing. I'm a rogue. In most online games, that's all I would be, and I would be just like every other rogue. In Endless Fantasy Online, it seems like I start out as a rogue but could end up being a one-of-a-kind stealthy backstabber class."

They all contemplated what Backstab was saying and eventually agreed that the system sounded fun.

"Regardless of our thoughts on the matter, this is important information that needs to be shared. Thank you Luke." Shrapnel extended his hand and Luke accepted the handshake. "I'll make sure people are aware and post it in the message board. We have a lot of people at level eight or nine, including myself, that really need to think about our next choice." The others nodded in agreement as they all appeared to be lost in thought.

Luke excused himself from the remainder of the festivities at the behest of his party members. He wanted to stay, but he wanted to speak with Rose more.

Heading through the streets, he was amazed at what the mages of the city were capable of. The damaged walls were already being restored with magic. Several robed figures were glowing with a variety of colors as stone flew threw the air and arranged itself. Additional mages and guards were creating and laying mortar as fire mages heated it up and air mages cooled it. The same treatment was happening with the ruined buildings. Mages were creating timbers as builders quickly put them in place and attached them.

I wonder why those mages aren't helping during the raids. I should ask Captain Holtz the next time I see him, Luke thought as he walked casually toward Rose's shop, with Ringo following closely by his side. When he arrived outside the alchemy shop, the candlelight was visible through the windows and he could see someone's shadow moving around inside. Mustering up the courage, he turned the door handle and went inside. Rose was in her office tossing items out of crates, clearly in search of something. "Rose?" Luke uttered nervously.

The gnome woman looked up from her current task and when she noticed it was Luke, she put on a warm smile. She met Luke at the counter as she climbed up the small staircase that was built into the back. "Come closer, let me get a good look at you." Rose pulled her trademark goggles over her eyes and they began to glow. "Hmm... I see... You went with Ranger. Ahh, and your nature's regrowth spell is coming along nicely." She paused for several moments in between sentences and Luke pumped out his chest. "And you're almost at intermediate levels with two skills. You seem to be growing just fine." She moved her goggles back to the top of her head before continuing. "I see you have a lot of unused skill points and attribute points. Why haven't you spent those?"

"I wanted to save them for when I decided what to specialize in. Enough of me. Where have you been!" Luke brushed off her questioning, in an attempt to get answers.

Rose turned away from Luke. "I've only been gone a couple of days, a week at most. Can't a girl go on vacation?" Peeking back, she saw that her answer wasn't going to satisfy him, so she huffed in disappointment before continuing. "I'm sorry. I left during an... inopportune time and I really appreciate you taking care of my plants while I was away." She paused, hoping that would be enough but Luke crossed his arms and nodded his head for her to continue. "Ok, Ok. I was on a mission for the King."

"The King? You know the King?" Luke uncrossed his arms, letting go of some of his anger over her sudden disappearance.

"The King and I were once part of the same party." Luke's eyes went wide at this latest revelation. "I was older than him and assigned as his healer and support mage. The previous King, King Henry's father, assigned me to his party. He thought my potion making and healing magic would ensure his son would survive." Her eyes went distant, and she had a playful expression on her face. "He didn't need my help though. Henry was an animal in combat. The King wanted me there to keep him alive but Henry was the one who kept the four of us alive. Those were some of the best times of my long life. After the previous King passed, Henry gave me this shop and asked that I stay in the city incase he needed me."

Rose pulled a crumbled sketch from her pocket and began to unfold it. She handed the sketch over and Luke examined it. The sketch featured a party of four adventurers laughing as they stood in the foreground with a massive monster lying dead in the background. Luke instantly recognized Rose in the photo, although she appeared a bit younger and sported the look of an adventurer with armor and weapons strung about her. He also recognized the King standing alongside her. He was much younger looking and didn't have the big beard that Luke associated with him.

Luke didn't recognize the short archer. He thought it was probably another gnome — or a halfling, if those existed in this world. What surprised him most was the fourth member of their party, their mage.

"Is that... Shadow Incarnate!" He dropped the sketch on the counter and Rose picked it up.

"We didn't call him that at the time. He adopted that silly name later in life, along with an insatiable thirst for power." She began to get choked up and her voice became hoarse from holding back tears. "We were all so close before Shadow Incarnate did something that could never be forgiven. We were forced to turn on him. The rest of us fought hard and ultimately stopped him." Her voice turned to one of anger and regret. "And that should have been the end of it! We defeated him and then Henry was supposed to kill him but he took mercy and banished him to the far reaches of the world."

"That clearly didn't work," Luke added.

Rose chuckled and her voice returned to normal. "The King came to me a few weeks ago and asked for my help. There were rumors of a dark uprising headed for the Phoenix Kingdom and he was concerned that it was his past finally coming back to bite him. He knew Shadow Incarnate would never reveal himself unless the royal family was gone, so he faked his death and the kidnapping of his wife and daughter. It worked like a charm and when most of the king's men were out of the city in fake pursuit, he invaded. You know how that ended." Rose looked at Luke for confirmation and he nodded. "Even when Henry came to me asking for my help, I never thought it could be him. I expected a lich lord or new necromancer, but never Shadow Incarnate. When I saw him approaching the city, I lost it. I gathered what I needed and waited for the King to confront him. When he fled, I took pursuit and have been following him ever since."

"Did you find him?" Luke asked.

She frowned. "No. I was able to track him through the outlying forests and mountain ranges but lost him a few days north of here. I did get glimpses of it though."

Luke gulped. "Glimpses of what?" He hesitantly asked.

"Glimpses of his army. They moved through shadow, travelers and monsters alike. There aren't enough high level people in the entire kingdom to stop that army. The king must have seen his army when he was hiding out. What other reason would he have to go to the Elk Kingdom but to ask for them to join forces."

"Wait, aren't the kingdoms already friends? I mean, I never see them attacking us or anything." Luke wondered.

"The primary kingdoms are all allies but tend to leave each other alone. If something threatens the Phoenix Kingdom, the Elk Kingdom wouldn't send forces to aid them. They would wait for the problem to be on their doorstep before taking action. Henry will plead with them to stand united against this foe before it's too late."

Luke pondered everything he heard so far, and a troubling thought crossed his mind. "Was the goblin raid tonight the start of war?" He asked with a tinge of fear in his voice.

"No. I'm not sure what tonight was. Something must have upset the local goblin population. Probably a group of stupid adventurers stepping into their territory." Luke's face went grim, and it didn't go unnoticed. "Luke? Please don't tell me you don't know what I'm talking about."

Luke explained what happened with The Den and with Xirx, the Goblin Warlord boss they defeated.

Rose had her head in her palms and was shaking it slowly in disbelief. "I leave for a couple of days and you start a blood feud with the goblins. By the sounds of it, we should be expecting many more attacks."

"What makes you say that?" Luke replied.

"You said the smiths were building crates full of weapons and armor?" Luke confirmed. "I didn't see a single goblin wearing armor or wielding anything more than a crude weapon. Tonight's attack was just an information gathering mission. They wanted to test how we would respond. I'll speak with Captain Holtz in the morning. For now, I suggest we get some rest." Rose's eyebrows shot up. "Speaking of which… I saw what you did to my storage closet."

Flustered and nervous, Luke responded. "I… I… I…"

Rose's eyebrows lowered, and she gave him a welcoming smile. "It's ok Luke. I should have given you a more permanent place to sleep after you started helping in the shop. Keep tending my garden every morning and help out around the shop and we'll consider that your rent."

"Thank you!" Luke smiled before his expression turned to one of worry. He gazed down at Ringo before speaking. "It's ok that she stays here too, right?" Luke grabbed Ringo and placed her on the counter.

"Hmm..." Rose rubbed her chin in thought. "As long as she doesn't make a mess and you keep her from causing trouble with the customers, I don't mind." Rose began to pet Ringo gently on the head. "Now then, it's late and I'm exhausted from my travels so I'm going to bed." Rose began down the staircase leading from her counter to her workshop. When she entered the workshop and began shutting the door, she gave Luke one final gaze. "Thank you for watching my shop and garden Luke and I really appreciate your concern for me. I'm glad to be back and see that you're ok." With that she shut the door and retired for the evening.

*100 **Reputation Gained** with **Rose.***

Luke retired to his small closet of a room. Opening his pack, he put the heavy bestiary on his desk, relieved to get rid of the extra weight. He also unpacked the uncommon class weapon box and most of the pet supplies. He kept some nutrient pellets in his bag incase he needed them on the go, along with his brush in case he got downtime in the field. He kept his meager fifty-one gold on him and decided not to open the class weapon box for the time being, rather saving it for when he specialized.

Luke placed a few handfuls of nutrient pellets on the ground and began taking his armor off. Realizing he had no place to properly store his armor, he stacked it as neatly as he could in one corner of the small room. Luke laid in the bed, while Ringo ate her food, and pulled up his character sheet. When he realized that he had nine unused skill points, he decided he could afford to spend a few to get some more immediate gains, especially if more goblin raids were forthcoming. Distributing five skill points he confirmed his choices.

Skill up: **Nature's Regrowth**, *Intermediate 0. New rank achieved. Additional effect added based on your use of the skill up to this point.*
Nature's Regrowth *(Intermediate 0): Grasping a better understanding of the healing powers of nature, you can harness this energy quicker than before. Harness the power of nature to speed up the natural healing and growth speed of the target. Cost: 4x mana. Effect 1: Heal for 2x every 5 seconds for 15 seconds where x = skill level. Effect 2: Additional 10% health restored when the spell is used on someone other than you. Cooldown: 45 seconds. Range: 10 feet.*

Skill up: **Short Bow**, *Intermediate 0. New rank achieved. Additional effect added based on your use of the skill up to this point.*
Short Bow *(Intermediate 0): You have become familiar with short bows and no longer are looked at as a beginner by others. Increasing this skill will increase the damage dealt with a short bow. This is a passive skill and requires no activation. Effect 1: +10% short bow damage. Effect 2: +x% damage when attacking targets distracted by an ally.*

Amazed by the boons he received when a skill hit the intermediate levels, he had to hold himself back from spending the rest of his skill points. He winced slightly at the increased mana cost of nature's regrowth, now only being able to cast the spell three times before he ran out of mana. He contemplated spending his four unused attribute points in intelligence, but again held himself back as he reviewed his updated character sheet.

Name: *Luke, Wolfsbane.*
Class: *Ranger*
Primary Profession: *Herbalist*
Animal Companion: *Ringo (Alpha Wolf Pup)*

Level 5: *Exp 4632 Exp to next level: 368*
Hit Points: 70/70
Mana: 130/130
Mana Regen: 1.75/sec
Stamina: 110/110
Physical Resistance: +15
Elemental Resistance: Water +10, Earth +10

Attributes *Base (Modifier) .*
Strength: 1
Agility: 7
Intelligence: 6 (+3)
Wisdom: 2 (+2)
Constitution: 3
Social: 4
Luck: 1

Skills, Spells and Abilities

Short Bow *(Intermediate 0): You have become familiar with short bows and no longer are looked at as a beginner by others. Increasing this skill will increase the damage dealt with a short bow. This is a passive skill and requires no activation. Effect 1: +10% short bow damage. Effect 2: +x% damage when attacking targets distracted by an ally.*

Herbalism *(Beginner 8): This skill allows you to identify various plant life.*

First Aid *(Beginner 0): Basic knowledge on how to apply basic first aid and use basic bandages. Increasing this skill will increase your knowledge of first aid techniques and increase the speed at which you can apply this skill.*

Nature's Regrowth *(Intermediate 0): Grasping a better understanding of the healing powers of nature, you can harness this energy quicker than before. Harness the power of nature to speed up the natural healing and growth speed of the target. Cost: 4x mana. Effect 1: Heal for 2x every 5 seconds for 15 seconds where x = skill level. Effect 2: Additional 10% health restored when the spell is used on someone other than you. Cooldown: 45 seconds. Range: 10 feet.*

Alchemy *(Beginner 1): Knowledge of basic reagent combinations. Increasing this skill will increase your knowledge of alchemy and increase your chances of combining new reagents successfully.*

Bartering *(Beginner 2): Trading is a craft and you have taken the first steps in learning that craft. You will receive small bonuses when attempting to barter. Effect: +x% bartering results where x = skill level.*

Inspect *(Beginner 2) Knowledge is half the battle. By focusing on your opponents you can now gleam basic knowledge of them. Leveling up this skill will grant you more information and allow you to inspect a wider range of enemy levels. Effect: Gain basic knowledge of enemies up to double your level.*

Sneak *(Beginner 0): While others try to be honest and fair, you sneak around in the dark, looking for opportunities to strike. What are you really doing hiding in those bushes? Cost: 1 stamina per second. Effect: +x% chance to sneak and +1x% chance to perform a sneak attack when attacking while hidden, where x = skill level.*

Water Shot *(Beginner 4): Infuses your arrow with water. When shot it will fire off like a water jet and do increased water affinity damage. Cost: 25 + x mana. Effect: Increases arrow travel rate by 10% and adds 1x water damage where x = skill level. Range: Touch arrow.*

Resurrect Companion *(Class Skill): Resurrects your animal companion if they have unfortunately died. Allowing your animal companion to die will negatively affect your relationship and they*

may choose to break their bond with you. Cost: 100% max mana.
Effect: Channel this spell for 10 second to resurrect your animal
companion at full health. Cooldown: 24 hours. Range: Self.
Beast Mastery *(Beginner 4): You have bonded with a beast and*
taken a baby step in befriending the animal kingdom. Improving this
skill will increase your bond with your animal companion and
increase their proficiency in battle. This skill also scales based on your
social attribute. Effect: +2% animal companion's attributes.
Rapid Fire *(Beginner 1): Most people take careful aim at their*
targets to ensure they hit but not you. You just keep shooting until
something sticks. Cost: 2 stamina per second. Effect: Increase arrow
firing rate by $X + 2\%$ and decrease your aim by $x + 5\%$ while
channeling the spell where x = skill level.

Proud of his progress, he called Ringo to bed. Jumping up, Ringo began to go around in circles until she laid down near Luke's feet. Smiling, Luke blew out the candle near his bed and drifted asleep.

Luke woke up to Ringo scratching the door to be let out. Thinking back, Luck couldn't recall a time that his animal companion went to the bathroom. Not sure what to do, he lead Ringo out back to the garden to take care of business while he tended to Rose's plants. Luke carefully retrieved Ringo's droppings in a spare planting pot and carried it outside to one of the bins that were located in front of each of the homes.

Rose explained to him once that the bins were all connected underground with earth magic. Once a day, the mage's guild would collect all the contents, using the underground tunnel system, into a large waste facility at the edge of town. Fire mages would burn all the trash while light and air mages would purify and disperse the toxic cloud it created. Luke never saw the system activate but every morning the bin was empty and he didn't have a reason to doubt what Rose told him. All in all, Luke thought the system was a smart way to deal with trash and waste — it also explained why the city always smelled worse toward evening and better in the morning.

Going back inside he found Rose rearranging shelves while several beakers of liquid were boiling on a workstation nearby. Ringo was following Rose around, sniffing each herb and flower that Rose was arranging. "Morning Rose." Ringo sneezed as she got too close while smelling some red flowers.

Rose and Luke giggled before she returned his greetings. "Morning Luke. Any plans for the day?"

Luke was put off a little by her casual demeanor. "Are you forgetting our talk last night? There is a war with goblins headed our way. Shouldn't we be preparing or something?" He was getting worked up by the time he finished speaking.

She smiled and started petting Ringo before responding. "No, I didn't forget but a few days or weeks of me training won't make much of a difference in the upcoming battle. I won't see much of any return for such a small training session. My time is best spent brewing potions." She gestured toward the brewing stands spread out across the room. "You, on the other hand, could use as much training as possible. You have made some good progress in the couple of days I have been gone but you are still lacking and would see great returns from rigorous training."

Luke opened his mouth to argue but rethought it. Rose was right, her time would be better spent preparing potions and healing items for everyone. "Well... any suggestions for me then?"

"I just gave you a suggestion, train." She replied curtly.

"Yeah, I get that but how? Should I just go out and kill things or is there a better way for me to be training?"

"No, no, no. Fighting monsters will give you some experience in battle but it's not good training. You need to train your body and mind." She pointed a finger at Ringo. "You too little one. Find a trainer in town that suits your goals and follow his instructions. I could teach you how to brew some more potions but that wouldn't help you in the upcoming fight." She thought for a moment and added, "Why don't you visit a friend of mine. Her name is Ursa, and she uses animal companions like you. But be warned. She is one tough broad and good at whipping people into shape, if she likes you."

Where had Luke heard that name before? He started scratching his head before things clicked. Pulling up his quest log with a thought, he found what he was looking for.

Passion of Beasts: *Edmund, the local owner of Critters and Creatures Pet Haven, has expressed his interest in you becoming a Beast Tamer. Take his letter of recommendation to Ursa the Beast Tamer to learn more about the class specialization. What harm could there be in learning more? Reward: Knowledge of the Beast Tamer specialization and increased reputation with Edmund.*

"Ursa is the beast tamer trainer right?" Luke asked.

"You know Ursa?"

Luke shook his head. "Not exactly. A shop owner named Edmund thought I would make a good beast tamer, so he gave me a quest to speak with her," Luke responded.

Rose nodded. "You have been busy. You can find Ursa toward the west side of the city. She owns several large stables and warehouses in that district."

"What does she look like? I'm not familiar with the west side of the city and hate to wander around."

"Oh, you didn't know? She was the woman wrapped in

bandages from the goblin raid last night."

Luke recalled last night. Adrenaline filled him as he replayed the life-and-death battle in his head. *Where did I see someone wrapped in bandages?* He tried recalling but came up empty. After a few moments of not saying anything, Rose continued with her description of Ursa.

"You seriously don't remember? It was the woman riding the massive gorilla."

"The one who broke the ogre's neck with a single punch!?" Luke sounded concerned, thoughts racing through his head about being trained by such a monster.

"She's much nicer and gentler to people than she is to ogres." Rose waved her hand to help dispel Luke's worry.

"Oh, really? That makes me feel better."

"No. She's ruthless to everyone she meets, I just wanted you to feel better." Luke began to protest but Rose started ushering him out of her store. "I have work to do and so do you. Now go train!" She shut the door as soon as he was fully out.

Luke looked down at Ringo. "I think we're in for a rough day."

CHAPTER THIRTEEN

A New Teacher

Luke stopped at the guild before heading off to find Ursa. He told the party members what Rose said about the goblins, his party wincing when he implied it was their fault. His party stuck to their plan, following Luke's example. They all went in search of trainers to prepare for the battles to come.

It took him more than an hour to reach the west part of town, guided only by the marker Edmund put on his map. In a normal game he would have a digital map and likely a marker on the ground to guide him, but in Endless Fantasy Online, they took a more realistic approach. Luke had a rolled up paper map with incredibly crude landmarks drawn on it. He could buy a more detailed map that had more buildings and landmarks on it, but they were expensive, and he had better things to do with his limited gold.

Pulling out his map one last time to verify he had reached his destination, or as close to it as he could determine, he rolled it up and placed it back in his bag. Luke looked around and took in the sights in front of him. There was a large barn-shaped warehouse, approximately thirty feet high and seventy or eighty feet long. Surrounding the large barn-style warehouse were several one-story stables.

The lack of sound and light coming from the buildings concerned him. The entire facility looked abandoned. If he had come at night, he would have thought it was haunted. Ignoring his concern, he proceeded.

The large double doors at the front of the warehouse stretched from the ground to the thirty-foot roof. The larger doors had a smaller, human-sized door built into them, so Luke began knocking on it. He waited a few moments and then knocked again. On his third attempt, he knocked as hard as he could and the door creaked open.

Luke peeked his head in and hesitantly called out. "Helloooo." His voice echoed slightly in the open chamber, but there was no light and no response. "I'm gonna come in now." After waiting a moment and getting no response from the darkness, he entered.

He took a few steps in before hearing a low rumbling growl. He turned to leave but a blur of motion shut the door after it passed him, throwing a blanket of complete darkness over Luke. "Hello? I'm looking for Ursa. Edmu…" Luke was forced to the ground by a giant paw. When he struggled to get out from under the paw, the pressure intensified. It was so much pressure that he was losing hit points. In a matter of a few moments, he was down to 80% health.

"You're looking for Ursa?" a faint voice came from around Luke asked.

A glowing orb of dim light formed above him and he could see a massive wolf's mouth bearing teeth only inches from his face. Instinctively he looked away, pushing his head as far away from the creature as he could. Drool dripped from the creature's mouth onto Luke's face and the ground near it. The light didn't illuminate the wolf, and Luke couldn't see far enough to determine who was speaking to him.

Remembering he wasn't alone, he called out for his companion. "Ringo! If you can hear me, run!"

"Hmm…" The mysterious voice began again. "Your companion is with me now."

Luke looked up and noticed the voice was coming from the wolf. "Did you just talk?" His voice filled with surprise and lost any traces of fear or panic.

Taken aback by the sudden change of mood, the wolf hesitated before smiling. "I don't get to use this on too many people, so I apologize."

In an instant, the room lit up, orbs of bright light forming around the ceiling. The large paw holding him down retracted and the large wolf started panting and acting like a dog. Luke slowly inched away and stood when he was out from under the beast.

The first thing he noticed was the sheer size of the animal. The creature made the alpha wolf look like a puppy. The head of the wolf alone was almost the size of an old Volkswagen bug and the body was the size of a city bus. The creature had to be forty or fifty feet long, not including its large tail that was swinging slowly behind it.

Looking around, he spotted a woman, completely wrapped in bandages with clothes draped over her. She was holding Ringo and petting her. "Hello Luke," she stated in a flat monotone, muffled slightly by the bandages over her mouth.

Luke inspected her. It appeared to him that only her eyes and hair were unwrapped, both of which were a dark brown, almost black. Her hair ended at her shoulders in a bob. "You must be Ursa?" he asked hesitantly.

She put Ringo down and then ran over to stand by Luke's side. She began to walk in a circle around Luke and Ringo, eyeing them up and down before stopping in front of Luke, facing him. She rested a hand on the wolf's body, stroking it slowly before speaking. "Why should I train you, Luke?" still speaking in a dull flat monotone but at a normal speed.

Luke was taken aback by the question, remembering his first day in the Phoenix Kingdom. He grabbed Edmund's letter and handed it to her. "I met a friend of yours, Edmund. He recommended you to me. I think you also know Rose?"

Ursa raised a single eyebrow at the mention of Rose. "So you're him?"

"Him who?" Luke responded confused.

"The brainless kid that Rose started teaching. She said you have something special. What was the name again? Puke?" Ursa answered dryly.

"The name is Luke and yes, I'm the one helping Rose out for a bit," he responded through gritted teeth.

She took another look up and down at him and started walking down a hallway that led deeper into the barn. "Aren't you coming?"

Luke picked up Ringo and followed Ursa down the hall. She stopped at a door before glancing back to make sure he was following her. When she saw that he was, she removed a large wooden beam that was acting as a lock on the door. When Ursa opened the door, a wave of sound filled the space. Clucking, wing flapping and the occasional sound of fire could be heard as Ursa entered the space. When Luke caught up with her and looked into the room, he was stunned.

The doorway opened into a room so massive, he thought the hall must have led them to another building outside. What amazed him most were the creatures running and flying around. They appeared to be baby dragons with long, thin tails and chicken heads. Not knowing what he was looking at, he inspected them.

Inspect Successful!

Name: *Cockatrice*
Level: 1
HP/MP/Stamina: 25/25/50
Status: *Neutral*

"What's a cockatrice?" Luke asked.

Ursa was halfway into the large space and surrounded by cockatrices, some at her feet and others circling above her. She was tossing out handfuls of seeds for them. "You don't know what a cockatrice is? I help raise them for the kingdom. They breed like rabbits, eat very little and are tasty when fried. Their scales are also used in the low level scale armor that a lot of the guards wear. You're looking at the king's primary source of protection and food for his army."

Luke's jaw dropped. "Aren't you a beast tamer? Isn't this against your nature or something? Raising all those creatures to die sounds... cruel."

Ursa approached him and locked eyes with him. "First thing, I'm more than a beast tamer so show respect. Second, if you want to learn more about being a beast tamer, here is where it starts." She gestured at the cockatrice. Some were playing, while others loafed around. Still more of them were eating seeds or hunting for worms in the open grass. "Everything is connected. You have to consider the natural cycle of life. When we die, we become nutrients that feed the soil. The soil grows plants that produce seeds to feed the cockatrice and eventually we eat the cockatrice. It's all about balance and surviving as long as you can before you become part of the circle again." She scoffed, the first sign of emotion or change from her monotone she had expressed. "You will learn." She scooped up Ringo and walked out the door, turning around from the other side.

"I'm sorry. I didn't mean to offend you or anything," Luke quickly added.

"Lesson one: Survive." She picked up a small pebble on the ground and threw it at one of the cockatrices. "And don't kill my birds." She shut the door and Luke could hear the board being put back in place, locking him in.

Luke turned around and saw a furious-looking cockatrice with a rock by its feet. Smoke began to trail from the corners of its mouth as other cockatrices cocked their heads, smoke trailing from their mouths as well.

"Good birdie, goooood birdie. No one wants any trouble now." Luke had his hands up trying to calm the animals.

The cockatrice who had been struck started to run toward him, flapping its wings and eventually gaining flight.

"Shit, shit, shit." Luke started to run as quickly as he could in the opposite direction.

Fireballs started landing near him. They came slowly at first, but their numbers quickly increased as more of the cockatrices joined in. Luke leaped, rolled and dodged as much as he could, but multiple fireballs were hitting him in various places. It was lucky that the cockatrice were low level as their fireballs seem to only be taking a few percentage points of health per hit, and his nature's regrowth spell could keep his health full.

Luke continued to run as more and more cockatrices joined in. With the increased numbers, his healing spell was having trouble keeping up, so he scrambled to dodge as many fireballs as he could..

*New skill acquired: **Dodge**, Beginner 0. Why take damage or wear heavy armor to prevent it when you can simply dodge it. This is a passive skill and requires no activation. Effect: 1 + x% added to your reaction time when attempting to dodge an attack. Note: The reaction time and chance to dodge is linked to your agility stat and requires the use of stamina.*

Luke waved away the message as soon as he was done reading it. He began to duck and roll out of the way of the attacks as best he could. He didn't notice the effects of the dodge skill at first. After an hour of sweating and running away from rabid cockatrices, he swore he missed some attacks that looked for sure as if they would hit him.

The only issue with this tactic was his limited stamina bar. After running around and dodging for twenty minutes, he began taking more hits as he slowed because of his stamina bar depleting. When this happened, it forced him to use nature's regrowth to heal himself. He stood still while his stamina bar recovered, enduring multiple fireballs and pecks from cockatrices beaks.

He repeated this process for what felt like hours. The cockatrices never let up until the door to the room opened. Ursa walked in and raised a hand. Green energy pulsated like a wave from her palm and the cockatrices began to calm. After a moment, their rage abated, and they all returned to their normal selves.

Luke, panting and taking big gulps of air, walked over to Ursa, his face turning red. "What is" pant "wrong with" pant "you?"

"Hmm. It appears you have passed my first stage of training," she said as she put Ringo down. Ringo was soaking wet and looked lifeless.

Luke, recovering some stamina and no longer panting, responded by shouting at her. "You could have killed me! I'm about to level up and I would have lost all my experience! I'll repeat myself, what's wrong..." He was cut off by her throwing a punch at him.

Luke leaped to the side and attempted to roll. He had depleted his stamina with the leap, so he just fell on his side.

"It appears you learned the basics of survival. Come back at first light tomorrow for stage two. We need to beef up your body if you are going to survive the later stages of training." She bent down, leaned close to him and made deliberate eye contact. "Don't make me wait for you tomorrow or, trust me, you will pay for it." With that she left the room and was gone.

Luke wiped sweat from his brow and looked himself over. His new fur armor was in tatters, desperately needing repair, and he was sore in places he didn't know he could be sore in. Ringo was panting heavily and staggered toward him before she collapsed, resting her head on Luke's leg.

A blinking icon distracted Luke. The icon meant he had delayed notifications that needed review. Since he was stuck on the ground recovering stamina, he pulled them up.

Skill up: **Dodge***, Beginner 4.*
Attribute point increase: +2 **agility***.*
Attribute point increase: +1 **constitution***.*
Attribute point increase: +1 **luck***.*

Luke still thought Ursa's methods were crazy but he couldn't complain about gains like that. "Did she torture you too?" Ringo let out a low howl before resuming her panting. "Should we go home?" A loud growl came from Luke's stomach. "Maybe we should stop and get a bite to eat?" Ringo's ears perked up at the mention of food, causing Luke to chuckle.

After letting his stamina regen to half he sat up. He looked at Ringo, who still refused to move, and decided to carry his furry companion home. Scooping her up, Luke left Ursa's facility in search of food, surprised that it was already dark outside and that he had been training all day.

It didn't take long for Luke to find a grilled-meat booth on the street and he rushed over to it. "Hello. Can I have five skewers please?" Luke started fiddling through his coin purse in preparation for paying.

"That will be ten gold," the vendor spat out as he smelled Luke, held his nose and offered the meat with an outstretched hand.

"Ten gold? The other places only charge three gold for five pieces," confusion crossing Luke's face.

"Then go to the other places. Seriously, please go. You smell terrible and you're driving away my other customers," the vendor spat out.

Luke sniffed himself and Ringo, instantly pulling his head away from his body. They both reeked and Luke noticed that flies were gathering around him instead of the trash that was scattered around. His gaze went over to his status bars and he noticed a new debuff showing a cartoon style poop with flies swirling around it.

Odor II. You have accumulated so much stink that you have an almost visible bad odor. People will treat you differently when you stink and you should take care of this as soon as you can. Seriously, you should bathe. -10 social while effect is active.

"If you give me the meat for five gold, I'll walk away right now," he countered the shopkeep.

"Fine, fine, just go." The man handed over the meat in exchange for five gold and Luke hastily walked away.

Luke removed the meat from two of the skewers and fed them to Ringo, polishing off the remaining three himself. Smelling himself again, and having just finished eating, he gagged and had to hold down bile that was threatening to come up. "Ok buddy, we need to find a bathhouse."

Luke asked for directions and got rude looks and curt responses from several people, but he finally made it to a bathhouse. The freshly clean people leaving the bathhouse gave him a wide berth as he entered.

There was a long counter with several people manning it. Behind it, hanging on the wall, was a list of services and prices. Luke decided to go for a private hot bath, and elected to add on clothes washing and armor repairing service. All said and done he was in for twenty-five gold. They also charged an additional fee for his current status, but Luke didn't mind. He understood that with his extreme odor, they would have use extreme effort to clean his clothes and armor.

He was directed to a small room and told to undress and then proceed to the bath. He followed the instructions except that he took his coin purse and bag in with him as he entered the next room. The room was a ten by ten foot square that had water streaming from a hole in the ceiling, filling a large smooth stone basin that covered most of the room. There was a variety of bottles, brushes and cloths stacked neatly on a shelf.

Luke jumped into the hot water and Ringo quickly followed. The two bathed, swam and generally enjoyed each other's company for some time before cleaning themselves. He felt incredible with the warm water doing wonders for his sore muscles. This was exactly what they needed, and they took it slow, wanting to enjoy it, not wanting it to end.

When they were eventually done, Luke opened the door to find his clothes and armor cleaned and repaired on hangers. *I could get used to this.* He thought as he donned his armor and Ringo shook the excess liquid from her fur.

When he left the room, there were several attendants waiting with large brushes and cleaning supplies. They went into the room after he left, hanging an "out of service" sign on the door. Luke didn't think he smelled that bad, but he felt a ton better now. He checked his status to make sure the odor debuff was gone and was pleasantly surprised by what he saw.

Pampered. *You have taken good care of yourself and clearly enjoy the finer things in life. You will receive +1% exp for the next 30 minutes.*

He laughed at the buff and headed for Rose's shop. By the time he arrived, the moon was almost half way up. After locking the door he headed straight for his bed, ready to collapse, Ringo trailing behind him.

After her entered his small room, he opened his interface and scrolled through it in search of an alarm clock. He found an alarm app and set several alarms for the next morning, knowing that he would snooze through the first few. The moment he confirmed his alarms, he fell onto his bed and slipped into a deep sleep.

CHAPTER FOURTEEN

Resolve

A loud buzzing caused Luke to sit up in bed. Grunting, he rubbed his eyes and mentally clicked the alarm's off button. He turned off the other alarms settings and swiped away his interface. He slumped over, sheer will being the only thing preventing him from laying back down.

"Time to get up Ringo." Hanging his feet off his bed, he stretched and rubbed the crumbs out of his eyes and looked for his furry pal. Instead, he saw a large wolf's head resting on his leg, eyes gazing up at him. Looking down, Luke jumped to his feet and grabbed the closest thing he could find to fend off the wolf.

"Step back! I know how to use this!" Luke was holding one of his fur boots in his shaking hand.

"Papa?" Luke heard a faint, young-sounding girl's voice.

"Huh?" His eyes started roaming the room, looking for the source of the sound.

"Papa, it's me." Luke didn't respond but attempted to find the girl speaking to him. "Papa, do you have any food?"

"Ri... ri... ringo?" Luke responded through jittering teeth.

"Yes, papa." Luke inspected the dog-sized wolf sitting in front of him. The wolf had thick gray fur and Ringo's sporadic sky blue spots around its body. It had to be Ringo. Luke noticed, for the first time, that Ringo's underbelly was more white than gray and that her fur became darker the closer it got to her back.

"How is this possible?" he asked.

"I don't know. I have always been talking to you, but this is the first time you have responded," Ringo answered.

"This is the first time I've heard you." He reached his hand out and began petting her. "You grew so much so suddenly." Ringo wasn't as big as the larger wolves in the Howling Forest but she was three or four times the size she was when they had fallen asleep. She was now the size of a large dog. She sort of looked like a slightly large Siberian husky. "What could have caused this?"

"Are you unhappy Papa?" Ringo asked with a hint of concern in her voice.

"No, no, of course not." Luke put his boot down and sat facing Ringo, petting her with both of his hands. "You just surprised me. I really wasn't expecting to wake up to this." Luke pulled up his character sheet to see if he could find any answers. A new system message came into view.

*Congratulations! Your animal companion, **Ringo**, has grown past the baby stage. This can be accomplished through age, natural growth, strength of your bond, or reaching a certain level of minimum stats. Now that your companion is past her baby stage, she will begin to grow at her specific natural rate. You have also gained access to your animal companion's character sheet. Would you like to access your animal companion, Ringo's, character sheet now? Yes No*

Luke mentally selected yes and a new character sheet opened up with Ringo's name on it.

Because this is the first time you are viewing this sheet, additional information has been provided. This information will not be displayed upon future viewings. To see this additional information again, focus on something specific.

Ringo, *Alpha Wolf*
Level 5 – *Level shared with master and 3 attribute points awarded per level up*
Favorite Foods: *Meat (any), Fruit (apples)*
HP: *100 (Base 100 + 10 per point in Constitution)*
MP: *0*
Stamina: *150 (Base 100 + 10 per point in Agility)*

Abilities Base *(Modifier)*
Strength: *5*
Agility: *6*
Intelligence: *2*
Wisdom: *1*
Constitution: *1*
Social: *3*
Luck: *1*

Skills, Spells and Abilities
Confusing Howl *(Beginner 1): A high pitched howling sound wave that pierces the eardrums of all enemies who can hear it, causing them to become confused. Cost: 2x Stamina, where x = skill level. Effect: 100% chance to add the confused debuff. This percentage decreases by 10% for every 5ft the enemy is from you.*

Pounce (Beginner 0): Building up energy, you leap onto an opponent, dealing bonus damage. Cost: 1x stamina, where x = skill level. Effect: Add 1x damage to your attack or 2x damage if used while unseen.

Tracking (Beginner 1): Being a wolf, you have enhanced senses that lend themselves to tracking and hunting. Effect: +1x% increased chance of finding and following the scents, tracks, sight or sounds of your enemy, where x = skill level.

Luke swiped away the messages, happy that Ringo was growing up strong. This made his decision to train with Ursa easier. If Ringo was going to gain more abilities, beast tamer must be the right specialization.

As the messages about Ringo vanished, another system message came into view, this one pertaining to his own skills.

*Skill up: **Beast Mastery**, Beginner 6.*

*New Skill! **Companion Telepathy**, Class Skill. By strengthening your bond with your animal companion and having them reach a certain stage in their life, you have gained the ability to speak with your telepathically. The range of this skill is increased by your Beast Mastery skill level. At the current level the range is sight only.*

This is incredible, thought Luke as he cleared all the messages.

"What's incredible papa?" Ringo's voice echoed in his head.

"Wait, can you hear all of my thoughts?" he said aloud.

"Unless you block our connection, I will hear everything." Luke began experimenting with sending thoughts to Ringo and then closing their connection. He was pleased that he could still hear Ringo when he closed his thoughts off to her. He would only allow his own thoughts through to Ringo when he chose.

Luke looked at the time and began to panic. He should have left at least fifteen minutes ago if he wanted enough time to get to Ursa's warehouse. "Ringo, we have to hurry!" he sent telepathically to her as he bolted from the room. He thanked the gods that he slept in his armor the night before.

He stopped for nothing as he raced through the city against the sunrise. He knew he still had some time because none of the shops were open, not even the ones that served breakfast.

Luke ran so fast that his stamina bar was completely depleted when he reached Ursa's warehouse. He knocked on the door as he slowly turned to check if the sun was peeking over the mountains yet.

"You made it with no time to spare." Luke spun on his heels to see Ursa holding the door open for him. Luke and Ringo entered the lit warehouse, Luke noticing Ursa's gaze being drawn to his wolf.

"What's next?" He asked with more than a little hesitation in his voice.

Ursa gave him a warning glance before speaking. "She has grown past the baby stage I see." Ursa's hand began to glow green as she laid it on Ringo's back. "Hmm… I will have to change the training plan slightly to compensate. I planned on separating you two again today but I think it would be better if I separated you for only part of the day."

Luke raised his hand, scared to speak out of turn again. Ursa gave him a slight nod of her head, so he decided it was safe to speak. "I don't want to doubt you, but why does her growing larger change your plan for us?"

"Good point. Let me ask you a question then. Are you sure you want to be a beast tamer? And I mean sure."

Luke really thought it over. He loved casting spells and shooting arrows but in their short time together, he was really growing attached to Ringo. His thoughts went to their time in The Den and Ringo jumping in and defending him against the Goblin Warlord. "If I choose to be a beast tamer..." he paused and looked to Ringo before returning his gaze to Ursa. "If I become a beast tamer, will Ringo get stronger? Will she be able to defend herself better?"

"Yes. Ringo will grow regardless of what path you choose. But choosing the path of a beast tamer will increase her growth and her potential. More than that, it would increase the bond you share and enhance it with special abilities." She hesitated as she thought of a better way to explain it. "If you choose a different path, Ringo will still grow to be a great wolf, with training and proper care of course, but if you choose to be a beast tamer, she will become a great alpha wolf. She will draw on your potential more and as your bond increases, the two of you will become a formidable force together."

Kneeling down, Luke gazed into Ringo's eyes. He never noticed just how blue they were. Resolve setting in, he knew his answer. "I'll become a beast tamer!" Bunching his hands into fists, his mind was made up.

Ursa gave Luke a genuine smile, the first time he had seen her show real emotion. "Do you have enough saved points to get your social skill to five and your beast mastery skill to intermediate?" she uttered as her face returned to its emotionless state.

Luke pulled up his character sheet. His social attribute was at four and his beast mastery skill was at beginner six. He had four unspent points for both attributes and skills. Knowing his future path, he decided to put all four points in social and beast mastery, confirming his choices when prompted to do so.

*Skill up: **Beast Mastery**, Intermediate 0. New rank achieved. Additional effect added.*

***Beast Mastery** (Intermediate 0): You have bonded with a beast and taken steps in befriending the animal kingdom. By improving this skill you can now feel the spirit of your companion and know where he or she is located by feeling their spirit. Improving this skill will increase your bond with your animal companion. This skill also scales based on your social attribute. Effect 1: +10% animal companion's bond rate. Effect 2: You know your animal companions general location from x+3 meters away where x = skill level.*

*Increasing your **Beast Mastery** skill to the intermediate levels has increased the range of your **Companion Telepathy** skill to sight or 6 meters without sight.*

After his skill increased, he sensed something in him change. It felt like a part of him was missing. Not like a missing limb, more like part of who he was. Looking over at Ringo he could sense that she was the vital missing piece in the puzzle that made him who he was. "I can feel you now." He mentally projected to her, and she began to wag her tail.

"Judging by the look on your face, you just entered the intermediate levels in beast mastery. That feeling you have right now is a soul connection. Bolstering that feeling will become important in your training and to becoming an effective beast tamer." Ursa walked over to Luke and placed her hand on her heart. A bright green glow of energy surrounded her hand and as she pulled it away from her chest, it remained connected by a green string of energy.

"What's this?" Luke asked as he stared on in amazement.

Ursa placed her hand on Luke's chest and his face turned beet red from embarrassment. He opened his mouth to say something but energy shot into him. His whole body started to warm up and his chest began to burn with pain. Ursa pulled her hand away and the string of energy was now going from her chest into his. Luke fell to one knee, grasping his chest. Ringo was saying something but Luke's head was swirling. He was unable to make out what came across as loud barking as Ringo also began to panic. System messages began popping up on his screen, but his vision was becoming too blurry to read them, so he tossed them aside to help him focus.

Then it was all gone. The feeling of warmth and pain poured out of him as quickly as it had entered. Panting and holding his head in a frail attempt to stop it from throbbing, he stood. Ringo's voice slowly became clear again.

"Papa, papa, are you alright? Papa. Say something Papa." She sounded worried and troubled.

He placed a hand on her to both calm her and steady himself. "It's ok... I'm... ok," he said aloud, not having the mental capacity to send it through their connection. "What the hell was that?" Turning his attention back to Ursa he saw the line between them still connected but slowly fading and becoming transparent.

"Look at your status." Ursa appeared to be in just as much discomfort as Luke. She was holding her head and was still down on one knee. It impressed Luke that she kept her signature monotone, not allowing the pain to affect her voice.

Luke waited a moment for his vision to be fully clear again and for his throbbing head to calm down before he pulled up his notifications.

Ursa, the Beast Master, has chosen you as her official apprentice. You are now connected and bound to the apprentice system.

The apprentice system allows for a higher level individual to take someone under their wing. The higher level individual, or master, may impart knowledge, such as quests, abilities, spells, or classes, onto the apprentice through various means like training. The apprentice system is limited to one person per master. Each apprentice can also only have one master at a given time. Warning! When a master chooses their apprentice, they bond their spirit energy with that individual. This causes them to lose a portion of their accumulated experience and may result in losing levels depending on what they impart on their apprentice. The master may set a goal for the apprentice, and if that goal is met, they will recover their lost experience and more. Failure to meet this goal will result in the permanent loss of that experience. Note: This is a one time system message.

Beast Tamer Conditional Specialization acquired. You have been awarded +1 agility, +1 intelligence, +1 social and the Beast Bond skill. Your new stats upon leveling up have changed to +1 agility, +1 intelligence, +1 social and 2 unallocated attribute points.

New title gained: Beast Tamer. This title gives you +1 agility, +1 intelligence, +1 social and bonding with beasts is 10% easier.

New skill acquired: Beast Bond, Class Skill. Through rigorous training and resolve, you have chosen to specialize as a Beast Tamer and unlocked the ability to bond with wild beasts. Successful use of this skill will cause a beast to become an animal companion. At your current specialization you are limited to one primary animal companion and two minor animal companions. Attempting to tame additional beasts will result in an automatic failure until you release one of your animals. Effect: Tame and bond with a wild best. The chance of successfully taming an animal is x/2% where x = social attribute limited to 30. Note: Other factors may increase or decrease this effect. Example, feeding or socializing with an animal may make it more perceptive to your bonding attempts.

Quest alert! **Passion of Beasts**. *Quest complete! Reward: + 100 reputation with Edmund.*

Quest alert! **Gift from a Friend**. *Quest Complete! Reward: 1,000 exp. Other rewards delayed until you speak with the quest giver.*

Congratulations, **Level Up!** *You have been awarded +1 agility, +1 intelligence, +1 social, +2 attribute points and +1 skill point, based on your class. Be careful with your decisions as they can not be undone.*

Luke staggered back in shock. "You did all this for me... why?"

"Well, I don't exactly have a line of people waiting to become beast tamers. You are the first person in a long time to even be interested," she answered dryly.

"Yeah, but I'm sure as more travelers start entering the game," Ursa cocked her head at the mention of this being a game. "I mean world," he tried brushing past his slip up. "That's bound to change."

"Maybe. Maybe not. Right now you are the only one, and you said you are resolved in your decision. Now I hope you won't regret it. Not with what I have planned for you." Ursa had a gleam in her eye.

Luke wasn't sure if he should be happy that he was chosen or scared. He pressed on regardless, "But I thought I had to be level ten before I could become a beast tamer."

Ursa placed her hand over her chest. "Traditionally, yes, but since you are my apprentice, I have given you enough experience to give you access to the class now. I need you to have the class in order for us to really start your training."

Luke thought over what she was saying. *If she had to give up the missing experience, does that mean she had to give up over thirty thousand experience to make this happen?* "Wait, you gave up thirty thousand experience for me?!" he said in shock.

Ursa cocked her head to the side again. "That sounds about right. I think it was a little more, though. The exchange was slightly over one for one. I only lost one level though."

Luke's jaw dropped. "I don't believe you." Ursa looked confused. "There's no way you gave all that up for me, a random traveler you barely know. What's the real reason."

Ursa opened her mouth and was about to brush him off but noticed the determination in his eyes for the truth. "Fine. Rose asked me to and I owe her more than I can ever repay." His eyes went soft at the mention of Rose. "She really sees something special in you or something." She approached Luke and lifted him by his fur armor. "Let us get one thing straight, though. You will listen to me and follow my orders. You will choose to be a beast tamer specialization when you hit level ten and I will get my lost experience back. If I get even the faintest hint that you are thinking about going back on this apprenticeship, I will kill you and I mean really kill you. I don't care if you come back to life a thousand times, I will be there waiting for you each and every time until I beat the beast master specialization into you. I don't care how much I owe Rose, I'm not doing all of this for nothing. Do I make myself clear?"

He swallowed before responding. "Yes ma'am." Ursa put him down and took a few steps back.

"Great, then we have an understanding. Now it's time to start today's training." Ursa walked down the hall and entered another doorway.

Luke took a few deep breaths to calm himself as he pushed up his glasses. Regardless of how their exchange ended, he was ecstatic about his class change and getting started as a beast tamer. Looking at Ringo he could tell she was sharing in his enthusiasm. The pair took off at a sprint toward Ursa and their next exciting challenge.

CHAPTER FIFTEEN

Beast Tamer

Luke collapsed from a mixture of exhaustion and being out of stamina. He gulped down air in long labored breaths.

"Not half bad." Ursa walked into the room, surveying his progress.

She had put Luke and Ringo to work in an underground mine. She gave him a heavy pick axe and told him to break apart the large rock wall to make a hallway. She tasked Ringo with digging out the chunks of rock buried in the compact dirt. When they filled their space, each of them would help fill bags and carts that they would drag back to the surface together.

They had been repeating the process for half a day and only made a few feet of progress. Luke tried removing his armor but was instructed to leave it on as extra weight. He would have found the task easier if there had been better light or better air quality but they had to work with hastily placed torches and thick hot air.

Luke followed Ursa out of their hole in the ground and reviewed his notifications.

*New skill acquired: **Mining**, Beginner 0. As this skill increases, so does your proficiency in mining. Proficiency lowers the amount of stamina required to perform this action. Effect: Proficiency +n% where n is skill level.*

*Skill up: **Mining**, Beginner 2.*

*Attribute point increase: +2 **strength**.*
*Attribute point increase: +1 **constitution**.*
*Ringo attribute point increase: +2 **strength**.*

Luke was pleasantly surprised to see Ringo's stat increases. Remembering his recent level up after becoming a beast tamer, he pulled up Ringo's character sheet and distributed her three stat points into agility, strength, and constitution. He also distributed his two points into constitution to help gain some survivability, electing, per usual, to save his skill point for later.

Ursa's large wolf walked in with a scroll in its mouth. She plucked it from the creature and read it before turning to Luke and stating, "I think that's enough for today. I have some urgent matters to attend to."

Luke's mouth went wide with a smile. "No argument here." Looking at Ringo he could have sworn he saw her smiling as well. Ursa began to leave before Luke remembered what happened last time he left her facility and called out to her. "Wait! Do you have a place where we can clean up? We really could use a wash before we leave."

Ursa eyed him, sniffing the air a bit. "Yes, you could." She whistled loudly and Luke could hear a distant rustling of noise. The noise got louder as it got closer, but he wasn't able to make out what it was.

Without warning a large gorilla, not as big as the one at the goblin raid, but still large, came barreling through the door. "Mook, please take these two to the lake so they can clean themselves." The gorilla leaned back on his feet, pushing out its chest. He hit his chest several times before returning his hands to the ground. "Good Mook." Ursa patted him on the head a few times before she jumped on her wolf.

Her wolf went down on all fours and a massive gust of wind pushed out from underneath it as it took off. It forced Luke to close his eyes from the sudden gust and by the time he opened them, only a moment later, the spot Ursa and the wolf had occupied was now empty. The gorilla beat his chest again and gestured for Luke to follow.

The gorilla took them through a back exit and down a short stone path. At the end of the path was a large lake surrounded by grass and wild animals. "It's pretty isn't it?" Luke telepathically sent to Ringo. She sent feelings of happiness toward him in return.

The group reached the lake and began to bathe. Luke did his best to clean his armor, and after some time the odor debuff disappeared from the gear's description. He wanted to go swimming for a bit, but large, ominous shadows in the water changed his mind. Removing his armor and doing his best to shake off the excess water, the pair were on their way out of the facility.

He exited the facility but wasn't sure where to go next. Missing his party a little, he wanted to check in with the guild and share his new information on apprenticeships. On his way through the city he stopped to get himself and Ringo more grilled meat which was becoming a favorite for the pair. Then he remembered that Edmund's shop was just around the corner and he had a quest to turn in.

The bell attached to the door frame rang as he entered Critters and Creatures Pet Haven. "Welcome to Critters and Crea..." Edmund stopping his normal greeting after realizing who had entered. "Oh Luke! Come in, come in."

"Hey Edmund." Luke gave Edmund a warm greeting as he shut the shop door behind him.

Edmund's eyes immediately went to Ringo. "Ohhh my. You've grown little one. Luke must be taking good care of you, huh?" Ringo barked in response. Edmund pulled out his monocle and placed it in his eye before it began to glow. "Hmm... yes you have grown little one and a primary animal companion." He said the last few words really slowly. "Does that mean..." His gaze drifted to Luke as the glowing intensified. Edmund jumped into the air and kicked his heels together. "My boy you did it! You're a beast tamer!" He started laughing from excitement and it was contagious, with Luke quickly joining in.

They moved to a small sitting area, grabbing a pair of stools to talk and catch up. Luke started and explained what happened to him after he met Edmund. He explained the goblin raid, being reunited with Rose and meeting Ursa. He spared no detail when it came to Ursa's rather unique training methods, garnishing him more laughs.

"Sorry about that. I knew she was a tough bird but didn't think she would endanger you like that." Luke waved away Edmund's concern. "Well, what can I do for the world's latest beast tamer today?"

Luke rubbed the back of his neck. "Well... you kinda gave me a quest that promised a reward..."

Edmund jumped up from his stool. "That's right!" Luke was startled and almost fell back out of the stool, his high agility saving him from making a fool of himself. "Come with me." Edmund grabbed Luke's forearm and pulled him to the back door.

Opening the door revealed a large, octagon shaped enclosure. Stone surrounded the space, but the middle had a small pond, a handful of trees, and grass everywhere. The top of the enclosure was open to let the sun in but was protected by a steel cage. There were a couple of doors leading out of the enclosure, and the space appeared to be a habitat of sorts.

"Wow. What is this place?" Luke asked as he slowly walked around.

Clasping his hands together, Edmund replied. "This is my personal wildlife enclosure that I let beast tamers use."

"I appreciate you showing this to me, but what would I need a habitat for? I plan on keeping Ringo close to me at all times." Ringo rubbed up against him at the mention of keeping her close.

"Of course you do, but this is for when you need to release your companions. You know how minor companions work, don't you? Luke gave Edmund a bewildered look. Edmund's eyes lit up. "I get to explain this to a beast tamer?" He let out a squeal of excitement as he rubbed his hands together. "It's been so long since someone has asked me to explain this. While it's true that you can keep all of your animal companions near you at all times, there are several occasions when you wouldn't want to. Imagine sneaking into an enemy base and you have your wolf, a bird, a ferret, a panther, and a lizard with you. Good luck with that. Also, feeding and caring for all those animals simultaneously can be troublesome. The other thing to keep in mind is that minor companions can't be used in combat. They are for utility purposes only."

Luke nodded in understanding. "So I can leave them here with you and you would take care of them for me?" Edmund nodded enthusiastically.

"Well, it wouldn't just be me. My wife and daughter would help out but it's also more than that. If you register yourself as a beast tamer with a habitat like this, you will gain the ability to release and summon your companions from any distance for nothing more than a little bit of mana. As you can see, with the lack of beast tamers nowadays, you would get exclusive access to this area."

Luke thought about it for a moment. Being able to summon more animal companions when he needed them would be really helpful. It would also be great for saving Ringo if he was in a tough spot. If he knew he wouldn't survive a fight, he could release Ringo here where it was safe, rather than letting her die along with him. "Well, how does it work?"

Edmund reached into his pocket and pulled out a small blue crystal, about the size of a salt shaker, and handed it to Luke.

Edmund's Habitat Beast Tamer Crystal (unique) x1 obtained. This crystal allows a beast tamer to magically summon or release his animal companions at will. Mana is consumed when using the crystal and the cost of each use is based on the animal's mass but can not exceed the user's maximum mana. This crystal is currently unbound.

"You will need to pour a little mana into the crystal to bond to it." Edmund explained.

Luke summoned his mana and directed it to the crystal. After a moment, the crystal gained a faint glow in its center.

*This item is soul-bound to **Beast Tamer Luke**. It can not be unwillingly taken from you and is not lost upon death.*

This was the first soul-bound item Luke had ever seen in Endless Fantasy Online. He was happy knowing that he wouldn't be able to lose such a valuable and heartfelt gift. "Thank you Edmund, this means a lot."

Edmund smiled. "I'm just happy to be in service to a beast tamer again. It beats selling pets to ungrateful travelers any day. Why don't you try using it?" He gestured toward Ringo.

Luke mentally asked Ringo if she was up for testing the crystal. She shrugged in response so he took that as an acceptance. They left the habitat and went back into the store space. Luke gripped the crystal and began pouring mana into it as he thought of sending Ringo through it. He was pouring mana slowly, ten, fifteen, twenty, but nothing was happening. He poured mana faster and the crystal greedily drank it in until he lost 100 mana, at which point the flow of mana abruptly stopped.

Ringo panicked when her feet began to turn translucent. The process continued up her body and flowed through her head and she began to howl. The howling stopped when her head, the last thing to fade away, vanished.

Edmund opened the back door and Ringo was standing in the center of the grass with her tail wagging. She began to walk toward the door but Edmund put his hands up for her to stop. "Let's make sure it works both ways." Ringo laid down, knowing it would be a minute or more for Luke to regain his mana.

When his mana was full again he repeated the process but instead thought of bringing Ringo to him. When the crystal was done draining his mana Ringo started fading into existence next to him.

"That's incredible! Thank you again Edmund. I honestly don't know how to repay you." Luke was genuine with his words and Edmund appreciated that.

Edmund shook his head. "No thanks needed. I'm just happy that you are keeping the beast tamer specialization alive. Repayment, on the other hand… I will require you to cover the costs of food for the animals, but we won't charge you for any care taking. That is my gift to you in honor of beast tamers past."

Luke's happy expression fell at the mention of money. *I will never have any gold, will I?* He thought as he patted his light coin purse.

Edmund made tea and the two continued to chat and catch up for an hour or so, until Luke decided it was time to leave. As Luke was on his way out, Edmund offered him one more piece of advice. "I highly suggest you find a flying animal and tame it. When you do, go see Ursa to learn the skill beast sight."

Making a mental note of Edmund's advice, Luke headed out of the store and toward the city's main gate. He stopped at the guild hall only to find it sparsely populated, as most of the guild members were out training. Shrapnel was one of those people, so Luke left a message for him regarding specializations and the apprenticeship system. He left another message for his party, asking if they wanted to grab a bite to eat, compare notes and catch up.

Since he couldn't spend time with his party, he decided to focus on the next best thing: attempt to tame a beast.

It didn't take long for him and Ringo to make their way into the forest. Wildlife was everywhere. "So what should we try to tame?" Luke asked Ringo.

"I don't know Papa, whatever you like, I suppose," she responded.

Luke looked around for suitable targets. There were squirrels, woodpeckers, robins, rabbits and a whole slew of other wildlife. "Edmund said we should get a flying animal but I don't think a woodpecker or robin would do much for us." Ringo nodded her head in agreement. "I wish there were hawks or eagles in this forest. It would be cool to have one of those."

The pair kept walking, checking the treetops for something

better than a robin, when Luke noticed large holes high up in several trees. He decided to get a closer look and attempted to climb the tree. After several failed attempts, and dropped hit points, he successfully got to the top of one of the trees.

*New skill acquired: **Climbing**, Beginner 0. You have learned the basics of climbing. Congratulations, you have the same climbing ability as a small child. Effect: 1+x% bonuses added to your climbing attempts where x is skill level.*

Chuckling at the system notification, he inched himself closer to the hole. Peeking inside he found a small white bird with brown and tan markings on it. Its head was oval and had a T pattern in its markings. Luke knew instantly what it was but inspected it to be sure.

Inspect *Successful!*

Name: *Barn Owl*
Level: *1*
HP/MP/Stamina: *25/0/50*
Status: *Neutral*

*Skill Up: **Inspect**, Beginner 3.*

"Ringo. I think I found a good animal to try taming." Luke received happy emotions in response. "I'm gonna give this a try."

Luke hoped that since the barn owl was sleeping he might get a bonus by taming it. He mentally gave the command to activate his beast bond ability, but nothing happened. *Maybe I had to be touching the animal*, he thought. Luke extended his arm and, as gently as he could, he placed his hand on the owl, barely making contact with its wing. He mentally tried to activate the ability again, but nothing happened.

"I'm not sure what I'm doing wrong?" He forgot to mentally project his words and instead spoke them aloud. At that time the barn owl woke up and freaked out.

The barn owl started flapping its wings rapidly and pecking at the intruding hand in its nest. The flapping was causing twigs and dirt to fly from the hole's opening and directly into Luke's face.

"Ahh!" Luke started rubbing at his eyes to get the dirt out. The owl leaped out of its nest and attached itself to Luke's face, pecking and scratching when it could. The whole ordeal looked like a scene out of a three stooge's film.

Startled by the attack and unable to see, Luke lost his balance, and he began plummeting toward the ground. Ringo sprung into action and leaped into the air, attempting to use her back as a softer platform for her masters descent. The three of them collided midair and bounced in different directions. Luke let out a grunt of pain and checked his health bar. He had lost over 30% from the stunt, and Ringo had lost almost 20%.

He pulled himself to his feet, grunted again and started dusting himself off. Ringo let out a small whimper but seemed to be fine as she began licking her wounds. It didn't take long for Luke to find the fallen owl. It was about fifteen feet away and struggling to stand. It seemed unable to lift its left wing, causing Luke to think that he may have broken it.

Luke tried using his beast bond ability again, and this time he felt strands of energy leap out of him and toward the owl. He could feel the energy meeting resistance and after only a few minutes, he felt the energy fade away.

***Beast Bond** failed.*

The creature must be conscious for me to attempt bonding with it, he thought as he stared at the owl. "Well… I don't think you want to bond with me very much, do you?" He received only cries of pain in response. "That looks like it hurts." Luke hesitated for a moment before getting a little closer. The owl reacted and tried to pull away. "It's ok. I'm not going to hurt you." Luke cast nature's regrowth on the owl and saw his magic take action. He heard a faint pop as bones moved back into their proper sockets and tendons began stitching themselves back together.

The owl stilled as the magic coursed through it. It looked shocked as it pulled its wing back into position and stood up. Luke took this opportunity to get closer to the owl. He closed his eyes and stretched an arm toward it. He heard the animal take flight and then felt a weight pressing down on his arm. Opening his eyes he saw the owl perched on his forearm and staring back at him.

Not wanting to lose this opportunity, he attempted his beast bond skill again. Feeling the strands of energy cascade outward toward the owl, he encountered the same strange resistance, but things were different this time. The resistance wasn't pushing back as hard as it was before and he could sense that some strands were breaking through.

As soon as one of the strands reached the owl, it became visible, represented by a semi-translucent green string. One end of the energy string was attached to Luke's chest and the other end led into the owl's chest. With that, Luke could sense and feel the owl's presence.

Beast Bond successful! Please name your new animal companion.

"Umm. How about Luna? It means moon and you're nocturnal,

right?" The owl screeched in response, but Luke could interpret it as happiness through his bond. "Well, doesn't sound like I can understand your words like Ringo but I'm still getting your emotions. Maybe after we bond more?" Luna screeched again before her eyelids started to look heavy. "You must still be tired, huh?" Luna was almost sleeping on her perch at this point.

Luke pulled out his transportation crystal and began pouring mana into it. His eyebrows rose with confusion when the crystal stopped accepting mana only a moment after he started the transfer. Luna had already faded away by the time he was done checking his logs. According to his system log, he only needed twenty mana to transport Luna from one space to another.

Luke was about to close his notifications and log when he noticed a pending traveler notification. He clicked the icon to open it and a new window opened up. The window showed a photo of Penny and the icon of a phone. There was a long blue line that moved in rhythm with her voice when she began talking.

"Hello?" Penny's voice seemed to come from the new hanging box, as if it was some form of speaker.

"Penny?" Luke responded.

"Where are we?" Taken aback by the question, Luke didn't know how to respond. "We're in a virtual world. Who leaves a paper note for someone when you can just call them?" She began to laugh loudly.

Luke joined in on the laughter before he responded. "Sorry, I forget we're in a game sometimes. You know, everything being so real and all."

"Yeah, I get it. Still funny though." She chuckled again.

"Yeah, yeah. Can't wait for you to slip up so I can give it to you." He commented.

"You want to give it to me eh?" Luke's face turned beet red.

"I… uhh… no… I mean yes, I mean no. Uhh, I didn't mean it like that." He was stuttering and barely able to get his response out.

"Luke, I'm fucking with you." Luke was happy this was only a voice call, otherwise Penny would see just how flustered that comment made him. "Anywho, we're all about to meet up at the guild hall for drinks if you want to join us."

Taking a few deep breaths, Luke responded. "Yeah, that would be great. I'm just finishing up now so I'll head back."

"Awesome. See you soon." The phone icon turned red and the system box disappeared moments later.

"It's time to head back Ringo, for a well-deserved drink."

CHAPTER SIXTEEN

Preparations for War

"Explain to me again how you have your specialization already?" Nanoc asked. Luke explained his time with Ursa and her choosing him as her apprentice for the second time.

"You really have a lot of NPC friends, don't you? What, can't get more travelers to tolerate you?" Penny barbed him.

"Ha ha ha. You're so funny," Luke commented in a joking monotone as the group all chuckled and downed their drinks. "This is nice." Everyone's attention turned back to him, causing his cheeks to flush. "I mean it's nice to share drinks with all of you again. I missed hanging out with you guys. Well, all of you but Backstab."

The group smiled and then broke into another round of laughter. "Hey! I resent that remark." Backstab shouted.

"Not as much as we resent hanging out with you," Nanoc added, feeding the laughing fire.

"At least I'm wearing a shirt. I see your body thinks it's cold tonight Nanoc?" Backstab put his hands under his shirt and used his fingers to make exaggerated nipples. Nanoc was mid gulp and laughed so hard that beer came shooting from his nose. "Still wielding that two-handed axe or have you decided to dual wield those two blades of yours." Everyone within earshot was now laughing and slapping Nanoc on the back in good jest.

System Alert! System Alert! Attention all travelers currently in or around the Phoenix Kingdom.

Luke looked around and everyone's eyes in the guild hall were distant. They all appeared to be looking at the same system message.

*Area Event Triggered! **The Great Goblin War!** The latest kingdom scouts have reported that a large mass of troops are headed for the capital. Current estimates place their arrival within the next 24 hours. Participation is not mandatory, but failure to complete this event will result in the Phoenix Kingdom's elimination, the loss of all Phoenix Kingdom resurrection points, the death of multiple key NPCs and a permanent debuff to any traveler who has chosen to play a human.*

Note: Traveler resurrection will be restricted during this event. Travelers will remain dead if defeated in combat. Travelers who are defeated may become spectators for the remainder of the event. Once the event is over, traveler resurrection rules will return to normal.

Rewards will vary depending on your level of participation. The top three players and top three guilds will gain bonus rewards. Prepare for war and good luck.

As people finished reading the system notice, panic erupted. Some people looked shocked and were trying to find somewhere to hide, while others were grabbing their weapons and shouting battle cries. The majority of people just looked concerned. After a few moments, people started to run for rooms or exits and then chaos set in.

"Enough!" Shrapnel slammed a large warhammer down on a nearby table, splitting it in half and sending wood shrapnel everywhere. "Calm the hell down! We are Travelers 4 Hire, not a guild of noobs! Everyone grab your weapons, armor, tools, potions, whatever the heck you need and meet back here in thirty minutes. Put messages on the boards and recall all your party members. If you aren't here in thirty minutes, find yourself a new guild!" Everyone was staring at Shrapnel, frozen in shock. "Did I stutter people? Move it!" People started scrambling but in a much more organized manner. Instead of panic and chaos, they were grouping up and arming themselves.

"Ok people, you heard the man, lets gear up!" Penny was taking charge of their party. "Luke, can you get some potions from Rose's shop for the guild?" Luke didn't answer, his eyes focused on the door. Penny snapped her fingers to gain his attention. "Luke, Luke. What's up with you? You need to focus here."

"What?" Moving his gaze to Penny, Luke noticed the anger and confusion on her face. "I'm sorry. I'm worried about Ringo outside."

"Listen Luke, I don't want to sound harsh here but you really need to focus on the battle coming up and your little puppy should probably stay home." Penny tried speaking in a firm but understanding tone. She ended up coming across more curt than she intended and Luke pulled back a little in response.

Luke scratched the back of his head nervously. "I'm not really sure how to say this. It's probably best if I just show you." Luke got up from the table and beckoned his party to follow him outside. "Now I was trying to tell you this before during my story but the system messages and chaos kinda got in the way." Luke opened the door as he finished speaking and the much larger alpha wolf was sitting and wagging her tail as she patiently waited for Luke to come out.

The entire party flinched when Luke approached the wolf without caution and wrapped his arm around it, stroking its neck.

Nanoc was the first to say something. "What the..." He spoke slowly, adding several syllables to each word and ending by leaving his mouth agape.

"Guys, this is Ringo." Luke explained.

Penny took a hesitant step forward and reached her hand out for Ringo to sniff. Ringo looked up at Luke for confirmation and he nudged her forward. She took a step forward, sniffed Penny's hand for a moment before pressing her head against her open palm. Penny started petting her slowly, and the others eventually joined in.

"This is great Luke, but we really need to..." Luke cut Penny off.

"Stay focused. I know, I know." He gave Penny a half smile.

"Well, Mr. Focus, can you get us some potions from the shop?" Penny asked again.

"I think so, I will have to ask. I know Rose has been brewing boxes full of them, but I think they are for the kingdom."

"I'll talk to Shrapnel but I'm sure the guild would authorize a large purchase of potions if she had them readily available. Please go check and I'll speak to Shrapnel to get it authorized," Penny added.

Luke nodded, grabbed his belongings and headed for Rose's shop, promising to return before Shrapnels deadline.

Pushing the door open to Rose's shop, he saw the short gnome equipping herself. Rose was slinging a bandolier across each shoulder and placing multiple potions in each. It reminded Luke of machine gun operators who slung ammo across their bodies.

"I take it you were notified that the goblins are approaching," Luke said as more of an observation than a question. Rose looked up and gave him a curt nod before returning to the task of arming herself. "I have to get a few things from my room, but my guild was wondering if you could spare some potions. I know it's short notice but…" Rose cut him off with a gesture, pointing at a small crate on the floor. Peeking inside, Luke saw health potions tightly packed in straw.

"You can have the whole crate. There should be at least a hundred minion potions in there. The rest of the crates," she gestured around the packed room full of boxes, "are for the kingdom."

"Thank you Rose." Rose returned Luke's smile as he scurried to his room. He grabbed a few potions he had been brewing and stuffed them in his bag. Looking around, he saw the uncommon class weapon box he obtained for completing The Den.

Uncommon Class Weapon Box *(Uncommon). When opened, this box will award you one uncommon weapon associated with your current class. Current class: Beast Tamer. Open? Yes No*

No time better than the present, he thought as he clicked Yes. A bright white light filled the room and quickly faded, leaving behind a pair of leather and metal gauntlets that appeared to be covered in wolf fur. They were fairly large and looked like they would cover Luke's entire forearm up to his elbows.

Not exactly the bow I was expecting. He disappointedly reached out and grabbed one of the gauntlets. A system message popped up, obscuring his vision, and he began to read. After reaching the end of the message, his expression changed to delight.

Wolf Claws (Uncommon). A pair of wolf fur and leather gauntlets, reinforced with iron where appropriate, including the knuckles. A sharp pair of retractable iron claws are hidden under the heavy fur padding on the forearm. When mana is passed through the gauntlets, the user can force the claws to appear or retract back under the fur. Adds +4 physical resistance. Adds 10-12 blunt damage with the claws retracted on strike. Adds 15-20 slashing or piercing damage when claws are out. Note: These can not be equipped over armor and take up your glove slot.

Luke quickly pulled his fur gloves off and tossed them aside, sliding both of his hands into the weapon. There were several leather straps and buckles on the underside of each gauntlet that he tightened as best he could. When he was done, the new weapons were firm against his arms, reminding him of a cast from when he broke his arm as a child. They seemed incredibly rigid.

He began shadow boxing in the room and testing the flexibility of his arms and hands. A large metal plate ran the length of his forearm, stretching from his wrist to his elbow, but his hands were only covered by thick leather. His knuckles and the top side of his hand also had small metal plates on them and reminded him of the brass knuckles thugs would use back in the day.

He pulled his bow from his back to make sure he still had the flexibility required to operate it effectively and was pleasantly surprised by the results. Returning his bow to his back he tried the feature that most excited him in the system message. He focused on his mana and pushed it into his arms and hands, only spending a point or two of his total mana pool. Without warning, three large, curved claws shot out from the topside of his wrists. He could hear them scraping slightly against the metal plate thathe now realized was there for his protection.

The claws only extended three or four inches past his fingers when he stretched his fingers out, but when he balled his hands into fists, they were impressively long. He took a few mock swipes at the air, getting a feel for the slashing motion he had to make to use the weapon effectively. After a few test swings with both arms he pushed his mana back into his hands and all six blades receded.

"I'm the wolverine!" he let out with excitement.

"What's that?" Rose said as she pushed the door to his room open. Luke looked down at her and took in the impressive sight. She was now fully equipped and her staff emitted a faint green light as she walked toward him. "Are you going to be ok?" She asked.

"Don't worry about me, I'll be with my guild." Rose looked at him, waiting for him to continue but Luke knew how powerful she was and asking about her safety seemed more like an insult than a sign of compassion.

Rose smiled in realization. "Good. The city guards will be here soon to pick up the shipment. I will make sure they drop off your guild's crate at your guild hall. If you need me, I'll be at the city gate, helping in the preparations." With that she turned to leave but hesitated. Turning to face Luke she pulled something from her bag. "Here, take this." She handed him a medium-sized potion bottle. The liquid inside was purple and bubbling.

Luke accepted the potion but when he tried to identify it, the system message was full of question marks. "What is it?" He asked.

"If you get in trouble, drink it, but be careful... it has quite the kick." She gestured for Luke to meet her eyes and get down to her level. Placing her hands on his cheeks, she continued. "Please boy, be safe. It would break an old gnomes heart if something happened to you."

He smiled. "Don't worry, I'm a traveler, remember? We pretty much can't die forever."

"Doesn't mean I want to see you die," Rose added and Luke's expression became more serious.

"I'll be careful Rose and..." he hesitated. "You be careful too, ok?"

"I'm too old to die." Rose chuckled before becoming serious. "Don't worry Luke, I will be fine." She patted his cheeks a few times before pulling away.

"Well, I should hurry back and see what my orders are," Luke added. Rose nodded, and the pair were off.

When Luke arrived back at the guild hall, it surprised him to find it stuffed with people. He didn't realize just how many guild members there were until all of them were gathered in one place. Pulling up his guild interface, he noticed the guild count of over a hundred, and they were all definitely present.

Leaving Ringo outside, he began looking around, quickly spotting his team. He began weaving and pushing through the crowd until he reached them.

"Luke! Are we getting some potions?" Penny asked.

Luke nodded. "The guards should be dropping off a crate of a hundred or so shortly."

"Good job." Penny was about to continue when Shrapnel started demanding everyone's attention.

"Everyone listen up!" he shouted and banged his warhammer against his armor. "I have spoken with the guards and have updates on the whole situation. The goblins have amassed a small army of themselves and their allies. They are all moving by foot, so it's taking some time for them to get here. They estimate that the full army should arrive in the morning, but an advanced scouting party will be here soon." People started whispering among themselves and someone in the crowd shouted a question.

"What do you mean goblins and their allies?"

Another person joined in. "Yeah, and what about this advanced scouting party?"

Shrapnel slammed his warhammer into the stone floor, leaving a visible indentation in its wake and causing cracks to splinter outward. "Silence! If you would let me finish, I would explain. Time is limited and I need to get people dispatched, so please keep your questions to yourself." The guild went silent and after scanning the room for anyone disobeying his command, he continued. "We have about one hundred combat players and a handful of non-combat players. We will form raid groups for various tasks. Raid groups can have five parties, or twenty players each, so we will have five raid groups of combat players and one raid group of non-combat members. I will post the group pairings after this, so party leaders please come see me. Raid groups one, two, and three will be with me behind the main gate on defense. Raid groups four and five will join a division of the city's guard to attack the advanced scouting party before they reach the city. Your goal is to wipe them out and if you can't, then delay them long enough for the city to build up defenses."

Heads were nodding around the room but no one spoke. Shrapnel pointed at the non-combat people in the guild. "Non-combat players, like our crafters, will have two main goals. First, you will help with building up the defenses of the city. Second, you will move around and give aid to the other groups. Bring potions to those who need them, pull people back to the healing tents, those types of things. Am I understood?" The group of smiths, potion makers, and gatherers all nodded in response.

"Good. Now to answer the other question that was rudely shouted at me." People around the room all looked in the man's direction who shouted out, causing his face to turn red. "The main army is primarily low level goblins. The king's scouts estimated their levels to all be below five. They should be easy targets for most of us but be careful, they are coming in high numbers. Besides the low level goblins, reports say they have orcs and ogres with them."

At the mention of ogres the room erupted in shouting and panic. Shrapnel had to raise his warhammer in the air for the room to become silent. "In addition to the orcs and ogres!" he shouted loudly, "reports said there are a few humans with them. The reports didn't specify if they were captured or working with them, we will have to wait and see." Much more quiet mumblings of confusion and suspicion filled the room. "Party leaders! Come see me so we can form raid groups. If any of you have questions, ask your guild leaders and they can come see me. Once you know what raid group you're in, get to work!" He turned his back to go through some paperwork and the crowd started splitting up into their groups.

"Not much of an inspirational speech, huh?" Backstab commented dryly.

"He has a lot to worry about." Penny was quick to defend. "I'll go find out what our assignment is. Why don't you all meet me outside. This place is getting kinda cramped." The group nodded and headed outside.

"I guess war is a great way to break in my new class," muttered Nanoc, causing Backstab and Luke to stare at him. "I was going to keep it a secret but..." He pulled his large battle axe off his back and started pulling it in opposite directions with his hands, as if trying to pull it apart. His hands started glowing red and as his right hand pulled his axe away to the right, a ghostly visage of his axe formed in his left hand. The ghost axe was completely outlined in red but quickly filled in and became less and less translucent. After a moment, he had an exact copy of his large axe in his left hand while his original axe stayed in his right.

"Wow! That's amazing!" Luke was genuinely amazed.

"Thanks. I hit level ten during training and became a Berserker. It lets me go into a crazy battle rage, gaining a ton of buffs to my strength and constitution. On top of all that, not only can I wield two-handed weapons with one hand, I can even create a copy of my main weapon purely out of my rage energy bar." Nanoc looked truly frightening. He still wore nothing over his chiseled chest but now wielded two massive axes, one in each hand. Each axe blade was the size of his torso, but he didn't seem to struggle at holding either of them.

Backstab huffed. "Am I the only one who doesn't have their class specialization?"

Luke looked puzzled. "Wait. Penny has hers also?"

Backstab nodded. "After your information dump the other day, she went and leveled up to ten and got her specialization from her trainer."

"Why don't you ask your trainer to make you an apprentice like me?" Luke questioned.

He huffed again before speaking. "Thieves and rogues are a greedy bunch. They don't give away their hard earned experience for the sake of someone else. No honor among thieves."

"Yeah, yeah. Hit level ten and you won't need handouts like Luke," Penny commented as she exited the guild hall.

"Hey! I resent that," Luke replied, causing the group to laugh. "So what specialization did you go with, Penny?"

"I specialized as a Crusader. It gave me some offensive spells but still lets me use a shield for defense," She commented with excitement.

"Hopefully it's enough." The group turned to see Shrapnel exiting the guild hall. "We will need all the help we can get to win this. The reports say there are hundreds of goblins headed this way."

"What about the King? He seemed pretty effective against the Crimson Shadow," Nanoc said.

"Too far away. Even if they could somehow get word to him, he would never make it back in time." Everyone's expression changed to one of concern. "The advance raid groups are heading out, why don't you all head for the city gate and help with the defenses."

The group all turned to Penny, and she nodded. "Don't worry, we are part of raid group two, we aren't going after the scouting party." An involuntary sigh of relief slipped out of the party's mouths. The group wished Shrapnel luck and headed for the gate to prepare.

"Hello there travelers." Guard Captain Holtz approached the raid groups assigned with defending the city. "Tonight's focus will be defense. I have the mage's guild reinforcing the walls and preparing artillery spells but that takes time. They won't be ready for the scouting party, but we should have enough time to prepare them for the main forces. I need any of you with range to join us on the walls and the rest of you to help defend the city gate. I trust that you all know your own strengths and weaknesses well enough to know where to go." The group of travelers all nodded and began to disperse, heading for where they would best fit.

"Where do you guys want me?" Luke asked.

Penny began rubbing her chin. "We really could use your help with healing down here, but I would be selfish to take you off the wall." Luke nodded but Penny stopped him from leaving. "Wait! Once the enemy breaks through the gate I want you to rejoin us. We work better as a unit."

Luke smiled. "You're assuming I'm going to let them get through the gate."

Backstab stared at Luke with a neutral expression before speaking in an almost mocking monotone. "Yeah… they're getting through the gates."

Penny let out an involuntary chuckle at Backstab's jab. "Just come join us when you can."

"Yeah, Penny would miss you too much if you didn't," Nanoc added.

Luke looked at Penny and her cheeks were turning red. Penny hit Nanoc in the shoulder and pushed the berserker toward the other raid members, leaving Luke stunned and confused. Shaking it off, he headed up one of the stairways toward the top of the wall. Ringo waited at the base of the stairs.

When he reached the top, he looked back at the city they were trying to defend. Catapults, large groups of armed soldiers, mages and citizens were all scrambling about. The city was in a full panic as they prepared for war. Looking around the wall, Luke saw several mages wearing a variety of colored robes glowing in many different colors. Every time they began to glow, the mages would move their hands in a complex set of patterns. Large spikes of earth erupted from the ground to rest against and reinforce the city walls. Some spikes had lines of various colors running through them. Luke guessed that the lines were runes of protection or counter measures of some sort.

With nothing to do Luke, got lost in his thoughts, so he did not notice the pair of men who approached him. One of them slapped him on the back. Luke turned on his heels, running magic into his hands and causing his claws to protrude toward the intruder. His claws stopped only an inch or two from a skinny man holding a lute above his head in mock surrender.

"Woah there buddy." Realizing the man wasn't a threat, he retracted his claws.

"Sorry about that. Little on edge I guess," Luke apologetically spat out.

"Don't worry about it." The man lowered his hands and strummed a few cords on his lute causing a calming sensation to fill Luke. Looking at his interface, Luke saw a new icon of a lute listed in his buffs. "It's a calming buff. It should help calm your nerves a bit." the man added.

"That's a neat trick." Luke extended his hand. "I'm Luke."

The man stuck his hand out but hesitated. "You're not going to cut my hand off with those claws are you?"

Luke let out a laugh. "No, I think you're safe."

The man took Luke's hand and introduced himself. "My name is Donny and the robed guy here is The Dunstin."

The robed man waved. "Call me TD, everyone else does."

A low growl came from behind the men as Ringo took slow, threatening steps toward them. The robed man yelped, turned around and began chanting. A fireball appeared in his open palm as he pulled his arm back to throw the projectile magic.

"Wait! Ringo, stand down." Ringo stopped her advance and sat wagging her tail.

"Sorry father, I felt your nerves rise, and I was concerned that these two might be attacking you," she mentally explained.

"It's ok girl. They're allies, but I appreciate your quick reaction. Why don't you stick by my side," Luke mentally sent back. Ringo casually walked forward, brushing up against Luke as she reached him.

"Guys, this is Ringo. She's my animal companion," Luke explained to the pair of men as he knelt to meet Ringo's gaze, scratching her chin as he descended.

"Ok, that is way cooler than my lute," Donny joked and TD's fireball extinguished. Donny pointed to the bow on Luke's back and asked, "So I take it you're an archer or something?"

Luke nodded. "I'm a beast tamer, but I started as a ranger. My bow is my primary weapon."

"I'm a fire mage. Thought I could roast some goblins as they tried to break through the gate," TD explained.

"And I'm a bard." Donny started strumming the tune of *the final countdown* on his lute. "I figure I can entertain you all while you fight." Luke raised an eyebrow and Donny gave in. "I can buff you all while cursing the enemies. I'm also decent with a rapier." Donny patted the sword tucked into his belt loop.

"It's nice to meet you guys. Are you with a guild or just coming to help?" Luke questioned.

TD chuckled. "Were in your guild, bro. Check your interface, we're in your raid group. That's how we found you."

Under Luke's party status icons were smaller bars for sixteen other players, separated into groups of four. Each one had the player's name, an icon for their class and a bar for their health, mana and stamina. After searching the list, he saw the icon of a music note next to the name The Dashing Donny and an icon of a fireball next to The Dunstin, Kaboom!

"Oh, I see you both now. How did you know who I was though?" Luke asked, still confused.

"We didn't know who you were exactly. If you click on one of the parties in the raid group they get highlighted in white around town. We just knew you were in that party, not which one in the party you were." Donny explained.

Luke clicked on the party that had Donny and TD in it and, sure enough, their bodies were highlighted in white briefly before fading.

"We just kept clicking on the various parties until someone around us was highlighted. We figured we should stick together, right?" Donny added.

"Makes sense I guess." Luke agreed. "I guess we wait now?" The pair shrugged and their conversation quickly devolved into idle chit chat. Occasionally one of them would go ask the guards or fellow guild members for updates, but no one ever had any.

"Well, I guess we should probably get some rest then. I mean, if we don't know when they're coming, we should probably be well rested," Donny explained. "I'll take first watch if you two want to get some shuteye."

"I don't know if I'll be able to sleep with all the anticipation," commented Luke. "What do you think Ringo?" Luke turned to see his wolf curled up into a ball on the floor, fast asleep. The sight of his snoring companion make him yawn. "I guess I could use a quick power nap." Luke curled up next to Ringo and his eyes became heavy. The last thing he saw was TD sitting with his back to the wall, using his pack for a pillow and closing his eyes.

CHAPTER SEVENTEEN

Battle for the Phoenix Kingdom

Luke was being shaken and he could feel Ringo's consciousness nudging him awake.

"Dude, wake up. Something's happening." Opening his eyes he saw TD shaking him.

"Papa, I can smell them." Ringo's voice echoed in his head.

"Whaa…" Luke rubbed his eyes and got to his feet. He stumbled a bit while getting his bearings and looked around. Everyone was awake or being awoken, and tensions were high. "What's going on?" Luke questioned the mage.

"A runner just got back to the city. He said the scouting party was on his heels. Time to man up and grab that bow of yours." TD pulled a large spell tome from his bag and opened it in one hand. Luke tried reading some words but they all appeared to be gibberish to him.

"Did any of the guild come back with the runner?" Luke asked. TD went still. "Only a single NPC runner made it back."

Luke opened his mouth to ask followup questions but he

stopped himself after seeing the expression on TD's face. Before he could contemplate the implications of their guild members being wiped out, he began to hear the faint tune of *Eye of the Tiger* coming from down the wall.

Donny was walking while playing his lute. The instrument was glowing a rainbow of colors as faint waves of musical energy emanated from it. When Luke could hear the sound more clearly, a new buff was added to his status bar. Focusing on the icon of lute prompted a system pop-up.

Bardic Inspiration, *Attack and Defense. You have been inspired by a bard's music or voice. You will receive an additional 10% to your attack and damage scores for the next 30 minutes.*

"Does the game let you play any song for your spells?" Luke questioned.

"Pretty much. I just have to hold a tune and have the mana required. I'm told that at higher levels I can give more than one buff, but this should work for now." Donny put his lute away and drew his rapier.

Following suit, Luke grabbed his bow off his back and pulled an arrow from his quiver in anticipation. He looked out into the darkness, not able to see a thing. *I can't see anything out there. How am I supposed to fight?* As if to answer his thoughts, he could hear Captain Holtz shouting something unintelligible in the distance. After a brief pause, glowing orbs were shot into the sky from various points on the wall. When they reached a fair distance in the air, they began to shine brighter, illuminating the fields below. They weren't as bright as daylight but they made a huge difference and shined enough light to reveal the surrounding area without further help.

It was just in time, too. A large force of several hundred goblins was running at a full sprint toward the city's walls. Scattered among them were larger, more muscular orcs with tusks jutting out of their mouths.

"Prepare your arrows!" Luke spun to see Captain Holtz taking command of the situation. The captain's voice seemed to be amplified by magic. "Take aim!" Luke pulled the arrow back on his bow and the captain raised his sword high into the air. Swiping his sword down he screamed, "FIRE!"

A hail storm of arrows was released from the wall, including those shot by Luke. The arrows raced into the air and the enemy forces made no effort to scatter. Several enemies in the distance began to glow red, orange and black. As the arrows started to descend, a barrage of fireballs and energy beams shot out from the glowing forms of their enemies. The variety of multi-colored spells collided with the storm of arrows, sending them flying off course or eviscerating them altogether. Several arrows still hit their marks. The struck goblins were slain, but the orcs just grunted in pain and annoyance.

"Again! Take aim!" The captain raised his sword and gave the command to fire.

Another storm of arrows flew across the field and was met with the same magical resistance. The defenders were barely making progress in their attempts to down the invaders, and the horde of monsters were getting dangerously close.

"Now hold!" Captain Holtz shouted to the men, his voice still being amplified by magic. "Mid-range mages, prepare to fire. Archers take aim."

The invading force was still spilling out from the distant forest and now clearing the outlying farms. As soon as the approaching army advanced within seventy-five yards, the captain gave the command for all of his archers to open fire.

Archers shot as fast as they could, and mages were now joining in. Fireballs, blasts of light, large stones and even lightning were raining down from the walls. Luke was firing arrows as fast as he could. It was easier to aim now that the enemies were closer.

Luke noticed that TD still hadn't fired. "Waiting for an invitation?" Luke muttered between ragged breaths.

"They aren't close enough. My fireball only has a range of about fifty feet before it dissipates."

Luke could see fear and frustration on the mage's face, but quickly focused his attention back to the enemy forces. Now that they were closer, the enemy's mages were more easily counteracting the defender's attacks, leaving most of their forces unharmed. The defenders on the ground were rattled as the city's gate began to creak and splinter from the barrage of attacks. Earth mages did their best to reinforce it with stone pillars and walls, but the enemy force was persistent.

Luke could hear a guttural shout from the enemy's lines. He focused on the area the shout was coming from and saw several goblins, wearing tattered robes, surrounding a group of orcs. The orc's bodies started glowing red with more and more intensity. Luke was confused as his vision of them started to blur. *Is that heat?* Before he could make heads or tails of the situation, the handful of orcs took off toward the gate at an amazing speed.

"Focus all fire on that group of orcs!" shouted Captain Holtz. Those orcs were not going unnoticed by anyone.

Every defender within range began focusing their fire on the sprinting group. It seemed that every time one of their attacks was about to make contact, the rapidly advancing orcs were protected by defensive skills and the bodies of their allies.. Finally, an arrow made contact with an orc's neck and he fell. A rogue fireball struck another orc down. Now there were only two glowing enemies left charging their gate. As the pair of orcs got closer, the enemy forces gave them room while staying close enough to protect them.

Before they disappeared under the gate's arching walls, Luke's and TD's combined attacks were able to slay one of the remaining two orcs, but a look of fear crossed their faces.

As the orc collided with the gate, he erupted in a massive explosion. The explosion was big enough to destroy not only the gate but also the connecting sections of the wall. Luke, Ringo, TD and Donny were sent flying from above the gate to the city streets below, landing alongside several guards.

Luke blinked away the spots in his vision as his body ached everywhere. Thinking quickly, he cast nature's regrowth on himself, watching his health refill slowly. As his vision cleared, he saw rubble and stones scattered across the street. Several guards were lying lifeless as the enemy army began charging through the newly created opening in the wall.

"Ringo? Ringo!" Luke projected his thoughts in all directions, panic starting to settle in when he didn't receive a response. He pulled himself to his feet and looked around. His eyes went wide and watery when he spotted Ringo trapped under a large piece of the destroyed stone wall. He ran over and tried prying the stone off of her but he could barely make it budge. The sheer act of lifting the stone caused Ringo to release whimpers of pain.

"Help! Someone please help!" He started shouting and pleading for assistance as he ignored his own injuries and knelt by Ringo's side.

He refused to take his eyes off Ringo, so he didn't notice the goblin sneaking up behind him. The goblin's war cry caused him to turn, but he had no time to react as a small blade came rushing down at him. Blood splattered across his face, obscuring his vision.

Numb to the pain, he began to frantically wipe his face with his sleeve. Nanoc was standing above him, holding his large, double-sided axes in both hands.

"Need a hand?" Nanoc dropped his weapons and grabbed both sides of the rock. "When I lift it, pull her out." Not waiting for a reply, he knelt into position and began to heave the collapsed wall off the ground. Luke grabbed Ringo and pulled swiftly before Nanoc lowered the stone again.

Ringo's chest rose and lowered slowly as he tended to her wounds as quickly as he could, casting nature's regrowth on her while force-feeding her a health potion.

"Papa?" The faint voice of his wolf filled his head again, and he released tears that he had been fighting back.

"You really had me worried there girl. Are you ok?" he asked in a soft-spoken voice.

"I... I think so."

"Let my magic finish its work before you get up." She started to protest, but Luke gave her a look that made her reconsider.

"I don't want to break up this reunion, but we could use some help." Nanoc gestured at a flood of goblins pouring through the gaping hole in the wall. Travelers and guards were colliding with the wave of enemies and fights were breaking out everywhere.

Luke looked around for his bow. After spotting it only a few feet away, he grabbed it and his grip was firm as he responded. "I'll back you up whenever you're ready," Luke said.

Nanoc grabbed an axe in each hand as he smiled. His body grew slightly and turned red as heat started radiating off of him in waves. Getting to his feet, Donny wiped blood from his brow and stood beside Nanoc, holding his rapier at the ready. Luke's back was becoming hot. He turned around and saw TD holding a large fireball in his hand. The mage gave him a curt nod as Ringo got to her feet and stood beside Luke. He nocked an arrow in preparation before Nanoc let out a massive battle cry, causing the surrounding goblins to shake slightly in fear.

Before Nanoc took his first step, an arrow whirled by him and struck a goblin in its forehead. The goblin spun around from the strength of the arrow and fell lifeless to the ground.

"Tomahawk!" Nanoc threw both of his axes at nearby goblins. The force of his throws caused the blades to cleave right through the goblins and land in the stone behind them. Nanoc continued to run, collecting his axes without breaking his stride before he encountered a much larger orc. He parried the first attack by the orc and quickly pulled his axes into position to stop a downward slash.

Before the orc could recover, a much smaller rapier blade had already pierced his gut. With a flick of his wrist, Donny opened the orc's gut and its innards starting spilling out. The orc dropped his blade and attempted to push his organs back in before blood spilled from his mouth and he dropped to his knees.

Whirling around, the pair of travelers faced a group of five goblins jumping at them. Before the two of them could get off the ground, a large explosion hit them from behind. Their eyes went white as their backs sizzled like bacon from the heat. The other three goblins leaped into the air. Another well-placed arrow killed one goblin before he could lift his weapon. A large dark form pounced sideways, catching one goblin in its fangs and the other in its claws as it drove them to the ground. Quickly finishing the one in her mouth with a sickening crunch, Ringo lifted her clawed paw and took a wide swipe at the remaining enemy. Several deep slash marks appeared on its chest as blood flowed freely out of the tiny creature. Ringo lifted her paw again and pressed it down hard, ending its life.

The group formed a tight circular formation and Ringo let out a loud howl. She was making it clear that she was on the hunt and that the goblins were her prey.

Goblins surrounded the group, snarling and growling as they circled the travelers. "Ready for round two?" Nanoc asked sarcastically.

Donny sheathed his rapier and pulled out his lute. Strumming *twinkle twinkle little star* as he began to sing along. "Twinkle twinkle little star, how I wonder what you are." Nanoc and Luke looked confused but TD conjured a large fireball in one hand while gesturing for the group to stay still with the other.

After just a few seconds, it became clear what Donny was doing. The goblins started to lean from side to side as their eyes began to open and shut. A few of them dropped their weapons as they slumped over, fast asleep.

"Tssk. I was hoping I could get them all with that." Donny surveyed the surrounding goblins. His spell put three of the six asleep, leaving the other three swaying and fighting back slumber. "Well, I did my part." He gestured at the goblins, suggesting that the other three start their attack.

"I like this one Luke." Nanoc grinned as he brought his axes down on one of the swaying goblins.

TD released his fireball on two of the sleeping goblins who were bunched up together on the ground, killing them both swiftly. Luke held his bow in one hand and drove his fist into the face of the last swaying goblin. As his fist connected with the goblin's face, he activated his gauntlets' special ability and claws shot out and through the goblin's unprotected skull. He quickly retracted them and a system message popped up.

Critical Hit!

Attacking weak spots on enemies will result in a Critical Hit. Critical Hits do increased damage.

*New skill acquired: **Claws**, Beginner 0. You have taken the first step in mastering claw weapons, a subclass of fist-based weapons. Congratulations, you know how to throw a basic punch. Effect: $1+x\%$ claw damage.*

By the time he finished reading the system prompt, Ringo had pounced on and killed the last goblin.

"What was that?" Nanoc stared at Luke's fist.

Stretching his hands out in display, he replied. "It's a new weapon I got, Wolf Claws."

"You're just trying to make Backstab jealous, aren't you?" Nanoc added, causing Luke and him to chuckle and their companions to just look confused.

Nanoc whirled around, raising his axes just in time to block a large bastard sword. An orc was pushing against Nanoc and slowly gaining headway. Before he had time to review the situation and counterattack, another orc ran his blade through Nanoc's side. TD threw a fireball at the two orcs, causing them to back peddle away from the group and to pull the blade from Nanoc's side. Once the blade was free, Nanoc fell to one knee, clutching at his wound.

Luke followed up on TD's attack, firing arrow after arrow. The orcs dodged and rolled out of the way, looking for an opening to close the distance again. Looking at his party menu, Luke saw that Nanoc's health was plummeting. The initial attack brought him below half and the bleeding debuff was steadily chewing away at his remaining hit points. He stopped firing arrows long enough to cast nature's regrowth on the downed berserker but the momentary lapse in ranged cover was the opportunity the orcs were waiting for.

Rushing forward, the orcs quickly closed the distance and swung their massive two-handed blades at Nanoc. Donny acted quickly, parrying one attack. His strength was not high enough to hold the massive blade back and it struck him, causing a large cut on his shoulder. The second orc swung down at Nanoc. Nanoc lifted the arm that still held an axe in order to block. In his weakened state, Nanoc wasn't able to prevent the sword from cutting deep into his upper arm muscle.

Luke released a water shot, striking one orc in the chest. The orc looked hurt but wasn't down for the count. He lifted his sword and prepared for another attack. As he swung down to finish the job a fireball hit him dead on and caused him to stagger back mid strike. Not wanting to leave anything to chance, Luke shot another water shot at the creature. The orc continued to stagger backwards before falling flat on its back. Ringo ran in its direction to finish the job.

Luke turned his attention back to their remaining foe and saw Donny struggling against the raw strength of the orc. He tried to parry the attacks and use the orc's strength against him, but with each attempt he found himself cut open by glancing blows. Running short on mana, Luke didn't want to use another water shot, so he fired a pair of regular arrows at the orc in an attempt to disrupt its battle rhythm.

The orc didn't attempt to dodge, he took both arrows and continued to advance on the bard. Donny was slowly being pushed backward as the orc gained the upper hand. Unable to take his eyes off the creature, Donny didn't notice the rubble around him and tripped on a large piece of stone. Falling backward, he saw the grin on the orc's face as the orc raised his blade high into the air above his head in preparation for a death blow.

Donny closed his eyes, accepting his fate. When he didn't feel the rush of cold steel across his body, he hesitantly opened his eyes. The orc was still standing over him, his blade raised but he was shaking and the grin on his face turned to an expression of disbelief.

"Backstab!" The rogue had jumped onto the back of the orc, driving his dual daggers deep into its upper back. When the orc tried to turn and pull the frail rogue off, a sword drove into its stomach, finishing the job.

"Stop playing around, Backstab, and go protect Nanoc. Luke! Give him another heal. We need potions over here now!" Penny was standing over Donny, taking charge and shouting out orders. Her orders were followed without hesitation. Backstab ran and stood in front of Nanoc as Luke swiftly healed him. Penny extended a hand to Donny, which he quickly accepted. "Are you ok?"

He patted the dust off and gave himself a once over. "Yeah, I think so. I'm at about 40% though, so I'm gonna need to heal up before we fight again."

"Donny! Sorry Bro, my magic has a long cooldown time. I tried jumping in to..." Donny raised a palm, cutting TD off.

"Don't worry, I get it. Things worked out in the end anyway." Donny gave the mage a reassuring smile.

"I hate to break up this love fest but there is a small army left to kill." Penny pointed at the goblins and orcs flowing into the city. "Follow my advance and give me supporting fire." She slammed her sword against her shield several times, triggering her taunt ability. Several goblins and orcs began moving her way in response. Everyone grabbed their weapons and followed Penny's lead. The fighting continued for a long time. The group would taunt a small patch of enemies, Penny and Nanoc playing the role of damage absorption while Luke, Ringo, TD, Donny and Backstab dished out damage. The whole guild was holding their ground. Then the city's full army arrived, making quick work of the remaining scouting party.

Exhausted and drained of mana and stamina, Luke collapsed to the ground. "That" gasp "wasn't" gasp "so" gasp "bad." Luke laid down flat on the cobblestone path and took in gulping breaths. They had fought back the advanced scouting party without losing more than a few members of the guild and the city guard.

"Maybe for you. I almost died at least three times," Nanoc added. Their core group all survived and worked well together while taking out a surprising number of enemies.

Backstab slapped Nanoc on the back. "Only almost?"

The group all laughed exhaustedly and immediately collapsed alongside Luke, using the last of their stamina reserves in their laughing fits.

Unable to do much of anything while his mana and stamina recovered, Luke pulled up his notifications.

Skill up: **Nature's Regrowth**, *Intermediate 1.*
Skill up: **Water Shot**, *Beginner 5.*
Skill up: **Short Bow**, *Intermediate 1.*
Skill up: **Beast Mastery**, *Intermediate 1.*
Skill up: **Claws**, *Beginner 3.*
Skill up: **Dodge**, *Beginner 5.*

Simple Goblin Warrior *x17 defeated. 510 party participation exp gained.*
Goblin Scout *x14 defeated. 350 party participation exp gained.*
Orc Scout *x4 defeated. 140 party participation exp gained.*
Orc Warrior *x7 defeated. 350 party participation exp gained.*

Hmm, not bad gains, he thought as he mentally swiped away the notifications. Luke thought back on how he was forced to use his claws on more than one occasion when goblins tried swarming TD. He sat up and looked around. There was carnage everywhere, and bodies littered the city entrance and cobblestone paths. Forcing himself off the ground, he cracked his back and knuckles to release the tension in his joints.

"Man, nothing like a night full of battle to make you all stiff," Luke said to no one in particular.

Stretching beside him was Backstab. "You're telling me. If we get stuck in this game much longer, I'm going to open a massage parlor. I'll make a killing, I mean, imagine it. All these nerdy guys would pay fistfuls of gold to get a massage from a hot elven babe." He looked around for confirmation and was met with disapproving gazes from everyone but TD, who appeared to be holding back drool.

A cascade of arrows, engulfed in dark flames, rained down on the crowd. Everyone quickly jumped for cover. Some ran into alleyways or behind buildings, while others raised their shields in protest. Luke dove for a large piece of stone left over from the explosion, and Ringo followed his lead. When he heard the last of the arrows drop, he came out from behind his makeshift cover.

"Is everyone..." he froze. Backstab was on his knees and hunched over, a dozen or more arrows sticking into a variety of spots on his back. Luke cast nature's regrowth but got a system prompt in response to his efforts.

Unable to cast, *invalid target. Target must be alive in order to cast this spell.*

Penny slowly walked over to Backstab and closed his eyelids, his face trapped in an expression of utter shock. Even though he was several feet away, Luke could see the tears falling from her face.

Nanoc stepped forward and placed a hand on her shoulder. "He'll come back as soon as we end this. He'll probably be pissed that he was the one to die again." He let out a small chuckle.

Changing his priorities, Luke ran for the nearest set of steps that led up the wall. He looked out across the fields and saw a dark shadow far in the distance.

"They must have a few dark mages with them." Captain Holtz stepped beside Luke. "They were somehow able to hide their presence from our magic." He looked behind him, into the city, and saw several lifeless soldiers and travelers. "We lost a lot in that surprise magical attack." He noticed the grim expression on Luke's face. "Now is not the time for sadness, it's the time for vengeance! Mages! Light it up!"

A couple dozen massive light orbs flew into the sky, several of them exploding and causing glowing rain to come pouring down on the distant, dark shadows. As the rain fell onto the patch of darkness, it ate away at it like a parasite. It made quick work of the concealing spell and revealed an army of monsters. There were orcs, goblins, ogres and even some humans standing in large formations.

Luke couldn't even attempt to count their numbers. Looking back at the army of guards behind him he began to worry. He locked eyes with Captain Holtz before saying, "how the hell are we supposed to fight that?"

CHAPTER EIGHTEEN

All Hope Lost

"Prepare to launch artillery spells! Archers to the wall!" Captain Holtz was shouting orders, and people were flowing into position without hesitation.

Luke notched an arrow and turned to see TD running up the stairs and pulling his spell book out of his bag. Looking further behind the wall, he saw large teams of mages wearing matching robes standing on large complex magical circles. The circles were glowing and large elemental attacks started forming in the air. As they formed, large crates full of ingredients started to vanish around them. A wondrous display of magic filled the air with fireballs, glowing rocks, ice shards, and glowing balls of light. The elemental attacks continued to grow and grow until they were taller than the wall and the surrounding two-story buildings.

The enemy army wasn't idle during this time. The bulk of the army started charging toward the city at a full sprint while rows of archers and mages began preparing for attack.

"Mages, release! Archers, at the ready!" The captain gave the command to release the spells.

The larger-than-life elemental attacks launched into the air and over the wall. Enemy mages attempted to counterattack but the artillery spells were on a whole different level and the minor spells crashed ineffectively against them. As the artillery spells crashed into the ground, they splattered dozens before exploding and killing hundreds in their wake. Even several mighty ogres were eviscerated while charging into battle.

Captain Holtz gave the command for archers to launch their attacks. Hundreds of arrows flew into the air and, at the command of the captain, mages enchanted the arrows. As the arrows reached their peak and began to descend, they ignited. Flaming arrows now rained down on the approaching forces. Pockets of corpses appeared in the crowd where the artillery spells and arrows hit most frequently. Any gaps were soon filled in as the enemy army marched over the bodies of their fallen allies.

As the army readied another round of arrows, the enemy archers and mages fired. Hundreds of arrows, enchanted with black flames, flew toward the city and descended upon the defenders. The city's mages attempted a counterattack, but most of them were focused on preparing another round of artillery spells, so the flaming projectiles flew unimpeded.

Men fell from the ramparts as flaming arrows crashed into them. They slew several mages who were focused on preparing their spells. Luke ducked behind the wall as best he could in order to avoid the attack. Ringo stood over him, not wanting her papa to be struck. When the barrage was over, Luke pulled away from the wall and saw that Ringo had a flaming arrow sticking out of her side. He quickly pulled it out as Ringo let out a loud roar and Luke cast his healing spell on her.

"You all right?" Luke questioned mentally.

"A warning before pulling it out would have been nice," she replied.

Luke apologized as he stood to face the incoming army. Another round of artillery spells launched over the wall, crashing down and killing hundreds of monsters. But despite their best efforts, the enemy army reached the wall.

Dozens of orcs and goblins began flooding the open gate, while hundreds more struggled to find purchase on the reinforced defenses. As they made contact with the walls, defensive spells activated and explosions of magic shook the earth. Large blasts of fire, spikes of ice and explosions of lava burst forth from the magic wards placed earlier that night.

Luke was in awe at the power of the mages. That star-struck feeling quickly melted away when ogres reached the city. The ogres stretched their arms out, allowing dozens of goblins and orcs that were clinging to their body to jump on the ramparts before they began punching new entry holes into the city.

An orc landed only a few feet from Luke. Luckily, the orc stumbled a bit as it landed, leaving an opening that Ringo took full advantage of. Ringo rushed forward and sank her teeth deep into the orc's forearm. The orc pulled back its opposing arm to strike, but Ringo distracted it long enough for Luke to close the distance. Luke landed two punches in quick succession. As the blows stuck the orc, Luke sent mana to his fists and metal claws shot through its body, tearing through the orc's makeshift leather armor.

The orc fell to the ground and Luke took stock of his situation. Enemies were flooding the main gate, ogres were busting apart more openings in the wall, monsters were gathering on top of the ramparts and the enemy outnumbered them at least ten to one. It wasn't looking good for the Phoenix Kingdom.

"Luke! We need you down here, now!" A voice came screaming

from below. Looking around, Luke saw the origin of the plea. Penny and Nanoc were trying to fend off a party of orcs that had surrounded them.

Luke looked around and saw a shield leaning against the wall nearby. He grabbed it and placed it at the top of the stairs that led off the ramparts. *Time for my Legolas moment*, he thought as he jumped on the shield, attempting to ride it down the stairs while firing arrows at enemies. At least he could say he attempted it. As he jumped on the shield it flew out from under him, causing him to not only fall flat on his back but also to roll down the stairs. When he reached the first bend in the stairs, he fell over the edge and landed on a pair of goblins who were rushing for nearby defenders.

Scrambling to his feet, Luke had just enough time to dodge a dagger aimed for his abdomen. He pressed his back to the stone wall as the goblins prepared to lunge forward. Before they had the opportunity, a large wolf jumped from the ramparts and landed directly on the pair. Pressing down hard, Ringo crushed one of them while an arrow pierced the other's skull before it could counterattack.

"You have to be careful papa," Ringo cautioned.

"I know Ringo, I know." Luke responded telepathically as he dusted himself off and cast nature's regrowth to regain the embarrassing amount of hit points he lost in his stunt.

"Ahhh!" Nanoc screamed in pain. Luke spun to see an orc pulling his large bastard sword out of Nanoc's left shoulder. He dropped his axe as his arm went limp.

Luke fired arrows at the orcs as he ran, readying himself to cast nature's regrowth when the cooldown was over. With the enemy forces being so compact, he holstered his bow and focused on his claws. He simply didn't have the room to use his bow effectively.

Acting quickly, Luke delivered as many blows as he could to the backs of the orcs while their focus was on his party. The sudden jerk of pain in their backs caused the orcs to lose momentum and their attacks went wide. Nanoc and Penny capitalized every chance they got, slaying the handful of orcs who were around them and regaining their own battle momentum.

A sharp pain shot up Luke's side. Feeling around he felt something hard. He pulled on it to reveal a throwing dagger. Penny jumped in to shield him from additional daggers while he healed himself. Looking at his mana he noticed that he was down to about a third, only enough to heal a couple more times while maintaining his weapon's ability.

"Every time we think we're gaining ground something like this happens," Luke grunted out while getting back to his feet.

"They just keep coming." Penny bashed a goblin's head in with her shield while simultaneously stabbing another with her sword.

"The goblins are all low level but there's just so many of them." Nanoc was continually striking with his axes. He was disregarding any defense in order to slay as many enemies as possible. His rage numbed him to the minor wounds he was receiving. Luke cast nature's regrowth on Nanoc when the cooldown was finally up.

"Guys, we have a problem. I'm almost out of mana." It worried Luke. When he ran out of mana, the healing would stop. With the large number of enemies flowing in through the gate, his guild wasn't able to send runners to retrieve healing potions.

An ogre suddenly crashed through what was left of the main gate, sending more stone shards flying across the battlefield. Luke and his party fell to the ground in cover, watching large stone shards impale the travelers and goblins around them.

A large ape leaped off of a nearby building with its fists raised high. As it reached the ogre, the ape crashed its fist down on the hulking mass, sending it to the ground and cracking the cobblestone. The ogre crushed several goblins as it fell to its knees. Not giving up its advantage, the ape picked the ogre up and started spinning it. The ogre spun around a few times before the ape threw it into a nearby building.

Several of the other ogres, who had now broken into the city, came to the injured ogre's aid. One of them attacked the ape with a club but the ape caught the club before it made contact. While the ogre distracted the ape, another ogre landed a combo of punches to its lower back, forcing the ape to release his grip on the club. Now free, the ogre with the club pulled back to swing again but a large wolf, the size of a minivan, tackled it to the ground. The wolf wrapped its large mouth around the arm of the ogre and began to drag it around like a makeshift chew toy.

Ursa ran across the rooftops, leaping over the ogre that had previously crashed into a building. Before she could land, the ogre swung its fist at her. She crossed her arms to block the blow but the sheer strength of the attack sent her flying several dozen yards, over the wall and into the ranks of the enemy's army.

The ape launched an uppercut at the ogre, knocking it off its feet and onto its back. Before it could stand, several of the mages sent waves of attacks against it. The ape put a foot on the ogre to keep it on the ground, beating its chest in a display of dominance.

A massive black fireball crashed into the ape's back. The following concussive blast sent him flying through several nearby buildings. The enemy mages finally made it to the battle. Dark-robed goblins began to flood the city's walls and fire down on the defenders. Those who were able to, took cover. Many were too slow and now lay slain by the onslaught.

Luke hid behind some rubble and noticed a shift in the battle. The orcs and goblins around the city gate started running past him and the other defenders. The monsters were no longer stopping to fight their opposition. Captain Holtz suddenly flew out of an alleyway. He was covered in white flames and made quick work of the first few rows of enemies who ran by the city's defenses.

"Don't let them into the city! Stop them at all costs. We have to protect the citizens." Captain Holtz dashed through the lines of enemies, taking another few dozen down before engaging the ogres.

The captain's attacks created an opening for the defenders to recover without enemies surrounding them. The enemy mages capitalized on this and rained down their area of effect spells on the wide open space. Despite them hiding behind cover, the mages destroyed a third of the defenders' forces with their back-to-back assaults of magic. Defender after defender fell from a barrage of fireballs, ice storms, chain lightning and rays of pure darkness.

After a few rounds of attacks, the mages switched focus and began protecting the ogres. They cast heals and buffs to empower the hulking beasts. Captain Holtz, the city's mages, Ursa's ape and various high level NPCs were having trouble keeping up with the enhanced creatures.

Two humans, wearing thick black robes, appeared on top of the wall. One of them had two ropes strung across his chest in an X shape. Several black crystals were strung from them. At their sudden appearance, the bulk of the enemy forces stopped their advancement.

"Hello and good evening everyone." The man with the robes spoke in a deep booming voice. It was clear to Luke that the man's voice was being empowered with mana as it was loud enough to reach across the entire battlefield. "My name is Iron and I'm here representing the joint forces of the Crimson Shadow and these monsters." The man gestured at the army of monsters surrounding him. Luke gritted his teeth in anger at the mention of the Crimson

Shadow.

"I'm here to make all the travelers an offer. Join the Crimson Shadow. All we ask is that you swear your allegiance to us and Shadow Incarnate with your mana. In exchange, we offer you power. The power to take what you want, the power that releases you from the chains of society. We can make you gods!"

There was a long pause before someone shouted out, "you're all mad! It's your fault I can't see my kids right now!" Luke couldn't locate the person who was shouting, but they sounded extremely upset.

"I understand your confusion. I was confused at first too. Crimson Shadow didn't trap you in this game. We evolved your minds to a higher plane. Think about it. You will no longer be trapped in a nine-to-five job, no longer insulted or picked on. You will no longer be the outcast, the geek, the loser. In here you will have power! Real power! You can write your own destiny and you will not be confined by society's rules. You can do anything and everything you want. It truly is an Endless Fantasy." The man chuckled slightly at his unintentional pun. "We are legion, we are one, we are power!" The man clenched his fists and black flames began to surround them. "Join us and you will have this power too!"

There was another long pause before someone else shouted. "Yeah... Sounds kinda like a cult if you ask me." Several travelers started laughing, washing away any power or strength Iron may have gathered from his speech.

Iron spoke slowly and emphasized each word. "We are not a cult."

"Exactly what someone in a cult would say," another traveler shouted and this time it caused all the travelers to erupt in laughter.

Iron grinned. "Clearly I haven't shown you enough of the power

I was referring to." He grabbed one of the black crystals attached to his garment and ripped it loose. Holding it in his hand, the crystal drained in color as thick black lines began coursing up his arm. The black lines covered his entire body in tattoos that represented dark power. When the crystal was fully clear and drained of its pigment, it crumbled into dust.

Iron looked through the crowd, eyeing the people who shouted at him. He lifted both of his arms and pointed a hand at each traveler. At first, nothing happened but soon a black ball formed in both of Iron's open palms. Without warning, a torrent of black flames exploded from each of the black balls. The flames flew outward, expanding into a large cone.

The flames traveled fast and quickly reached their intended targets. Besides hitting the two travelers, the cones expanded outward and encompassed an area about fifteen feet wide. What scared Luke the most was the sheer power of the flames. They destroyed travelers, stone, goblins, walls, rubble, virtually everything in their path. As the flames flew from Iron, the black tattoos slowly drained away from his body and into his palms. When the tattoos vanished, the flames abruptly stopped.

Luke stood in shock. That single attack destroyed at least thirty travelers. There were large indentations in the ground showing the path the flames took toward their intended targets. The flames were powerful enough to tear up and melt the cobblestone path. Luke had to do something, or else they would all be dead.

Iron looked down with an evil grin dawning on his face. He grabbed another crystal and allowed the power to course through himself. He let out a grunt of pleasure. "Now." He paused a moment to allow the power to fully course though himself as the crystal crumbled in his hand. "What was I saying? Oh, that's right. Who wants to be on the winning side?"

The travelers shuffled uncomfortably, no one wanting to speak up and face Iron's wrath. "Don't make me repeat myself." Iron's eyes emitted an ominous black light as he shouted into the crowd. Orcs and goblins were cheering while the travelers all jumped in fear.

Someone in the crowd said something faintly and Iron shouted at them to speak up. "I said, go to hell!" Shrapnel emphasized his words as he stepped forward, travelers parting and giving him a wide berth. "No one here will join you. You trapped us in here and cut us off from our friends, our family, our lives! I think I speak for everyone here when I say, you can take your offer and shove it!" Shrapnel raised his war hammer in defiance. Other travelers soon followed, raising their respective weapons and preparing for battle.

Iron started laughing. "Well. What can I say?" He shrugged his shoulders and raised his hands up questioningly. "I was hoping you would say that." He grabbed another crystal, and the power flowed into him. Another set of black patterns started appearing on his body, in addition to the patterns that were already present. His body was now emitting a visible aura of darkness. It was as if his body couldn't contain that much power so it was leaking out of him.

Iron took a few steps forward until he was on the edge of the ramparts. The monsters around him took several steps back in anticipation of the upcoming magical release. The shadow aura coming from Iron made his grin more intimidating and sinister as he raised his palms into the air. "Die to my power." Large black fireballs began to form in each open palm and Iron began cackling as the fireballs grew in size.

The cackling abruptly stopped. Iron looked down at his chest, his face showing a mixture of shock and pain. Three holes appeared in his chest and blood was slowly running down the front of his robe. As people looked closer, they noticed three lines of dripping blood coming from the holes. The lines appeared to be floating in midair as if held up by an invisible force. Slowly fading into existence were three metal claws.

"In the words of a friend, Backstab!" The other robed man shouted in fear as Luke materialized next to him, with a clawed gauntlet through Iron and an empty potion bottle in his other hand. Luke had consumed the invisibility potion he had brewed from the ghostshrooms he found in The Den, using it to sneak into position. Iron fell to his knees and his hands flew to grab at his stomach. The fireballs his hands had been holding fell toward the ground.

It didn't take long for the fireballs to come in contact with the stone below and the instant they did, they exploded. The concussive force of the blast sent everyone flying. Luke tried to leap out of the way but Iron's limp form crashed into him and sent both of them soaring over the walls.

The explosion sent splintering flames in all directions. The flames engulfed traveler and monster alike. Since the travelers were farther away, it caught only a few of them but the monsters weren't as lucky. The blast killed several waves of goblins and orcs before dissipating.

The explosion was loud enough that they could hear it all over the battlefield. It created a temporary ceasefire while both sides struggled to locate the source of the noise. It didn't take long for them to find it and continue their respective attacks.

Several yards away from the wall, outside the city, Luke was groaning as he struggled to stand. Opening his eyes, he discovered that he was in the middle of the enemy army. Goblins and orcs were pushing each other aside to be the first to taste his blood. Not knowing how he would survive, Luke raised his fists in preparation for the fight to come.

A loud noise, sounding like a crack of thunder, came from the middle of the city. Dozens more followed it in quick succession. Luke turned to see what was happening. Large flashes of light were continuously going off, as if someone was shining a flashlight in your eyes and then turning it off.

Luke could hear a loud commotion coming from the ruined city gate. Without warning, the enemy forces started fleeing from the city. Goblins were running to regroup outside the city walls and large groups of travelers were following them with their weapons drawn. Luke tried to find his own party but didn't recognize any of the advancing travelers.

He heard Ringo's voice ring in his head. "Papa. Papa. Travelers are here. Hundreds of them."

CHAPTER NINETEEN

Travelers

The booming lightning continued, showing that even more travelers were arriving. Luke's eyes lost focus as a searing pain ran up his back. Looking down, he saw a blade protruding from his stomach. He tried to spin around and counterattack but the motion caused the blade to move around inside him, sending another round of pain coursing through his body. A goblin ripped the blade out with a grunt from behind him.

Luke fell to his knees and more enemies began closing in, blades rising and at the ready. A goblin slashed across his chest, and blood was gushing from the deep gash. Ringo screamed for him as his guild mates tried to reach him, but they were still too far away.

The slash from the goblin cut the strap holding his bag to his chest. This caused the bag to fall to the ground and its contents spilled out. Luke's face fell, his hit points reaching five percent and falling. Looking around the ground, he saw the contents of his bag rolling around. He saw health potions, some arrows and food sprawled about. Luke's eyes were drawn to the medium-sized bottle containing a bubbling purple liquid.

Rose's emergency potion! he thought as he tried to think of a way to get the potion. An orc took a swing with a large battleaxe in an attempt to decapitate him but, thinking quickly, he fell flat on his stomach. The motion and falling caused him to lose three percent health but his face was within inches of the bubbling liquid.

The orc staggered sideways as a result of missing his blow, but was quickly recovering. Luke reached for the emergency potion, removed the stopper and downed the liquid. As the cool liquid raced down his throat, he could feel sparks of energy coursing through his entire body as a system message crashed into view.

__Major Empowerment__. You have received the major empowerment buff. You have received the following effects for the duration of the empowerment: +300% max hit points, +300% max mana, +300% max stamina, +300% hit point regeneration, +300% mana regeneration, +300% stamina regeneration, +25 to all attributes, and +25% movement speed. This effect will last for two minutes.

__WARNING!__ Skill, attribute, and experience gains are disabled during the duration of your empowerment.

__WARNING!__ You will receive a Major Weakening for 24 hours after the major empowerment's duration is over. Major Weakening will give you the following effects: -75% max hit points, -75% max mana, -75% max stamina, -75% hit point regeneration, -75% mana regeneration, -75% stamina regeneration, -25 to all attributes, reduced to a minimum of 1, and -75% experience gain.

His flesh began to stitch itself back together at a rapid pace. Before he knew it, the cut on his chest had vanished and the hole in his stomach was reduced to nothing more than a bruise. The orc had recovered and was swinging his battleaxe from overhead, but Luke noticed something: the orc seemed to move in slow motion. Looking at his hands, he realized that the orc wasn't moving slowly, he was moving fast!

Easily dodging the orcs attack, Luke rolled to the side and delivered several punches to the monster's stomach. He watched as the orc flew backwards in slow motion. Weighing his options, he headed for the city to help the travelers repel the invaders.

He bent down and leaped into the air with all his strength. He leapt fifteen feet up at the peak of his arc before landing. As he landed he extended his hands with his claws out and crashed into several goblins. He took several jabs to clear a space large enough to leap again.

With one more impressive leap, he landed among the charging travelers. Ringo rushed through the crowd to reach him.

"Papa…" she asked questioningly as she slowed and stopped several feet away from him. She cocked her head in confusion. "Why are you on fire?"

"What!" He looked down at himself and, for the first time, noticed the purple flames covering his body. Looking at his buffs he noticed '*purple aura*' listed as a side effect of the potion. He also made a note that he only had about one minute left before he would become useless.

"Ringo, help the travelers push the monsters back. I'm going to try to help with the ogres." Before Ringo could protest, Luke leapt into the city and began a full sprint toward the nearest ogre.

There was an ogre near the city's wall, and a group of new travelers was taking its chances fighting the monster. It was a foolish attempt, and every swing of the ogre's club killed several of them, sending them to respawn once the conflict was over.

Luke ran at the ogre, using his increased speed to dodge a swing of its club. The club crashed and sent cobblestone rubble into the air. Luke jumped on the club and ran up the ogre's arm. The ogre panicked and swung his other arm at the advancing threat. Luke pushed off the arm, propelled himself toward the ogre's stomach and launched a combo of attacks. His claws could just barely break through the ogre's tough skin, thanks only to his enhanced stats.

The ogre swung his club down at Luke. Since Luke was falling through the air, he wasn't able to dodge the club and it made contact with a sickening crunch. Luke crashed into the nearby city wall and, as he made contact, the wall gave way, throwing Luke out of the city. Rolling to his feet, Luke held his side as he cast nature's regrowth. Aided by his buff, his ribs healed and the large bruise was steadily decreasing in size.

The ogre looked concerned when Luke came running through the hole in the wall. Luke threw another combo of attacks at the ogre and he was gaining ground, forcing the monster back. Not giving up his advantage, Luke pressed the attack with combo after combo.

In the middle of throwing several punches, he felt a sharp pain and could barely stand. He was panting and his body felt sluggish. Looking up, he noticed a red icon of a sickly man in his status bar and the empowerment buff was gone. He was out of time.

The ogre was covering his face with his hands and moving backward. Once he noticed the attacks had stopped, the ogre uncovered his eyes and grinned at the sickly visage of Luke below him. He raised his club, and it came crashing down with alarming speed.

Before the club impacted Luke, Ringo jumped in and took the blow. She let out a loud cry of pain as she went flying across the battlefield. Luke saw her health bar reach zero and her status bar grayed out, signifying her death.

Filled with rage, Luke clenched his fists. "I swore to her I wouldn't let her die, you bastard!" The ogre chuckled at the tears flowing freely down Luke's face. "I will kill you! I will end you! I don't care if it's the last thing I do but you will die!"

Class skill unlocked! **Tamer's Vengeance.** *Watching your animal companion die after swearing to keep her alive has filled you with the vengeance and power of beast tamers past. This skill is auto-triggered when either the beast tamer or animal companion is killed in battle within view of the other. You are filled with the power of the beast tamers before you and can concentrate that power into a single attack. Effect: Buff your next melee or ranged attack, adding 5x its normal damage. Note: If the attack does not instantly follow the triggering of this effect, this buff will last until the beast tamer and animal companion are reunited or five minutes, whichever happens first.*

A picture of Ringo with a broken heart surrounding it appeared in Luke's status bar, but he paid it no attention. Luke charged headfirst at the ogre before it could recover. He pulled back a fist and a glowing green light emanated from it as he screamed in anger.

Luke slammed his fist as hard as he could into the ogre's gut, sending out his claws as he made contact. Green light shot through his claws and out the back of the ogre. The ogre pulled its head back and released a roar of pain and anger as Luke fell to the ground, collapsing from a mixture of exhaustion and overexertion.

The ogre gripped its stomach with its free hand and its face contorted in anger. It tightened its grip on the club and pulled back to deliver the final blow. The club came down swiftly and crashed on top of Luke, the sheer force causing a cloud of dust to raise off the ruined cobblestone.

Something was off with the ogre's attack. Glancing down, the ogre noticed that his club was several feet off the ground. The dust began to clear, and the ogre saw an unharmed man lying on the ground and a bandaged figure stopping the club from making contact.

"Rose would kill me if I let you die." Ursa's hand began to glow with energy and she punched the club.

Her punch was strong enough to send the club soaring back at the ogre. The club crashed into the ogre, knocking it on its rear. Ursa leapt at the ogre and delivered a quick combo of three punches, each punch making a cracking sound on contact. Ursa pulled away, ready to fight, but the ogre had had enough. It fell back and its eyes rolled into its head. It was dead.

"Since you're unconscious, I can say this. You made me proud as a beast tamer, kid." Ursa pulled a healing potion from her pouch and force-fed it to Luke.

He was slow to respond, but he began to open his eyes. By the time he could get his eyes fully opened, Ursa was gone, and he was none the wiser. He sat up with a grunt and saw the dead ogre in front of him. It had multiple stab wounds from his claws and three mysterious deep indents on its body.

Looking around the city, Luke saw a surprising lack of enemy forces. There were still ogres but only a handful of mages were still with them. There was a clear absence of orcs and goblins. He sadly noted the large number of dead guards and travelers.

He pulled himself to his feet and slowly walked toward Ringo's lifeless body, casting nature's regrowth on himself. With the major weakening debuff on, his health was a fraction of what it normally was, but the cooling energy took some of his exhaustion away.

He sat next to Ringo and pulled her into his lap as he cried. "I failed you again." He wiped Ringo's face. "I know I promised I wouldn't let you die, but I wasn't able to keep that promise and I don't know if I can keep it moving forward. We're gonna face some tough enemies in this world but I promise," he stopped to chuckle. "I know my promises probably aren't worth much at this point, but I promise things will be different. We'll train together and become unstoppable! We will be the strongest in this world!" Luke was stroking Ringo's fur as he began casting resurrect companion.

Unable to cast, you do not meet the mana requirements for this spell.

Luke was failing Ringo yet again, unable to bring her back. He wouldn't have the required mana until his debuff was gone in twenty-four hours. He got up and pulled her under a tree in the city's courtyard. Looking around, he spotted what he was looking for. He got up and walked toward a group of dead travelers.

He whispered his apologizes as he pulled a cloak off a dead rogue traveler and walked back to Ringo. He covered Ringo with the cloak before he kissed his hand and laid it on her for a moment. "I've got to go now, girl. I have to see if I can help, even if I can barely stand." He muttered the last few words under his breath and began heading for the castle wall.

After an exhausting amount of effort, he made it to the top of the ramparts. Looking outward he saw that the travelers and guards were gaining ground. Even the enemy mages and ogres inside the city were dropping like flies. The city's mages and guards could focus all their effort on the enemies after the travelers pushed the main enemy force outside the city. Luke smiled, they were winning!

The city and surrounding area started getting dark again. All the light was being pulled to the center of the battlefield. Looking for the source, Luke spotted the robed man who originally appeared with Iron. The man had his robe off and was wearing nothing but cloth pants. He was pulling something off of Iron's corpse and pushing it into his exposed chest.

Focusing his sight, he knew exactly what the man was doing. He was shoving all the remaining dark crystals against his body and absorbing their power. There had to be a dozen or so crystals left after the handful that Iron used and the man seemed hellbent on using all of them. The man's entire body was turning black and seemed to be absorbing all the surrounding light as his power continued to grow.

Letting out a loud roar that echoed across the battlefield, the man began to grow in size and morph. His muscles grew larger, his skin turned black as it began to resemble cracked stone. Large curling horns grew from his head and a large pair of wings sprouted from his back. His wings had bones running through them and were covered with a thin black membrane.

The man, or more accurately, demon, stretched his massive wings out and began flapping them. His wings had a wide, fifty or sixty foot wingspan and they kicked up dust and stone as he flapped them. He quickly gained altitude and was now hovering thirty or forty feet in the air.

Opening his mouth, he pulled a vortex of shadows in and formed a massive ball of shadow energy. The energy ball grew to twenty feet in diameter before he took aim at the city and released it.

The ball flew quickly towards the city's castle. Several mages shot at it with their respective energies in an attempt to knock it off course or destroy it, but their attempts were futile. The shadow ball hit the castle with a deafening boom. All light vanished from the world for a moment, being consumed by the shadow ball's explosion.

Luke blinked rapidly to clear his eyes as light flooded the world again. When he regained his vision, his eyes went wide. The castle was in ruins. The shadow ball caused an explosion big enough to wipe it from existence. The only remnants were some castle towers which were engulfed in black flames.

"Ha ha ha." The demon's deep and booming voice filled the battlefield. "We told you we had true power. All of you deserve to die for refusing us! We are the Crimson Shadow and you are all dead." A large shadow ball started forming in front of the demon's mouth and crackles of black lightning sparked between his two large horns. He let out a loud cackle as the shadow ball reached its full size.

As he started to release his attack, a torrent of orange and red flames hit him dead center and sent him sailing across the battlefield. His shadow ball began to shrink and fade from existence without the demon channeling it.

"You will pay for that!" The demon stood and began looking for whoever dared to attack him.

A bright light was coming from the ruined castle. It was so bright that it looked like the sun had risen early. The figure in the distance started rising into the air and growing in size until it was just as large, if not larger, than the demon.

It was a giant bird, made entirely of flames. When the light died down a little it became clear. It was a Phoenix!

CHAPTER TWENTY

Rise of the Phoenix

The phoenix took flight in a straight path toward the recovering demon. In anticipation of the phoenix reaching him, the demon grew jet-black nails as long as Luke's entire body from his fingers. The demon bent over, ready to jump forward and strike, but the phoenix changed trajectory and flew straight up into the air.

The phoenix climbed another hundred feet before slowing its rapidly flapping wings and hovering in the sky. Its flames were so bright that it made the night look like midday. The phoenix opened its mouth and its eyes began to emit white light as a woman's voice came out.

The voice was regal and firm as it spoke. "My name is Queen Samantha, and I have stood by watching long enough. You are threatening my people and I will not stand for it!" The phoenix's light grew in intensity as the queen got angry. "Let this be a lesson to you and to all who dare threaten us. You will find nothing but defeat and death when you threaten the Phoenix Kingdom!"

The phoenix's eyes stopped glowing and it let out an ear

shattering bird caw. It began to flap its wings faster and faster but it didn't move. Instead, it rained down a symphony of fireballs into the enemy forces. Their mages acted quickly and threw up magical barriers but the barriers shattered after a few attacks landed. The attack devastated the enemy's army. The phoenix wiped out a third or more of the enemy force in a single moment.

Luke was cheering alongside the other travelers and guards when he spotted Captain Holtz nearby. Green blood covered the captain and he had a worried look on his face.

"Captain!" Luke's voice was hoarse, desperately needing some water. The captain didn't register his voice, so Luke walked over and grabbed the man's shoulder. "Captain?" Captain Holtz turned to him and Luke instantly noticed tears streaming down the normally stoic face.

"This is bad son, this is really bad." The captain could barely get the words out. He was a train wreck, as if he had just lost someone close. "She has to stop, she can't wield this power, it's too dangerous."

A large black bastard sword, the length of a building, crashed into the chest of the phoenix and the bird screamed in pain. The scream caused Luke and the captain to refocus on the fight that was vastly out of their league, the fight that would determine the war's victor.

The demon was grinning as the phoenix came crashing down. The bird landed among allies and enemies, but its flames only seemed to affect the monsters. Travelers and guards caught in the flames seemed to be unaffected and began running away. The flames instantly set the monsters aflame as the intensely hot fire stole their lives from them.

The demon leaped toward the struggling bird with its black bastard sword in hand. It landed on top of the phoenix and plunged the blade into its wing. It grabbed the blade in both hands and began to twist the dark metal. Deep red flames began to pour from the wound as the phoenix cried out in pain.

"Die you dumb bird!" The demon pulled its blade free and attempted to plunge it in again.

Being freed from the blade, the phoenix released a shock wave of fire. The fire tore into the demon and several chunks of dark energy fell from him. The demon took a few steps backward and screamed. Black energy began to refill the holes and missing chunks of flesh, making him whole again. The phoenix was on its feet and quickly healed itself as flames filled the holes in its body.The two giants stared each other down, each hesitating and not wanting to make the first move. "Screw this," muttered the demon before it charged forward.

The phoenix flapped its wings and shot several large fireballs toward him. The demon acted quickly, slicing the fireballs and deflecting them with its blade, all the while advancing.

Captain Holtz jumped over the ramparts and was running toward the fight. Luke called out to him but the captain ignored him and sped up. He was muttering something that Luke couldn't hear and the captain was soon emitting a white and purple aura as his speed increased. He was moving fast enough that Luke was having trouble following him with his eyes, partly because of his weakened state.

He heard a rattle and looked down. There was a medium-sized potion bottle rattling around where the captain was standing. Inspecting it closely he saw trace amounts of a purple liquid bubbling inside. "Oh no... Captain, what have you done?"

The demon tossed his sword into the air and caught it in the same motion. He was now holding it like a spear and tossed it at the phoenix. He shot a shadow ball from his open hand. The explosion caused the sword to propel forward.

The phoenix stopped flapping its wings and instead sent a torrent of flames out of its mouth in an attempt to stop the blade from reaching it. The flames began slowing the blade, but the flames obscured the demon from view.

When the torrent of flames stopped, the sword fell harmlessly to the ground, but it revealed the demon channeling a shadow ball larger than the previous ones. The attack was growing so large that the demon appeared to be pouring every ounce of its strength into the attack. The energy that made up its body was being drained as the attack grew in size.

As the phoenix opened its mouth to release more fire the demon resumed its attack. As soon as the shadow ball released from his hands, he flew into the sky. The phoenix released another torrent of fire but it only slowed the shadow ball and did not destroy it. The attack got closer and closer as the phoenix's flames began to eat into it.

Descending quickly from the cloud cover, the demon landed and slashed his recovered blade across the bird's back. The flames momentarily subsided as the shadow ball picked up speed and collided with the phoenix's body. A ring of fire surrounded the bird as it created an invisible heat shield at the last possible moment.

"Why won't you die!" The demon lifted its blade in both hands and sent energy coursing up the hilt, transforming the sword into a large two-handed axe.

As the axe finished forming, a white and purple streak of energy flew past the demon's arms and landed on the adjacent ground. Captain Holtz held his blade up in defiance and the demon's arms slid off his body at the elbow, landing on the ground with a heavy thud.

"Who the hell are you?" the demon barked in anger. Black

tentacles of energy shot from the demon's stubs and connected with its lost appendages. The tentacles pulled up his lost arms and reconnected them. After a moment of healing, one couldn't tell where the captain had cut them off.

"Let the gods of light and fire empower me, so I may strike this foe down. Holy Fire!" The captain's rapier ignited in white flames. "Let me protect the city I've sworn to protect, the people I care about and the Kingdom I love!" The flames began to spread past the tip of his blade and extended outward, increasing his blade's effective range significantly.

The demon laughed and raised a palm. Smaller shadow balls began shooting out of it at a rapid pace. Captain Holtz jumped from side to side, dodging the attacks and occasionally deflecting or slicing through one with his rapier.

"You are an annoying bug." The demon leaped at him to crush him under his massive foot but the captain stood his ground and thrust his blade upward, releasing a white energy blast that tore the demon's foot apart.

Struggling to balance on one foot, the demon fell forward onto the ground. The captain was on him instantly, delivering blow after blow with his rapier. Every blow exploded with white flames shortly after being made. The flames ate away at the demon, creating large gaps in its body as the dark energy struggled to reform its demon-like body.

A sweeping punch hit the captain, and the punch sent him ricocheting across the ground like a stone skipping across the surface of a lake. The demon lifted itself into a plank position as its arms and its leg reformed, in an attempt to be able to stand. Dark flames filled the missing chunks of the demon's body and soon the demon was once again whole.

"Impressive for an NPC but how long can you keep that up? Me, on the other hand, I have an endless source of dark power."

Captain Holtz stood but didn't bother to brush off the dirt and dust. He coughed and spit out a mouth full of blood. His body was covered in gouges and scrapes from his trip across the battlefield. Wiping his mouth, he grinned as the healing effect of the potion took over.

"You won't be alive long enough to see." The captain bolted forward, cracking the earth beneath him as he closed the distance.

The demon attempted to slice through the captain with its newly formed axe, but the captain dodged it and sent a wave of white fire at the demon's chest. As it burned away the dark energy, the captain saw what he was looking for.

The hole in the demon's chest revealed a man with dark tentacles coursing out of his body and dark crystals clinging to his chest. The captain shot a single attack at the man but the energy reformed quickly enough that the attack missed.

"It seems I know your secret traveler," the captain said between labored breaths.

"I will kill you!" The demon shot another barrage of shadow balls from his palms, this time using both hands and doubling the effectiveness.

The captain struggled to dodge them all but eventually collided with one. As it hit his body, it exploded and caused a chain reaction. All the shadow balls began to explode, creating a dust storm. As the dust cleared, the captain was on one knee, holding himself up with his rapier and laughing.

The demon took a step closer and was hovering above the guard captain. "What's so funny?"

The captain smiled. "I'm just a distraction."

The demon turned on its heel but was too late. A wall of fire crashed into him and quickly ate away his shadow energy. The demon attempted to fly away, but the fire destroyed his wings. The phoenix then flew into the body of the demon.

The demon let out a torrent of curse words as it panicked, looking for a solution, looking for salvation. The flames continued to eat away at its body, revealing the screaming traveler inside. The dark energy tried to heal itself but was failing to keep up, the flames being too much for it.

As the fire faded, the phoenix faded with it, leaving the traveler standing there with black energy still coursing through his body.

The demon gasped and gulped down air. "You…" Gasp. "Failed…" The demon lifted both arms into the air and began forming a shadow ball. The energy started smaller than before but was quickly growing.

Captain Holtz wasn't healing anymore. His time limit was up on the empowerment potion, leaving him significantly weakened. "Gods, I beseech you one last time. Please give me the strength I need to smite this wrongdoer." A faint aura surrounded the captain. The aura quickly concentrated on his feet and he dashed forward.

The demon anticipated this and the shadow ball faded as he dropped one hand. The man's hand shot outward and formed a large black spike. It impaled Captain Holtz as he drove his rapier through the traveler's heart. The shadows covering the man melted away, and he returned to his normal shirtless form. Captain Holtz fell backwards, a visible hole in his stomach. Both sides of the conflict stood in awe. Horns were being blown, and the monsters began their retreat, having suffered major losses.

The human army didn't pursue, instead, it stopped at Captain Holtz. A small form was bent over him pouring a variety of liquids on his wounds. The liquids were bubbling and oozing as they combined on the captain's chest. The captain's chest was smoking, but he still wasn't moving. The figure tried force-feeding the captain healing potions, but he remained unresponsive.

Luke met up with his team and Nanoc helped him to the field.

"Rose?" Luke called out to the shop owner.

"He's... he's dead." Rose stood and turned to him. Her eyes were watery and red.

"Can't someone resurrect him? There has to be some form of resurrection spell!" Nanoc pleaded.

Rose shook her head slowly. "The gods limit resurrection to travelers only. We only get one life."

The gravity of her words sunk in. Luke frowned and tilted his head down, partially in respect and partially to hide his own tears. Rose's hands began to glow green as she placed them on the captain's chest. "I will miss you, Rupert." She wiped her brow as she took a few steps back and the energy surrounded the captain's lifeless form.

The ground started shaking and small roots began sprouting out of the captain and into the ground. The roots began to grow, getting larger and spreading out. The captain's body began to transform into wood as a tree trunk broke through the ground. The tree pulled the captain's body into its trunk as it grew.

The tree stopped growing after it was thirty feet tall and six feet wide. The side of the tree that faced the city began to shift and move as the bark formed the visage of Captain Holtz. It was a spitting image of him holding his rapier to the ground in a knightly pose.

Rose stepped forward and placed her glowing hands against the base of the tree. A square wood plaque formed under the image of Captain Holtz. The plaque read:

Here lies Captain Rupert Holtz, protector of the Phoenix Kingdom.
Remember him as he lived, a knight of the highest caliber and an even
better man.

She stepped away and bowed her head. Others joined in, and soon all members of the army were bowing their heads in respect. The new travelers, unsure who the captain really was, paid their respects. They all knew they were alive now because of him.

After a long moment of silence, the crowd broke up and began heading for the city as a new day's light began to dawn.

"Rose?" Luke approached the gnome and placed a hand on her shoulder. "We should head back now."

Rose cleaned her face and took his hand. The pair walked slowly back into the city, heading straight to their shop to sleep away their sorrows. Luke made sure Rose was situated before heading for his own room. When he made it to his bed, he collapsed into unconsciousness.

CHAPTER TWENTY-ONE

Aftermath

Luke's door was thrown open and Penny walked in. "You aren't up yet? We've been waiting for you."

Luke covered his eyes, shielding them from the light that was flooding the room. Groaning, he asked, "What time is it?"

"Time for you to get up, clean up and get to the castle."

"They destroyed the castle, didn't they?" He responded.

"They rebuilt parts of it and they asked for all the noble guilds to be there, so let's go." She tried pushing him along, but he wasn't having it. "Just get to the castle please."

Luke waved her off. "Ok, ok, I'll meet you there."

Satisfied, she left, allowing him to wake up and get his bearings. He sat up in his bed and paused, still feeling sluggish from the major weakening debuff. The bottom of his view was blinking rapidly, so he pulled up his notifications but chose to see only the condensed version. It was too early to be bombarded with system notifications.

Multiple enemies slain. 2,675 party participation exp gained. Focus here to see a full breakdown.

Multiple skill increases. Focus here to see a full breakdown.

Area Event Complete: **The Great Goblin War!** *Multiple stat increases, new title and 15,000 event exp rewarded. Focus here to see a full breakdown.*

Phoenix Kingdom, *New Status:* **Friends.**

Congratulations, **Level up x2!**

Luke was shocked. How did he get that much experience? He focused on the area event.

Area Event Complete: **The Great Goblin War!** *Congratulations, you ranked 3rd among travelers and have been rewarded 5,000 exp, 100 gold, and 100 Phoenix Kingdom reputation. Congratulations, your guild, Travelers 4 Hire, ranked 1st among guilds and all members have been awarded 10,000 exp, 150 gold, and 150 Phoenix Kingdom reputation. All members of the guild, Travelers 4 Hire, have also been awarded +1 to all attributes. You have also been awarded the title Defender of the Phoenix Kingdom. While this title is equipped, you will receive +25% reputation gain with the Phoenix Kingdom and receive a 10% discount in all Phoenix Kingdom shops.*

That's an impressive haul, he thought as he got to his feet. The pain of survivor's guilt hit him as he thought of his personal gains. Still feeling sluggish, he cast nature's regrowth on himself to get a morning boost of energy.

300

Not bothering to equip his armor, he left his room and his focus turned to the closed door behind the counter. He considered waking Rose but decided against it and instead left for the castle.

It took him longer than normal to reach the castle, his mind running through last night's events over and over. His eyes became watery as he held back tears when his thoughts turned to Captain Holtz.

"Hey kid." He looked up to see Ursa sitting on top of a nearby building. He waved, and she jumped to the ground. She also appeared to be holding back tears. "How is Rose?" Ursa pointed down the walkway in the direction Luke had come from.

He shrugged. "I'm not sure. She wasn't up when I left and I didn't want to bother her."

"And how are you?" She added.

Luke shrugged. "Not sure the full weight of things has hit me yet but I'm surviving, you? I was a little worried when you got tossed over the wall."

Ursa thought he was deflecting, but she brushed it off, not wanting to push him on the topic. "Yeah, that wasn't my proudest moment but I'm surviving." She hesitated, unsure what to say next. "I think I might go check on Rose. Stop by later so we can talk, ok?"

He nodded and continued toward the castle. When he finally arrived, he saw that they had erected a small stone building outside the ruins and people were gathering outside it. Dozens of mages were making good progress on erecting a new castle. Crude barriers of rock were being summoned from the earth while other mages set about transmuting them to polished stone walls.

Luke was shocked to see Robert Xanders sitting behind a small counter, speaking with several travelers and handing out scrolls with different names written on them.

"Rob?" Luke questioned, not believing what his eyes were

showing him.

"Luke!" Rob began shuffling through a crate and pulled a letter out with Luke's full name written on it.

"What's this?" Luke grabbed the letter confused.

"It's a letter from your mother."

It shocked Luke to see Rob, but he was downright bewildered at seeing a letter from his mother. The scroll had a wax seal on it and as he grabbed the seal, a system message popped up.

Identity confirmed.

The wax seal then burned away in blue flames, leaving the scroll undamaged and unraveling in his hand. He pulled it open and began to read.

Hello Lucas,

Didn't you promise to call me after your first day at this job? You're a little late kiddo.

I honestly don't know what to say or how to share my concerns about this whole situation with you. Vortex Industries promised me that you're ok and I guess I will have to cling to that.

I stopped by your apartment and packed up your things. I can't really afford your rent, so Vortex Industries paid out your lease, and I stuck your things in your old room at the house.

They also said I could stop by their headquarters if I wanted to login to one of the "VR Stations" to see you. I don't know what that all means but after you got stuck in there, I have no intention of trying it for myself. I want to see you, but someone has to pay the bills around here.

I miss you Lucas and I hope you're safe and well. Please write back soon and remember that I love you and, even though I'm not physically there with you, I'm always with you in spirit.

Love, Mom

After composing himself, Luke approached Rob again. "Thank you." Rob nodded. "She asked me to write her back, is that possible?"

Rob nodded and pointed to the far end of the counter. There were stacks of paper with ink and quills next to them. There was also a small bowl of hot wax and several seals lying around.

Luke wrote several pages, explaining most of what had happened to him. He described meeting Rose and his guild, getting trained by Ursa, summoning Ringo and the late Captain Holtz. He left out most of the gruesome bits but tried to leave in all the important parts. He signed off the pages with love and rolled them together. Grabbing a seal, he dipped it in wax and pressed it against the paper's fold.

Basic mana seal created. *This document can not be opened by anyone other than the intended recipient.*

Luke wondered how they could enforce that considering that the letter was being delivered outside of the game, but he wasn't bothered by the thought of somebody else reading it. He wasn't sharing any deep, dark secrets or anything.

"Can you deliver this to my mom, please?" Rob took the scroll and placed it in a box at his side. The letter burned up in blue flames and vanished.

"Don't worry." Rob saw the look of concern Luke was giving him. "The box sends it to the Vortex Industries mailing program and e-mails it to the designated recipient if there is one in the database. If there isn't an email address for the person, then it will reject it. We have everyone's family email address on file from when we explained the..." he hesitated, "current situation to them."

"Speaking of which, what's the deal? I mean, I assume all the new travelers are the ones you spoke about in your announcement, but what's the news on getting us out of here?"

Rob grimaced a little. "Unfortunately, we don't really have a time frame for that. The FBI is working the case the best they can. They have some leads but they haven't filled us in on much of the day-to-day investigation. I know they are making it a big priority and treating it like a mass kidnapping."

Luke opened his mouth to ask more questions, but Rob cut him off.

"Listen Luke, I would love to explain it more but I can't right now. Just know that the top brass is working on getting you guys home but, for now, I can't give you a timeline. To help bolster good relations we're offering all family members of beta players free access to login and meet up with their family. We are also going to buy one of the local buildings near the castle and set it up as a customer relations building. If you have questions, you will have to speak with whoever they assign to that building. I'm only here today to hand out letters and connect people with their families as a sign of good faith from the company." Rob gestured behind Luke at the large line that had formed behind him. "As you can see, everyone is trying to connect with their families at the moment, and

I really can't spend too much time with anyone in particular." Rob gestured to Luke in a way that suggested he should move along.

Luke gazed around and saw a lot of players hugging kids and kissing what he assumed to be their spouses. Not wanting to get in the way of families being reunited, he stepped aside and made a mental note to come back and visit the customer relations building when it opened.

"Hey Luke!" Turning he saw Penny shouting and waving him down.

As he approached he noticed Shrapnel, Nanoc, Backstab and several other guild members gathering in front of a large red and orange tent with guards surrounding it.

"What's going on?" Luke questioned.

Shrapnel slapped Luke's back. "We did it! I'm assuming you read the system message about us ranking first during the Goblin War?" Shrapnel paused and after Luke realized he was waiting for a response, he nodded. "Good. Well, Princess Kira has asked for a meeting with our guild. I invited the officers," he gestured around at various guild members, "and your party because you've met the King before and I also noticed you ranked third for personal contribution."

Penny, Nanoc and Backstab all looked at him with wide eyes. "When were you going to tell us that little bit of information?" Nanoc asked.

Luke blushed and shrugged. "Didn't want to seem like I was bragging or something. I assumed you all ranked high." They all lowered their heads.

"I don't know about them, but I placed second," Shrapnel continued. "As I was saying, before someone interrupted me," He shot them all a dirty look, "Princess Kira wants to meet with us. She has some news regarding the queen and a new guild quest!" He waved them all forward and approached the guards, informing them that Princess Kira was waiting for them.

"Hmm." The guard wearing all plate armor was staring down Shrapnel. He lifted the tent's flap and an elderly man in orange robes stepped out.

"Hello travelers." They all waved. "Let me get a good look at you." He moved his fingers and hands into a complicated series of patterns and symbols as a small orb of orange light formed on his pointer fingers. He placed the fingers against his eyelids and when he reopened his eyes, they were solid orange and glowing.

He spent time looking at each of them, moving from one to another. After he was done, he returned to the front of the tent and closed his eyes. When he opened his eyes they had returned to normal, and he held the tent flap open.

"Please go in, I sensed no ill intent from any of you. The princess has been expecting you." He gestured with his free arm for them to enter.

The group entered the tent and took in their surroundings. The tent was incredibly elaborate with a variety of colored fabric strung from the ceiling. The floor was covered in decorative furs and rugs. The room was well lit with candelabras and floating orbs of light. In the center of the room was a woman lying in a long bed, surrounded by mages continuously casting spells on her. In front of the bed was an ornate chair raised up on a platform, holding a young woman who was sitting straight.

Luke's group recognized the woman lying in the bed as the queen and the woman on the throne-like chair as the princess. When their group approached, they all went to one knee to show respect. The robed man followed them in and took a seat on a small simple chair next to the princess.

"Before we begin, the princess requires you all to take a mana binding oath of silence." The man began but stopped when the travelers all gave him confused expressions. He raised an eyebrow before continuing. "I can see by your expressions that none of you know what that is. Please allow me to elaborate. When you make a mana binding oath or contract, you imbue your words with your mana. Your mana will hold you to your oath and if you break your agreement, it will kill you."

The group all looked at each other and did not show any sign of concern before they returned their gaze to the robed man, their expressions neutral.

"I don't believe you're understanding the full magnitude of my words," the man added.

Shrapnel shrugged. "We're immortal, death really doesn't bother us too much. I mean it hurts, a lot, but it's not the end of the world." Realizing what he just said, he quickly added, "but you don't have to worry, we will keep our word."

The man began to grin as he put on a dark expression. "That is where you are wrong. Soon after the travelers started popping up we discovered that death doesn't burden you much. So, we developed a way of punishing you if you were to ever get out of hand. We have the ability to change the bind point of any travelers who are sent to respawn within our city. What's more, we can change the bind points of absolutely anyone so long as they have been physically captured."

These last words finally got a rise out of the travelers. They began murmuring amongst each other and concern clearly showed on their faces.

"And in case you were wondering, the Phoenix Kingdom dungeons have several bind points ready for travelers who misbehave."

Shrapnel started to speak but was stopped when Princess Kira stood from her chair. "Please travelers, I need your help. Please swear on your mana that you will not repeat what I'm about to tell you to anyone other than the souls in this room and the King himself."

They all looked at each other for a few moments before nodding, agreeing to the oath. Shrapnel spoke up. "We agree." After Shrapnel finished speaking Luke noticed a few points of mana drain from his status bar and he felt a pain in his head that quickly subsided.

Mana Oath Issued. You have agreed to keep your silence about the princess's request. If you attempt to speak about this to anyone other than the souls present during the oath's agreement or the King, you will be struck down before you are able to speak a word and your bind point will be changed to the Phoenix Kingdom's dungeon.

Clearing away the message, Luke saw the others doing the same. Returning his sight to the princess, he noticed her warm smile and newly relaxed shoulders. It was as if a huge weight had been lifted from her.

"Thank you." The princess looked back at her mother. A team of mages were continuously casting a variety of magic spells on her as she slept. When the princess turned around, she greeted them with a frown. "My mother is in danger. Very few people know this, but the phoenix that fought last night was an ancient summoning spell reserved for the royal family. The spell is extremely taxing and from the moment my mother summoned it, her mana and life force were being drained. I believe that's why the late Captain Holtz charged into battle." The guards in the room shifted uncomfortably at the mention of their deceased captain. "He knew the truth of that spell and I believe he wanted to finish the fight as quickly as possible to save my mother."

The princess paused for a moment to look back at her mother and to allow the gravity of her words to sink in.

"I'm sorry to interrupt, princess, but where do we come in?" Shrapnel questioned.

"I need you to retrieve my father. He should be powerful enough to restore my mother back to good health."

Shrapnel furrowed his brow. "I don't mean any disrespect, but can't you send some runners from the city guard?"

"I can not. The enemy army is still in the forests and hills that surround our kingdom. If they got word that the queen was injured and that we were sending runners to fetch the King, they would attack again in an instant. I need to send travelers. We still don't know a lot about you, but the inhabitants of this world know that you seek adventure. Our enemies wouldn't think twice if they saw a group of travelers exploring the neighboring lands."

Shrapnel opened his mouth to argue but quickly shut it. Thinking about it for a moment, he knew she was right. It would be a strategic plan to send travelers. Monsters expect to see us roaming the outskirts in search of adventure. City guards, on the other hand, would be suspicious to anyone.

"I offer you this quest. Go to the Elk Kingdom, find my father and bring him home," the princess pleaded.

Quest Alert! **Return the King**. *Princess Kira has requested that you travel to the Elk Kingdom to find her father and bring him home. Rewards: +250 reputation with the Phoenix Kingdom and 100 gold. Exp: 25,000. Accept / Decline*

Luke's jaw dropped at the amount of experience offered for this quest. That was more experience than every other quest and event reward he had seen before combined.

"This is an urgent quest. The enemy army is still retreating, but I ask that you leave as soon as possible. Please only send a handful of people. I don't want the enemy to think we are on the move. I also need travelers to help rebuild the city's defenses. We lost a lot of good men and I will offer anyone in your guild a quest to join the city guard on a temporary basis while we recruit and train replacements."

The queen groaned in pain and the princess ran to her, taking the queen's hand in hers. The man in orange robes ushered them all out of the tent. When they were all outside and the tent was closed again, he spoke in a hushed tone so that no one else would overhear him.

"Go now and carry out this request. We need the King here as soon as possible."

He disappeared into the tent, and Shrapnel signaled all of them to follow him. They all walked back to the guild hall and gathered in one of the large meeting rooms. The door shut behind them and one of the guild officers cast a spell that caused a circle of fast-moving air to surround them before giving Shrapnel a nod.

"Thank you SilverFox. No one outside this bubble of air should be able to hear us now." Shrapnel looked intensely at Penny. "I need your party to handle this."

It took Penny aback. "Sir... I..."

"There are no ifs ands or buts about it." He cut her off. "You are the only full group that has worked together and has this quest. I can't pair people who have the quest with those who don't have it. We could end up breaking our oaths. The other officers and I don't make a compatible enough party to survive the trip together. Most of us are damage absorbers and we have no healing or damage dealers. It has to be your group."

Penny shifted her eyes back and forth in thought. She gave each of her party an inquisitive look and they all gave her a nod. Penny returned her gaze to Shrapnel and nodded her acceptance.

"Thank you, Penny. When you're ready to leave, I'll send other parties out to the surrounding forest to help camouflage your departure. I think that's all we have to discuss. This request seems urgent, so I suggest you leave tomorrow." The group began to break apart and head off to prepare. Shrapnel turned to the party and said, "Good luck in the Elk Kingdom."

The End

EPILOGUE

Iron respawned on a stone circle in a dark and damp cave. Various magic carvings were etched into the floor beneath him, and they were glowing as his character came back from the dead. Appearing next to him was the robed man who had transformed himself into a formidable demon during the battle of the Phoenix Kingdom.

"Bruce! You were a maniac back there!" Iron was excited to see his friend.

"Shadow's going to kill us." Bruce didn't share Iron's excitement at the situation.

Iron looked at him, confused. "Dude, you were perfect. You almost destroyed the entire city! So what if we failed? Shadow can finish the survivors easily." Iron walked down a set of stone stairs that led out of the small resurrection chamber. "You worry too much," he called back as he left the room with Bruce running after him.

Iron entered a much larger chamber, deep underground. There were stalagmites and stalactites covering the bulk of the massive opening. There was a raging river near the opposite wall. The sound of rushing water echoed throughout the chamber. The room was well lit with floating black fireballs casting an ominous light over the space. Several robed and armored figures were bustling throughout. Iron looked around for Shadow Incarnate and approached when he spotted him.

"Hey, Shadow!" Iron called out.

Shadow Incarnate turned slowly to face Iron. "You have returned. Is the Phoenix Kingdom no more?" He raised a single eyebrow.

"Well, not exactly," Iron began to explain. "We put on a great fight but couldn't manage it with the troops we had. We'll get them next time though."

Shadow Incarnate approached Iron and put his arm around him in a friendly embrace. "That's ok, Iron." Bruce looked confused. He had never seen Shadow Incarnate act friendly, especially with the travelers, but now he had Iron in an embrace? "As long as you brought back my crystals, we're all peachy."

Iron and Bruce blanched at the mention of the crystals. "Well, you see... about the crystals." Iron began to explain, but Shadow Incarnate raised his hand to stop him.

"I remember asking you to attack the Phoenix Kingdom with my crystals in order to cause them some damage. I remember saying that I would give you one or two crystals for the task. I remember you saying that if you had more of my extremely rare and powerful crystals," Shadow Incarnate emphasized the importance of the crystals as he spoke, "that you could destroy the Kingdom." Shadow Incarnate walked around Iron to face him, placing his hand on the traveler's shoulder.

Iron began to sweat, and his next words came out with fear clearly in his voice. "Well... there were some complications. There was a Phoenix and then tons of trav…"

Shadow Incarnate drove his free arm through the traveler's stomach and out the other side. When he pulled his arm out, fiery shadows burst from the wound. The dark magic traveled over Iron's body until it covered him from head to toe. The shadows began to deform and reshape the traveler. Large curved horns jutted out from his head, his feet became hooves and his fingernails and hair grew long. The entirety of his new form was jet-black in color, save for his pure blood-red eyes.

Shadow Incarnate put a hand over the traveler's mouth. Iron's body began shaking and it responded as if it was being tanned like leather. All the moisture was being drained, and as his flesh shriveled it became leathery and dry. As Shadow Incarnate pulled his hand away, an orb of light pulled out of the creature's mouth and sat in his palm. The orb had a purple swirl of energy inside it.

Shadow Incarnate pulled a bottle from his belt. The bottle had multiple marbles with energy of various colors swirling inside them. As he pulled the cork stopper from the bottle, a storm of begging pleas came rushing out.

"Help! Please! I want to go home!" One voice called out.

"I can't respawn! I thought this was a game, someone please help me!" Another screamed.

Shadow Incarnate closed his hand over the baseball-sized orb in his hand and it condensed, stopping when it was marble sized. He placed the orb in the bottle and replaced the cork stopper before returning the bottle to his belt.

"Now." Shadow Incarnate approached Bruce. "Care to tell me what happened?"

Bruce flew to his knees in worship. He told Shadow Incarnate everything that had happened, pleading with the man to spare him.

"Ha Ha Ha," Shadow Incarnate laughed briefly. "I like you

traveler. You're much more direct than the last one." He patted Bruce on the shoulder and helped him to his feet. "Don't worry, I never intended for you to destroy the Phoenix Kingdom." Bruce looked confused but didn't dare speak out, afraid that he would be next to face Shadow Incarnate's wrath. Sensing Bruce's hesitation, Shadow Incarnate continued. "See, you've already proven to be smarter than your friend." He looked over at the ghoulish form of the previous traveler. "He just needed to be punished for taking most of my crystals and wasting them. He insisted that he could get the job done if I just gave him more crystals." He returned his gaze to Bruce. "You have to know your limits and your place."

Shadow Incarnate turned around and walked to a raised altar made entirely of bone. The surface of the altar displayed a large ritual pattern. The pattern had several intricate symbols and words carved in lines into the bone. The lines made up two large triangles with oval indentations at each of the six points. Another set of magical writing encircled the ritualistic diagram.

When he reached the altar, he pulled a large orange oval piece of amber from his pocket. A raging cascade of flames was burning inside the amber and it cast a visible heat in the air. As he brought the amber above one of the six indentations, black tentacles shot from the altar's surface and grabbed the gem from his hand. The tentacles slowly pulled the amber into place until a faint click was heard.

Shadow Incarnate took a step back to take in the scene. He now filled two of the six indentations, leaving four empty sockets. Joining the orange amber was a jet-black onyx. "I don't need to bother the Phoenix Kingdom again. With the help of your distraction, I was able to slip in and get what I desired." Shadow pulled his head back and let out a manic laugh.

AFTERWORD

Thank you for reading Endless Fantasy Online: The Phoenix Kingdom! I really hope you enjoyed reading it.

Please leave a review!

I would love it if you could spare some time to leave a review on Amazon. Reviews really go a long way in sharing my stories and encourages me to write more. I love to hear and learn from your feedback, good or bad.

If you don't want to miss updates on this saga or want to learn more about my other series, think about joining my newsletter:
http://eepurl.com/guWgvv

For more updates, check out my official website:
http://www.devinauspland.com

Also consider joining my Facebook group:
https://www.facebook.com/devinausplandbooks/

If you want to show the utmost support, you can donate to my Patreon page. You can gain early access to future chapters and special rewards by becoming a member:
https://www.patreon.com/devinauspland

Again, I would just like to thank you, the reader. Thank you for your support of my writing journey. It's because of you that I'm able to bring my stories to life.

A special thanks to both Heart of the Game and WNY Gaming for hosting book releases with me on their Dungeons & Dragons nights. For more information on either of them, please check out their Facebook pages.

(https://www.facebook.com/heartsofthegame/)

(https://www.facebook.com/wnygaming/)

Check out GameLit on Facebook for more great GameLit reads.

(https://www.facebook.com/groups/LitRPGsociety/)

Check out LitRPG Books on Facebook for more great LitRPG reads.

(https://www.facebook.com/groups/LitRPG.books/?ref=boo kmarks)

To learn more about LitRPG, talk to authors including myself, and just have an awesome time, please join the LitRPG Group.

(https://www.facebook.com/groups/LitRPGGroup/)

LUKE'S CHARACTER SHEET

Name: *Beast Tamer Luke*
Class: *Beast Tamer*
Primary Profession: *Herbalist*
Animal Companion: *Ringo (Alpha Wolf)*
Level 8: *Exp 6,657 Exp to next level: 1,343*
Hit Points: *110/110*
Mana: *170/170*
Mana Regen: *1.50/sec*
Stamina: *180/180*
Physical Resistance: *+15*
Elemental Resistance: *Water +10, Earth +10*

Attributes *Base (Modifier)*
Note: You have 4 unallocated attribute points.
Strength: *3*
Agility: *13 (+1)*
Intelligence: *10 (+3)*
Wisdom: *2 (+1)*
Constitution: *7*
Social: *12 (+1)*
Luck: *2*

Skills, Spells and Abilities
Note: You have 3 unallocated skill points.
Short Bow *(Intermediate 2): You have become familiar with short bows and no longer are looked at as a beginner by others. Increasing this skill will increase the damage dealt with a short bow. This is a passive skill and requires no activation. Effect 1: +10% short bow damage. Effect 2: +x% damage when attacking targets distracted by*

an ally.

Herbalism *(Beginner 8): This skill allows you to identify various plant life.*

First Aid *(Beginner 0): Basic knowledge on how to apply basic first aid and use basic bandages. Increasing this skill will increase your knowledge of first aid techniques and increase the speed at which you can apply this skill.*

Nature's Regrowth *(Intermediate 1): Grasping a better understanding of the healing powers of nature, you can harness this energy quicker than before. Harness the power of nature to speed up the natural healing and growth speed of the target. Cost: 4x mana. Effect 1: Heal for 2x every 5 seconds for 15 seconds where x = skill level. Effect 2: Additional 10% health restored when the spell is used on someone other than you. Cooldown: 45 seconds. Range: 10 feet.*

Alchemy *(Beginner 1): Knowledge of basic reagent combinations. Increasing this skill will increase your knowledge of alchemy and increase your chances of combining new reagents successfully.*

Bartering *(Beginner 2): Trading is a craft and you have taken the first steps in learning that craft. You will receive small bonuses when attempting to barter. Effect: +x% bartering results where x = skill level.*

Inspect *(Beginner 3) Knowledge is half the battle. By focusing on your opponents you can now gleam basic knowledge of them. Leveling up this skill will grant you more information and allow you to inspect a wider range of enemy levels. Effect: Gain basic knowledge of enemies up to double your level.*

Sneak *(Beginner 1): While others try to be honest and fair, you sneak around in the dark, looking for opportunities to strike. What are you really doing hiding in those bushes? Cost: 1 stamina per second. Effect: +x% chance to sneak and +1x% chance to perform a sneak attack when attacking while hidden, where x = skill level.*

Water Shot *(Beginner 5): Infuses your arrow with water. When shot it will fire off like a water jet and do increased water affinity damage. Cost: 25 + x mana. Effect: Increases arrow travel rate by 10% and adds 1x water damage where x = skill level. Range: Touch arrow.*

Resurrect Companion *(Class Skill): Resurrects your animal companion if they have unfortunately died. Allowing your animal companion to die will negatively affect your relationship and they may choose to break their bond with you. Cost: 100% max mana. Effect: Channel this spell for 10 second to resurrect your animal companion at full health. Cooldown: 24 hours. Range: Self.*

Beast Mastery *(Intermediate 2): You have bonded with a beast and taken steps in befriending the animal kingdom. By improving this skill you can now feel the spirit of your companion and know where he or she is located by feeling their spirit. Improving this skill will increase your bond with your animal companion. This skill also scales based on your social attribute. Effect 1: +10% animal companion's bond rate. Effect 2: You know your animal companion's general location from x+3 meters away where x = skill level.*

Rapid Fire *(Beginner 1): Most people take careful aim at their targets to ensure they hit but not you. You just keep shooting until something sticks. Cost: 2 stamina per second. Effect: Increase arrow firing rate by X + 2% and decrease your aim by x + 5% while channeling the spell where x = skill level.*

Dodge *(Beginner 6) Why take damage or wear heavy armor to prevent it when you can simple dodge it. This is a passive skill and requires no activation. Effect: 1 + x% added to your reaction time when attempting to dodge an attack. Note: The reaction time and chance to dodge is linked to your agility stat and requires the use of stamina.*

Companion Telepathy *(Class Skill): By strengthening your bond with your animal companion and having them reach a certain stage* *in their life, you have gained the ability to speak with your companion telepathically. The range of this skill is increased by your Beast Mastery skill level. At the current level the range is sight or 6 meters without sight.*

Beast Bond *(Class Skill): Through rigorous training and resolve you have chosen to specialize as Bast Tamer and unlocked the ability to bond with wild beasts. Successful use of this skill will cause a beast to become an animal companion. At your current specialization you are limited to one primary animal companion and two minor animal companions. Attempting to tame additional beasts will result in an automatic failure until you release one of your animals. Effect: Tame and bond with a wild best. The chance of successfully taming an animal is $x/2\%$ where x = social attribute limited to 30. Note: Other factors may increase or decrease this effect. Example, feeding or socializing with an animal may make it more perceptive to your bonding attempts.*

Mining *(Beginner 2): As this skills increases, so does your proficiency in mining. Proficiency lowers the amount of stamina required to perform this action. Effect: Proficiency $+x\%$ where n is skill level.*

Climbing *(Beginner 0) You have learned the basics of climbing. Congratulations, you have the same climbing ability to climb as a small child. Effect: $1+x\%$ bonuses added to your climbing attempts where n is skill level.*

Claws *(Beginner 4) You have taken the first step in mastering claw weapons, a subclass of fist-based weapons. Congratulations, you know how to throw a basic punch. Effect: $1+x\%$ claw damage.*

Tamer's Vengeance *(Class Skill): Watching your animal companion die after swearing to keep her alive has filled you with the vengeance and power of beast tamers past. This skill is auto-triggered when either the beast tamer or animal companion is killed in battle within*

*view of the other. You are filled with the power of the beast tamers
before you and can concentrate that power into a single attack. Effect:
Buff your next melee or ranged attack, adding 5x its normal damage.
Note: If the attack does not instantly follow the triggering of this
effect, this buff will last until the beast tamer and animal companion
are reunited or five minutes, whichever happens first.*

Ringo, *Alpha Wolf*
Level 8
Favorite Foods: *Meat (any), Fruit (apples)*
HP: *110*
MP: *0*
Stamina: *160*

<u>**Attributes**</u> *Base (Modifier)*
Note: You have 6 unallocated attribute points.
Strength: *8*
Agility: *7*
Intelligence: *2*
Wisdom: *1*
Constitution: *2*
Social: *3*
Luck: *1*

<u>Skills, Spells and Abilities</u>
Note: You have 3 unallocated skill points.
Confusing Howl *(Beginner 1): A high pitched howling sound wave
that pierces the eardrums of all enemies who can hear it, causing them
to become confused. Cost: 2x Stamina, where x = skill level. Effect:
100% chance to add the confused debuff. This percentage decreases by
10% for every 5ft the enemy is from you.*

Pounce *(Beginner 4): Building up energy, you leap onto an opponent, dealing bonus damage. Cost: 1x stamina, where x = skill level. Effect: +1x damage or +2x damage if used while unseen.*

Tracking *(Beginner 1): Being a wolf, you have enhanced senses that lend themselves to tracking and hunting. Effect: +1x% increased chance of finding and following the scents, tracks, sight or sounds of your enemy, where x = skill level.*

ABOUT THE AUTHOR

Devin Auspland

I live outside of Buffalo NY with my wife, 2 dogs and 2 cats. By day I work in an office, but at night I become a writer!

After enjoying countless Fantasy and LitRPG books, I decided it was time to create my own cast of characters and world to put them in. It has been a huge investment of time and a lot of late nights, but I'm incredibly humbled to share my story with the world and with you, the readers.

I hope that you get as much enjoyment out of it as I have had writing it. Minus the late nights of course.

If you want to know more about the Endless Fantasy Online series or other books I'm working on, please visit my website here:
http://devinauspland.com

I love to hear from my readers and engage with them, so please reach out to me at devinausplandbooks@gmail.com

Made in the USA
Monee, IL
05 July 2023

38691928R00198